My Heart Belongs in Fort Bliss, Texas

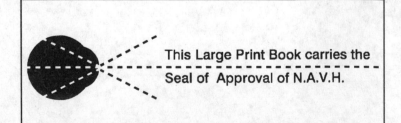

This Large Print Book carries the
Seal of Approval of N.A.V.H.

My Heart Belongs in Fort Bliss, Texas

PRISCILLA'S REVEILLE

Erica Vetsch

THORNDIKE PRESS
A part of Gale, Cengage Learning

GALE
CENGAGE Learning·

Farmington Hills, Mich • San Francisco • New York • Waterville, Maine
Meriden, Conn • Mason, Ohio • Chicago

LIBRARY OF CONGRESS CATALOGING-IN-PUBLICATION DATA

Names: Vetsch, Erica, author.
Title: My heart belongs in Fort Bliss, Texas : Priscilla's reveille / by Erica Vetsch.
Other titles: Priscilla's reveille
Description: Large print edition. | Waterville, Maine : Thorndike Press, 2017. |
    Series: Thorndike Press large print Christian romance
Identifiers: LCCN 2017004704| ISBN 9781432838294 (hardcover) | ISBN 1432838296
    (hardcover)
Subjects: LCSH: Large type books. | GSAFD: Love stories. | Christian fiction.
    Classification: LCC PS3622.E886 M9 2017 | DDC 813/.6—dc23 LC record available
    at https://lccn.loc.gov/2017004704

Published in 2017 by arrangement with Barbour Publishing, Inc.

Printed in the United States of America
1 2 3 4 5 6 7 21 20 19 18 17

DEDICATION
To my parents,
James and Esther Bonam,
with all my love, and as always, to
Peter the hero of my real-life romance
every day.

CHAPTER ONE

Trans-Pecos Territory of West Texas, 1874

Only the army would think a place like this worth defending.

Priscilla Hutchens clamped her teeth together to keep them from rattling right out of her head. Grabbing the wagon bow, she sought to find an anchor as the converted military ambulance jounced up a slight rise. The howling wind, which a cheerful enlisted man had called a "freshening breeze," tore at the canvas cover overhead. That same enlisted man had rolled up the stained fabric along the sides of the ambulance, and as a result, Priscilla had an unfettered view of . . . pretty much nothing.

She'd had no idea when embarking on this rescue mission that so much "empty" existed anywhere. Miles and miles of brush, sparse clumps of grass, cacti, and bare ground stretched away to the edge of the world. In the distance, a humpbacked ridge of mountains poked up from the desert — a dusty, purplish lump on the otherwise flat expanse. The small company of soldiers, horses, and wagons she traveled with could be the last inhabitants on earth.

How had her brother stood this everlasting openness? After the bustling, busy, and varied life of Cincinnati, how had he survived the tediousness of a frontier military post? And not only him but his wife and children?

Fort Bliss. One of a string of forts along the San Antonio–El Paso Trail, and until now, a place Priscilla had never thought to visit. Only the twins' need of her could've gotten her out of the city and to this forsaken desert. And the sooner she accomplished her purpose and returned to civilization, the better. Fort Bliss. There was nothing blissful about this awful place.

A particularly fierce gust yanked at her bonnet, and she let go of the wagon bow to grab it before it tumbled to the dirt. Opposite her on the other bench, Fern Perry gave her a sympathetic smile.

"That hat is going to take wing and fly away." She had to speak over the rattle of the wagons and harness and the tramping of dozens of boots. Boots that raised puffs of dust to swirl around them, land on their

8

skin and hair, and work their way into their clothing. Priscilla had never felt so gritty and dirty in her life.

Fern braced herself against the lurch of the wagon. "When we get to the fort, the first thing you should buy is a sunbonnet. The sutler's store is bound to have some, or you could hire one of the laundresses to make one for you. The sun will ruin your skin otherwise. Your hat's so stylish, but it's rather impractical out here."

"I don't anticipate remaining at the fort long enough to need to change out my wardrobe." Priscilla anchored her hat once more, arranging the netting and hoping the silky black feathers adorning the left side of the royal-blue brim were sewn on tightly. The hat perfectly matched her traveling costume, and she couldn't imagine how ridiculous a slab-sided calico sunbonnet would look in its place. She'd rather battle the wind.

"Are you really only planning to stay a few days? It's such an awful long way to come to turn around and go back so soon."

"I have no desire to prolong my visit." Priscilla pressed her lips together. "Retrieving my niece and nephew is my only concern. And I must return to my job. The catalog will be getting woefully behind as it is." Though her employers had given her a generous amount of time off, twelve weeks in fact, she had no intention of using all of it. Her work was too important to her. She'd spent the last four years creating the overall look and design of the catalog, and if she was gone too long, they'd have to turn things over to another artist who might not have her same style and vision for the publication.

"I guess I never thought of where the artwork in mail-order catalogs came from," Fern said. "Fancy being an artist for the Carterson Ladies' Emporium Catalog. I guess that explains your pretty clothes. I've never seen anything as stylish as that dress." Her eyes traveled over Priscilla's clothing from collar to shoes. "My mother and sisters and I pored over every new Carterson's that arrived in the mail. They'll never believe me when I write to tell them I met the artist who drew all those beautiful pictures." Her expression took on a wistful look. "I wish my family could've come for the wedding." She shook her head as if ridding herself of unpleasant thoughts. "Still, it's enough that I'm going to be with Harry. I've missed him so much."

Fern had rhapsodized about her fiancé often and at length each night as they made camp. To hear her description, Lieutenant Harry Dunn was a saint, a knight in shining armor, a Byronic hero, and a brilliant scholar all rolled into one.

Yet, while Priscilla understood the bias with which Fern described her beloved, the girl's obvious happiness set up a longing in Priscilla's heart that lingered well after the lanterns were extinguished and the night watch set. Her spinster existence didn't have much to recommend itself. But the twins would solve that problem for her. She didn't need a man to be happy.

Not that she hadn't had offers. Why, even on this trip she'd been accosted by soldiers proposing marriage.

As if she would ever marry a soldier.

"We should be nearing the fort. The sergeant said at breakfast we should arrive in the mid-afternoon." Fern half-stood, peering over the shoulder of the enlisted man driving the wagon. "We might even be able to see the trees along the river."

Seeing trees again would be nice. They'd encountered few since leaving Fort Davis, the last outpost at which they'd stayed. The ever-present knot in Priscilla's stomach tightened. Soon she would see the twins, her brother's beloved children. She would hold them in her arms, and together they would grieve and heal and become a family.

Teresa — known as Tessa — and Timothy. The niece and nephew she'd never met. How had they coped in the month since their parents died? Tears smarted her eyes. Tessa and Timothy were her only two relatives left.

And they've suffered the same fate as you, made fatherless by the army. Only they've lost their mother, too. Though the argument could be made that the army cost you your mother, too. She died inside when your father was killed, and she spent every day of the rest of her life mourning him until she finally slipped away.

The army had taken her parents and her sibling, but no more. The army would never take anything away from Priscilla again.

"I see something." Excitement leapt into Fern's voice.

Energy rippled through the soldiers around them. Footfalls became faster, reins were shaken up, and expressions lightened. Priscilla craned her neck, espying a dark smudge on the horizon. Shapes began to emerge, sorting themselves out into various structures.

They drew nearer, and the closer they got, the farther Priscilla's hopes dropped. Given the starkness of their surroundings, she shouldn't have expected much, but the huddle of adobe buildings did little to meet even the basest necessity for beauty. Someone had planted a ring of straggly trees, and there were squares of parched vegetable gardens, but everything looked dusty and sad. Cracked earthen paths led to and around the buildings, and over all hung the odor of . . . stables.

In the distance beyond the fort were trees in a winding line. That must be the river, the Rio Grande.

How had Christopher stood it here? Even more, how had his wife? How did any woman?

Priscilla looked out on the post and felt nothing but loneliness, grief, and apprehension. The sooner she got the children away from here, the better.

They turned to cross a shallow gully, edging down between bare dirt walls. The horizon disappeared and then the wagon lurched, hooves scrambled, and the ambulance was dragged up the other side. Priscilla scrambled to keep her seat, banging her elbow on the side of the wagon and letting out a yelp.

The buildings grew larger as they approached. Though she'd never been to Fort Bliss, she recalled the standard layout vaguely from her childhood, the open parade ground, the barracks, the officers' quarters, and so on, all arranged in the manner prescribed by the military manual and carried out on every western post. But the forts she'd lived at in Kansas as a child had stone and wood buildings, sloped roofs, white-painted trim, glass windows. Here the adobe, flat-roofed buildings seemed to poke up out of the earth like square mushrooms. Everything was the same desert sand color. Window holes gaped like blank eye sockets with warped, wooden shutters or cheesecloth in the openings.

A guard stopped them with an upraised hand as they reached the northeast corner of the fort, spoke to the officer in charge of their caravan, and motioned for them to enter the square of buildings. In the center of the open ground, a flagpole pierced the blue sky, the stars and stripes snapping in the stiff wind. One of the adobe buildings was under construction, men setting the baked-clay bricks into place, others smearing straw-laced mud on the walls. One long wooden structure she assumed was a barracks was undergoing roof repairs, a work crew hammering away in the hot sunshine. The ambulance lurched to a stop in front of this building. The men on the roof stopped

14

working to stare at the newcomers.

Priscilla's gaze moved from building to building. Which one housed the children? The telegram informing her of her brother and sister-in-law's deaths hadn't said just who had charge of the twins, only that they were being seen to. Probably one of the officers' wives. She scanned the row of smaller, identical buildings, a shade nicer than the barracks. Officer quarters. The children must be there.

"Fern!" A lean, sandy-haired soldier broke from the knot of men on the end of the porch, vaulting a stack of crates, and skidding to a halt beside the ambulance. "Oh, Fern-girl, you're finally here." He reached up and plucked her from her seat, wrapping her in his embrace and knocking her bonnet askew.

"Harry, Harry, oh, Harry," she chanted his name as he covered her face with kisses. Her laughter drifted out, and several soldiers hooted and whistled, stamping their boots and clapping. The couple seemed to remember their audience, and he let her slide to the ground, though he kept his arm around her waist.

"Fellows, this is Fern. We're getting married tomorrow." Harry's voice rang with pride and deep emotion, and he never took his eyes from Fern's face.

Priscilla blinked back a tear and searched the crowd again. What would it be like to be met in such a manner? As if no one else on earth existed, and as if every moment apart had been sheer agony?

"Ma'am?" The burly private who had driven the ambulance looked up at her. "Can I help you down?" His expression asked if she was going to stay up there forever.

"Of course." Priscilla gathered her reticule and her box of art supplies. She had little faith in the ability of the United States Cavalry to transport her belongings safely and preferred to keep her precious inks and pastels and papers under her own watchful eye. Her trunk was somewhere among the other baggage in the wagon train, and she only hoped it had survived the journey undamaged.

Once her feet were on solid ground, she glanced at her dress. The navy poplin with an openwork silk stripe wore a covering of dust like a shroud. She slapped at her skirt, raising clouds. It had been the same with her burgundy silk yesterday, and her pink lawn the day before. She might as well purchase some burlap sacking and wear that, since it was the only thing that might

16

hide the infernal dirt that coated everything. How did women out here stand it? She glanced up and stifled a gasp. A dozen soldiers now stood within arm's length, staring at her with blatant curiosity.

A squat, bristle-chinned, sun-dried soldier stepped off the porch and elbowed his way into the group. "Ooo-eee! Ma'am, you sure are a sight for these tired old eyes. I know Miss Fern belongs to Harry here — goodness knows he's talked of nothing else but that gal for months — but, if you don't mind my boldness, who do you belong to?"

She jerked upright. The man's hubris was beyond the pale. "I don't *belong* to anyone, sir."

"That's all right then." Elbows jabbed into sides, and the men shifted.

He clapped his hands once and rubbed them together before turning to the assembly. "She ain't married nor promised from what it sounds like."

Grins aplenty, and the soldiers crowded around once more. While it was flattering to have the attention of so many men at once, Priscilla grew distinctly uncomfortable.

"Hey, don't you fellows make a move until we can get down there. It ain't fair to have us treed up here when a pretty lady shows up."

Priscilla turned to look up at the roof of the barracks. A red-haired man with a barrel chest started over the parapet, grinning and trying to keep ahead of the others. He grabbed the top of the ladder, but there was a tussle, and with a holler, the man missed his footing and plummeted to the ground, landing with a thud that traveled up through the soles of Priscilla's shoes and raised a puff of Texas dirt that obscured him for a moment.

She sucked in a breath and forgot to release it. Was he dead?

Time stood still as the dust settled and nobody moved. Then the man let out a low groan and squirmed, and her heart started beating again. The air trickled out of her lungs, and her muscles loosened. She'd thought he might've broken his neck. Men hustled down the ladder and sped toward him, and the soldiers who had been surrounding Priscilla left her to go to the injured man.

"I think he's busted his leg. Somebody go get the doc."

Priscilla edged away from the crowd, clutching her box and reticule in one arm and holding her hat on with the other. Shock and weariness leached the strength from her limbs. The poor man.

Something jolted her shoulder, and she spun, her art box and purse flying out of her arm. Her hat toppled into her eyes, and before she could right it, firm hands gripped her upper arms. "Beg pardon, ma'am."

Shoving her hat back onto her hair, she stared up into the most beautiful, silvery-gray eyes she'd ever seen. Eyes the color of a coming storm and fringed with dark lashes. Eyes that pierced hers and stole her breath away. Her heart hiccupped, and she felt as if she'd swallowed a goose egg. She took in the insignia on his hat and collar. A major. Medical Corps. For a moment everything froze, and then his hands fell away and he turned toward the injured man.

Priscilla found herself threading her way through the knot of men surrounding the fallen soldier.

"Glad you're here, Major." The patient grimaced. "Looks like I need a doc."

The major was slim and straight as a steeple. The yellow line down the outside of his light blue pants accentuated the length of his legs. His navy coat rode his wide shoulders like a second skin, and dark, slightly curling hair fell on his collar. He knelt beside the injured man. Fabric stretched taut over the major's thighs, and sunlight gleamed on immaculate black boots. Though his every movement spoke of power and manliness, his long, slender fingers were gentle as he examined his patient.

"What happened?" His low-pitched voice rumbled out, setting butterflies to flapping in Priscilla's middle.

I wonder if his mustache is as soft as it looks. That frivolous and disjointed thought scampered across her mind, and heat started building around her lace collar and chasing up her cheeks. Where on earth had that come from? She wasn't some silly schoolgirl. A grown woman had no business wondering such things, especially about a stranger. And a soldier at that.

"Well?" He scanned the crowd of men leaning in close.

"Matthews was trying to get down here quick to meet the pretty new lady. Guess he came down a mite quicker than he planned." The soldier who spoke up couldn't cover up a snicker, but the doctor quelled it with a steely glance.

"He's fractured his femur. You two" — he pointed to two privates — "go fetch a litter and tell Samson to prepare the surgery for setting a bone."

They sped away. The man on the ground groaned again, and the major thumbed up one of the man's eyelids. "He might have a concussion as well."

The major's eyes met hers, and Priscilla couldn't look away. She didn't miss the disdain and even accusation in his stare. Surely he didn't blame her for the man's injury? Her indignation brought her back to herself, and she realized her hands were empty. Looking back to where the doctor had collided with her, she saw her possessions on the ground.

Her supplies! Oh, no! The box had burst open, scattering its contents. One of the ink bottles had broken, spilling the precious liquid into the indifferent dirt in a black puddle. Kneeling beside the chaos, her hands flitted over the chalks and dusty pen nibs. Those supplies, the badge of her occupation, had safely traveled fifteen hundred miles in her possession, only to be jarred and upset by a careless officer looking for fault where none existed.

Someone touched her shoulder, and she found herself looking up into the sunshine. Dazzled, she couldn't make out more than a silhouette against the white-blue sky. Blinking, she shielded her eyes. "Ma'am, I understand you need to see the commanding officer? I'd be happy to escort you there."

A dark-skinned face looked down at her. She'd heard that there were Negroes serving in the cavalry, but this was the first whom she'd seen in uniform. He squatted and helped her gather her belongings, holding the box open for her as she laid the least damaged bits into the trays.

"You can just leave that broken glass, ma'am. I'll come back and clean it up."

Rising, she couldn't help but glance once more at the doctor. He was busy with his patient and didn't look up at her. But he didn't have to. She wouldn't soon forget those piercing gray eyes or the accusing expression they'd held.

That woman has no more business being at a frontier fort than a crystal chandelier in a horse barn.

Slender as a willow reed, with shining dark hair and amber colored eyes. A woman like that would wreak havoc among the enlisted men. Already had, considering Matthews had taken a notion to fly off the roof at the sight of her. A little garden pansy that would wither under the hot desert sun. This country called for hardy stock, and the new arrival was anything but hardy from the look of her.

And what on earth did she think she was

dressed for? A cotillion? This was the frontier, not some Boston drawing room. All
those frills and furbelows wouldn't last a
month out here. Was she staying at the fort
or just passing through on her way to
California? Regardless, she'd need to get
more practical about her clothing if she
wanted to last in this part of the world.

Major Elliot Ryder assessed his patient's
condition. Femur breaks were the worst.
Painful, and took a long time to heal. His
mind raced ahead to what he would need to
do to set the bone.

The litter arrived, and one of the sergeants
barked for the men on the roofing detail to
get back to work, retaining a handful of
soldiers to help transport the patient.

"Get hold of him under the shoulders and
lift him when I say." Directing the men, Elliot supported the injured man's leg near
the break. "Now."

A shriek erupted from Matthews's lips,
and he stiffened, clawing at the air. His
thrashing made him difficult to hold, and
the men stopped moving halfway to the
stretcher.

"Keep going. Get it done." Elliot spoke
through his teeth, straining to keep the leg
immobile.

When they had Matthews on the litter,

23

they all breathed a sigh, some mopping their brows. The patient shifted his grip to the poles of the litter, holding them so hard his arms shook.

"Easy, Soldier. I'll get you something for the pain soon."

The litter-bearers, one on each corner, hefted him up and started toward the adobe structure behind the barracks, one of the few original dwellings left at the fort since the building boom. Eventually, Elliot would have a new stone hospital to house his infirmary and surgery, but for now, the old adobe was good enough.

Samson met him at the door. His faithful helper and friend, Samson was a former runaway slave who had attached himself to Elliot's regiment during the War and was one of the most dependable men he'd ever met. Elliot didn't know what he would've done without Samson's help, especially over the last month. His gentle ways and wise, obsidian eyes were a comfort since Elliot's world had been dumped on its ear just four weeks ago.

"Everything's ready." Samson stepped back, rubbing his palm over his short, graying hair, his knuckles large and knobby. "Infirmary's empty fo' now."

"Good, because this won't be pleasant."

Elliot turned left into the room he used for a surgery, dispensary, and office all in one. "Let's get him on the table. Samson, support that leg." He turned to the well-stocked shelves and inhaled deeply the smells he loved — vinegar, antiseptics, and over all, the earthy, fragrant aroma of hundreds of different herbs. Row upon row of glass jars and bottles greeted him on ranked shelves from floor to ceiling, each containing dried leaves, flower heads, stems, roots, tinctures, elixirs, unguents, all collected and prepared by him at his various postings. Lined up like his own private army against pain, illness, and suffering. He gathered several of the jars, reciting the names as he worked. "Arnica, comfrey, sorrel. Snakeroot and elderberry."

The leather-covered surgical table creaked under Matthews's weight as he was transferred from the litter. He groaned, stirring. Elliot glanced at the tray of instruments Samson had laid out. Perfect, though he hoped they wouldn't have to use the restraints. Cuffs and rope lay on the workbench nearby, ready to be attached to the short posts on each corner of the surgical table if they should be needed.

"You men can go. Samson will give me all the help I need." Elliot arranged his medicines, smothering a smile at the relieved expressions on the men as they filed out. One man stayed behind.

"He's my buddy, sir. I'd like to stay." He twirled his hat in his hands, his brow scrunched.

"Then stay out of the way. If you feel faint, sit down against the wall and put your head between your knees. I won't have time to catch you if you pass out."

The young man paled but nodded, setting his jaw. He was tall and thick-bodied, not unlike Matthews, with the shoulders of a buffalo bull. Elliot had a theory when it came to strong stomachs. The bigger they were, the harder they fell. He'd been proven right often enough, especially during the War. Some of the brawniest men he'd ever encountered were the first to faint at the sight of blood.

"Matthews, I need you to drink this." Elliot leaned close and lifted the man's head, holding a glass to his lips. "Just a few sips. It will help with the pain."

Samson removed the boot on Matthew's good leg. "What you want to do about the other?"

"Don't cut it off." The words came from the patient through clenched teeth. "I just got these boots."

Gripping Matthews's shoulder, Elliot nodded. "As precious as footgear is out here, you know we'll do our best to keep them in good shape. We're going to have to set that leg, and I won't kid you — it's going to hurt. Do you want us to tie you down, or can you take it? It's going to feel like we're playing tug-of-war with you."

"I can take it, but let's get to it. I don't know how long my nerve will last. Can I have some whiskey?" A hopeful light burned through some of the pain in his eyes.

"Let's see how what I gave you works first. We'll give it a few minutes." Elliot was loathe to give medicinal whiskey, and he had better options in his pharmaceutical arsenal, though many men were slow to believe it. Within a quarter of an hour the drugs he'd administered began to take effect. Matthews was slurring his words, and his eyes had gone cloudy and unfocused.

Time to begin.

The next half hour was something Elliot would not soon forget. Halfway through setting the bone, Matthews's buddy sank to the floor, moaning and holding his head in his hands. Matthews squeezed his eyes shut and held onto the table edges. The medicines had taken the worst of the edge off the pain, but it wasn't pleasant.

Samson was a rock, following Elliot's orders, never questioning, never seeming to hurry, but anticipating Elliot's needs. For his part, Elliot braced his weight and pulled on Matthews's ankle until he was sure the broken ends of the thigh bone were in alignment.

"I'll maintain the tension and the angle while you get those splints in place and wrap the leg, quick as you can." Sweat rolled down Elliot's temple and along his jawbone. "Hold on, Matthews. We're almost there."

Though it was only about an hour from the time of the fall to when they had him splinted and moved across the hall into the ward, Elliot felt he'd aged a decade. He wiped his forehead, rolling the stiff muscles in his neck and shoulders.

"You did well." He patted his patient's shoulder. "Things will get better now. I've mixed up a draft for you that will help you sleep." After giving the dose, he straightened. "You sit with him, Samson, and I'll clean up."

Elliot returned to the surgery, startled at hearing a groan. He'd forgotten about Matthews's friend. The private still huddled near the wall, and Elliot stooped to check on him. "How are you doing, Soldier?"

The young man raised his head, his eyes wide and blank, his face pale as alkali dust. "That —" he broke off to swallow. "That was awful. I had no idea. When his leg started moving . . ." He wobbled.

"Soldier." Elliot put some iron in his voice. "Pull yourself together." He rose. "Attention!"

Muscle memory and discipline took over, as Elliot had known it would. The young man snapped to his feet, chest out, arms locked, eyes straight ahead, though still pale and trembling.

"You will return to your duties immediately. You aren't paid by this man's army to loaf around here."

"Yes, sir." He snapped a salute, turned on his heel, and fled.

Elliot turned to the shambles on the work bench and surgery table. Piling instruments and bandages onto a tray, he planned out and reviewed a strategy for caring for his newest patient, as was his method. As soon as he finished cleaning up, he'd write everything in his records and inform Samson of the regimen of herbs and medicaments. They would need to work out a way to keep that leg immobile and provide some tension on it to help it mend straight.

He had just put the last of the equipment

away when a clattering and pounding akin to stampeding buffalo sounded on the porch boards and two seven-year-old little whirlwinds erupted into the hospital.

As always, Tessa spoke for the pair in a rush of words, barely stopping to breathe between questions. "Is it true? Did Matthews fall off the roof and break his leg? Is he dead? Did you have to cut his leg right off? I can't believe we missed it all."

The words tumbled out one on top of the other. Silently, Timothy adjusted the canteen slung crossways over his narrow chest and shoved his white-blond hair out of his eyes, while his twin sister, Tessa, eyes bluer than the center of candle flames, peeked out from under the brim of her kepi. He had no idea where she'd gotten the battered forage cap, but it had been her constant companion for the past month. What would her mother have said at her disheveled appearance? Once more he was swamped with feelings of inadequacy and loss. Why, when it was his own family who needed him, had his skills been inadequate? Why hadn't he been able to save his sister and brother-in-law?

Tessa's pink little mouth opened to start another barrage of questions, and he fell back on the only way he knew to gain control.

"Ten-hut." He barked the order.

They snapped to attention, shoulder to shoulder, eyes staring straight ahead and narrow shoulders thrown back, just as the woozy private had done moments before. One shoulder of Tessa's pinafore drooped onto her arm, and Timothy's cut-down army coat, still miles too big for him, had been buttoned askew. But they imitated the recruits they saw every day, straight as stair rods.

Elliot clasped his hands behind his back and paced the open floor in front of them, considering what to tell them and what they might pick up from listening to the soldiers. "He did fall off the roof. He did break his leg. He is not dead. I did not have to amputate. Now where have you two been?" Since Tessa had straw in her hair, and the distinctive odor of horse drifted about the twins, he had a pretty good idea.

"Samson told us we could go visit our ponies." Tessa glanced up at him out of the corner of her eye. "There were lots of new horses and soldiers. A new company arrived, though they aren't staying for long. Dusty said they brought a couple of ladies with them. Not laundresses, but real ladies.

31

One of them is set to marry Lieutenant Dunn, but Dusty didn't know who the other one was." She frowned. "He sure talked about her a lot though, and he says a woman as pretty as she is won't go un-branded for long. He says it's a miracle she made it this far without someone throwing a loop at her. What does that mean? Is someone going to tie her up like a maverick cow?" Her little nose screwed up, and she tilted her head to the side before remembering she was supposed to be at attention.

"Unlikely. I believe Corporal Rhodes was referring to someone asking for the lady's hand in marriage."

"Dusty says a woman like that on a military post is nothing but trouble, but he said he'd die a happy man if he could suffer that kind of trouble every day for the rest of his life." Tessa rolled her eyes and shook her head. "I think he'd been nipping at his 'special canteen' again. He wasn't making any sense."

Elliot blew out a breath. The children encountered far too much gossip when hanging around the stables. He'd have to speak with Dusty again. The kids thought the world of the horseman, and Tessa in particular was prone to repeat everything he said, wise or not. Though he had to admit,

Dusty was probably accurate in his prognosticating this time. A beautiful woman was bound to cause trouble. And this one had already caused Matthews a bushel of pain.

Once more he found her image invading his thoughts. Skin smooth as porcelain, lips dusky as a summer rose, and eyes as big and liquid as a newborn colt — what was he doing? He shook his head and forced himself to stop that river of thought. He of all people should know better than to judge a woman by how she looked, and what on earth had gotten into him to rhapsodize about a girl he didn't even know? He scowled and smoothed one side of his mustache. She had no place in his thoughts or his life, and she certainly had no business on a military installation on the frontier. Still, by nightfall half the regiment would be besotted, and some silly fool was bound to marry her. It happened every time an unattached female landed at the fort. Though why this time it should bother him so much was beyond his ability to comprehend at the moment.

Tessa broke form, clasped her hands under her chin, and hopped in place. Timothy elbowed her, shoving his shoulders back and scowling to remind her they were supposed to be standing at attention.

"Stand still, Tess," he hissed. "What are you doing?"

She elbowed him back but resumed her proper stance. "Don't you see?" She spoke out of the side of her mouth, as if Elliot wouldn't overhear. "If she's going to get married to a soldier anyway, she can marry Uncle Elliot. He needs someone to take care of him, and then we'd kind of be like a family again."

The wistfulness in her voice stabbed Elliot's heart like a Comanche war lance, but he knew he had to stem her thoughts immediately. This wasn't the first time Tessa had hinted — more than hinted — that he needed to find a wife, something she'd learned from her mother, his sister. Rebekah had been after him for a long time to take a bride.

"Don't start spinning fairy tales, Tessa. I have no intention of getting married. I am a bachelor, and I intend to stay that way." He had no desire to stick his neck into that particular noose, especially not if the bride was the arresting beauty he'd collided with earlier. Tessa needed to face reality, and hearing it out loud wouldn't hurt him either. "And if I was to marry, it certainly wouldn't be to a decorative piece of baggage straight from the east. I'd want someone plain and sensible, someone who could take the two of you hooligans in hand and bring you up right." He held up his hand when Tessa started to speak. "I've said all I'm going to say on this topic. You'll just have to make the best of things, Tess. I'm not getting married, not to one of the laundresses, not to the chaplain's niece who visited last month, and certainly not to a stranger who has no business being west of the Mississippi."

A mutinous pout struck the little girl's mouth, so reminiscent of her mother when she was young that a pang of guilt and grief swept over him. But though her eyes brimmed with things she wanted to say, she held her tongue.

A miracle, that.

The strains of a bugle drifted on the air.

Timothy perked up. "Boots and Saddles. Can we go watch mounted drill?" Timothy loved everything to do with horses, and he never seemed to tire of watching the men drill on horseback.

"You may, but stay out of the way and stay out of trouble. In fact, it would be best if you stayed on the barracks porch. Don't wander off."

They were outside before he finished, their legs churning, feet kicking up dust. Neither had bothered to close the door, and he shook his head as he performed the task. Again the feeling of inadequacy swept over him. What was he — a bachelor of thirty — doing raising two children? *Raising* was rather too grand a term for it. They were running wild as tumbleweeds on the wind. In one thing Tessa was right. They needed a proper family. Too bad they were stuck with him.

CHAPTER TWO

"Standing orders, ma'am. All newcomers to the post must report to the colonel." The dark-skinned soldier walked along the path, keeping a respectable distance between them and his eyes straight ahead. Each time they encountered another soldier, he would stop and either salute or return a salute, standing straight as a yardstick and crisp as starched cotton.

Priscilla grew exasperated when this maneuver occurred for the third time in twenty paces. "How on earth do you get anything done with all this stopping and saluting?" Her nerves, already on edge, stretched thinner. She only wanted to get this meeting with the post commander over so she could see her niece and nephew.

"We're on the parade ground, ma'am." He glanced at her, clearly expecting her to understand. "Things are more formal on the parade ground."

Priscilla shrugged. She wouldn't be here long enough to relearn the rules and customs of the United States Army. When the next eastbound transportation left this pile of sand and creosote called Fort Bliss, she intended to be on it with the children and never visit another military post for the duration of her days.

"Officer country." Her escort gestured to the three buildings on the west side of the post. "Commander's house in the middle, officers' quarters on either side."

Her heartbeat kicked up. This must be where the twins were. Her brother had been a captain. He and his family would've been quartered here. Surely one of their fellow officers, or more likely an officer's wife, had stepped in to care for the twins until Priscilla could arrive and claim them. Priscilla owed whoever it was a debt for caring for the children in their fresh grief.

On the porch of one of the officers' quarters, Fern's boxes and cases had been piled. She emerged from the doorway with Harry, pointing and directing. Her face glowed. She would be a beautiful bride. Priscilla only hoped she didn't regret marrying a soldier.

"This way, ma'am."

Priscilla picked up her hem and mounted

the low steps to the commander's quarters. The door opened, and a young soldier stood back to allow her entrance.

"Visitor to see the colonel." Her escort left her.

The soldier holding the door asked, "Who is it I should say is calling, ma'am?"

"I'm Priscilla Hutchens. I've just arrived from Cincinnati." She eyed the long, narrow hallway bisecting the small house. Sunshine streamed in the back door at the end of the hall and doors opened off to the right and left. The tantalizing aroma of supper cooking drifted from the rear of the house. A proper supper, not the camp fare she'd eaten for so many days.

He led her into a small front parlor dominated by a large horse-hair-covered sofa. The floor was carpeted, a luxury Priscilla hadn't anticipated. She took a closer look, realizing that the carpet had been stretched over a dirt floor. Ugh.

Everything in the room was masculine save for a dainty rocker covered in needlepoint rose cushions and a sewing basket slung on a frame nearby. Whitewashed adobe walls with only a clock and a mounted deer's head to break up the plainness. After the busy wallpaper and clutter and knickknack craze of current décor back

39

east, it was almost restful.

The soldier waved to the settee and took her art box and bag to set on a side table. "Welcome to Fort Bliss. Please, have a seat. My name is Private Simmons. I'm the colonel's striker. I hope you had a pleasant journey. The colonel is working in his office across the hall. I'll tell him you're here."

"No need, Private." A tall, spare man with gray hair and whiskers entered the room before she could sit down. Gold braid and bright brass buttons decorated his navy tunic, and something about his bearing reminded her of a childhood memory . . . of her father, perhaps?

"I'm Colonel Bracken. Welcome to Fort Bliss."

She held out her hand. "Colonel. Miss Priscilla Hutchens."

His eyebrows rose. "Miss Hutchens, Captain Hutchens's sister, of course. Allow me to express my condolences." He took her hand between both of his. "The captain and your sister-in-law were wonderful people, and we miss them greatly. It was a shame, that fever catching them both."

"Thank you."

He gestured to the sofa. "Private, inform my wife that we have a guest. Please, Miss Hutchens, do sit down. I'm sure you've had a long journey. I'll confess, your arrival has caught me a bit by surprise. I had no idea you were en route to the fort."

Lowering herself to the hard sofa, she pressed her toes into the floorboards to keep from sliding off the slick horsehair. She smoothed her skirts and folded her hands in her lap. "I suppose I should've sent word ahead, but frankly, when I got the news, I had no other thought than to come to the children as quickly as I could. It took me several days to get my affairs in order and let my employer know I would be taking leave. With that and travel time, it's taken me a month to finally arrive."

A small woman breezed into the room, her eyes bright, and her smile quick. "My, my, my, look at you, dear." She held out her hands. "You're going to create quite a stir here." Bending quickly, she kissed Priscilla's cheek. "I'm so sorry for your loss, dear, but welcome to Fort Bliss all the same. You've come to visit the children, I expect? Of course you have. The little dears." She settled into the tiny rocker and set it into motion. Though gray streaked her hair and wrinkles lined her face, her eyes had a youthful sparkle.

"Thank you. I'm anxious to see them. How are they holding up?" These formali-

41

ties had Priscilla champing at the bit. All she wanted to do was to wrap her arms around the twins and draw them close. She'd come all this way and didn't even know where they were.

"Oh, as well as possible, I suppose. Children are so resilient. They have their moments, I'm sure, but they'll be fine. Especially now that you've come for a visit. They'll enjoy having a female family member, someone gentle in the midst of all this military masculinity." Mrs. Bracken laughed, smoothing back her gray-streaked brown hair. "How long can you stay?"

"Just until the transport headed east comes through."

"Oh? Goodness, they're through here all the time. They'd come even more frequently, I think, if they weren't afraid of Indian trouble. I hope this summer is more peaceful than the last few." She leaned over and patted her husband's arm. "Silly me, prattling on when she's come such a long way and must be tired."

The colonel smiled, as if he was well used to his wife's prattling and didn't mind it in the least. "There are just a few details to cover, Miss Hutchens, that I tell all civilians. I'm sure you'll have no difficulty." He stretched his long legs out and straightened the yellow line along the outer seam of his pants. "I must caution you not to leave the confines of the fort without a military escort. We are in the heart of Apache country, and they are an unpredictable people. Also, as my wife said, wagon trains come through here frequently. The San Antonio–El Paso Trail rolls right behind the quartermaster's warehouse. This means teamsters, traders, and emigrants headed to California. The emigrants don't give us much trouble, but the teamsters can be a rough crowd. If you go into town, be sure you have an escort along. And be back before nightfall. El Paso isn't exactly flush with choirboys, if you get my meaning. It's best to be in by nightfall." He smiled. "Other than that, I'm sure the children can fill you in on the rules. We do hope you'll enjoy your stay here and that you'll partake of some of the social activities."

Mrs. Bracken clapped her small hands. "Oh yes, there's the wedding tomorrow, and we're planning a dinner party here soon."

"Thank you, that's very nice of you, but I'm hoping not to be here too long. I only want to . . ."

"Yes, of course, the children must come first. I'm sure you're anxious to see them, and here we are keeping you." Mrs. Bracken's chair rocked harder. "We'll have Simmons take you to them right away."

Private Simmons entered the room before she could call. He must've been listening in the hall. Priscilla had the feeling that not much happened in this house without his knowledge.

"Take Miss Hutchens to the infirmary, Private." The colonel reached for his pipe and tobacco on the shelf beside his chair.

The infirmary? Her eyebrows rose and her heart tripped. "Are the children ill?" Fever had taken her brother and his wife. Had the children come down with the same malady?

"Oh, no, of course not. They're hale and hearty." He tamped the tobacco into the pipe bowl. "They're in the care of the post physician, Major Ryder."

A feathering of unease tickled her skin. The post physician, with the piercing gray eyes and accusatory look. If he'd been given care of the children, he must be married. Her disappointment at this information surprised her, and she took another firm grip on her imagination.

"They've been well looked after this past month, but I'm sure Major Ryder will appreciate you coming all this way for a visit. Private Simmons, let's not keep Miss Hutchens any longer." The colonel waved his long, lean hand. "We'll see you tomorrow at the wedding, I'm sure. Enjoy your stay at Fort Bliss, and if you need anything, Major Ryder will be able to help you, I'm sure. If not, come to me or my wife. We're all one big family here, and we look out for our own."

The private walked at a brisk pace, carrying her art box, and before she could gather her wits, they were crossing an open space behind two long, adobe buildings toward a rather ramshackle structure between the fort and the river. "The infirmary is this way. That's where the major is most days."

Priscilla picked up her hem and tried to keep up with the private's long strides. Dozens of mounted men had been wheeling and turning on the open square at the center of the fort accompanied by drums and shouted commands. The horses moved with such precision, and sunlight bounced off the metal bits of their harness. The dirt they kicked up rose above the buildings and drifted lazily toward the river to the south. If she wasn't in such a hurry to see the twins, she would've liked a few moments to watch the riders, but Private Simmons wasted no time in sightseeing.

He led her into the building and stopped her in the hallway between two open doors.

"Sickroom's here. Best not go in there without permission, what with the patients being mostly men. Wouldn't want to shock your sensibilities, ma'am."

"Of course." She tried to quell the color creeping up her cheeks, and knew she hadn't been successful when a smile teased the man's lips.

"Major? Got a visitor here for you, sir." Simmons stuck his head into the other doorway. "You can come in. He's alone."

Priscilla checked her skirts, straightening the folds, and patted her hair. Hopefully she didn't look too disheveled. She'd dealt with difficult men before. Not everyone at the catalog company had been happy when the board had hired her as the art director. After all, no woman had held the position before. She could surely handle one physician. In fact, he'd probably be so glad she'd arrived to take the twins off his hands he'd fall at her feet.

She stepped into the room, immediately hit with the smells of vinegar and herbs. Hundreds of glass jars lined the shelves on one wall. She blinked. How many medicines did one doctor need?

The major turned in his chair, a pencil in his hand. Once again she was struck by his handsome looks. The pale gray eyes were

46

even more piercing than she remembered. He stood, tall and masculine and totally sure of himself.

"Can I help you?" He had a deep, pleasant voice at odds with the frown that came over his face. "Are you ill, perhaps?"

"No. I'm fine." She swallowed. His stare pinned her to the spot like a gauche schoolgirl facing her headmaster. What was wrong with her, getting tongue-tied like this? She groped for some professional aplomb. "Actually, I'm here to help you. I'm Priscilla Hutchens. I understand you've had the care of my niece and nephew. I've come to take them off your hands."

Confusion clouded his expression. "Come to take them off my hands? What are you talking about?"

"The twins. Tessa and Timothy Hutchens, my late brother's children. I was given to understand you'd been looking after them since their parents died." Priscilla knotted her fists in her skirts. Had she misunderstood the colonel? "I came as soon as I could to get them. I'm sure you and your wife will be relieved someone of their own has finally shown up to take them."

He smoothed his mustache with the side of his finger. "You seem to be laboring under several misapprehensions. I *do* have care of the children, but there seems to be some mix-up. They're not going anywhere. They're staying here."

"There does seem to be a mix-up. I'm their aunt, their only living relative. My brother was their father. I've come to take them home with me."

The major leaned his hip against his desk and crossed his arms. "I'm afraid you're mistaken. You aren't their only living relative."

"Well, you can hardly count their second and third cousins in Pittsburgh. I haven't spoken to them in years."

"That isn't what I mean." He shook his head as if she was the one being dense. "What I meant was, they have other relatives. On their mother's side."

This gave Priscilla pause. "Have they contacted you about taking the children?"

"No. I mean, they don't need to. I have custody of the children. I am Rebekah's brother. The twins' uncle. I'm sorry you had such a long trip for nothing, but the kids are being taken care of quite well. You are, of course, welcome to visit them, but taking them won't be necessary."

His words hit like blows. He was their uncle? Her mind scrambled to assimilate this new information. "I had no idea. My brother never mentioned that Rebekah had a brother." Even if he had, Priscilla would never have assumed he would eagerly take on the care and raising of the children. She'd only thought of the twins in relation to herself, that they were somehow hers alone.

"She does. Did." A shadow passed over his face. "Not to mention, we also have two more sisters, and our parents are still alive in Wisconsin."

"Do you have plans to send the twins there then?"

"No. They stay with me. It's what their parents wanted." His voice was firm.

"They left a will?" Her hopes began to fade. If her brother had put his wishes into writing, she'd have no chance of changing this man's mind.

"No. There was nothing official. But my sister begged me on her deathbed to take the children and raise them as my own. She loved army life and wanted her children raised here. I intend to honor her wishes."

"What about what my brother wanted? Did he ask you to care for the children?"

"No, I'm sorry to say there wasn't time. The fever took him too quickly. He dropped down in the middle of a drill, and beyond a few mumbles, never really came to his senses again. But he obviously wanted his children raised here, or he wouldn't have been in the army."

She groped for any foothold. Surely her claim was as strong as his. He was their uncle, but she was their aunt. It was up to her to make sure the children didn't suffer out here a day longer than necessary. "Perhaps your wife might feel differently, raising children not her own? Might she prefer me to take them?"

"Sorry, but that is another mistake you've made. I'm not married. No wife to consider. Besides, any woman I married would be more than happy to raise the twins because it's the right thing to do. Not that I have any plans to marry." He crossed his ankles, his knee-high boots gleaming.

"Surely being raised by a bachelor on the frontier isn't optimal. They would be better off with me back in Cincinnati in a stable environment, with security and good schools and opportunities. They need a home and a family." She found herself clutching her purse and forced her fingers to relax.

"I take it you're not married then? You introduced yourself as Priscilla Hutchens." He ran his finger down his temple.

"No, I'm not married."

"Then how is what you're offering them

any different than me?" He spread his hands and shrugged, tilting his head. "Neither of us is married."

"You *are* married."

"Excuse me? I've just explained to you that I don't have a wife." His eyebrows went high.

"You're married to the military. The cavalry will always come first. No matter where they send you, you will go. No matter the danger or the crude accommodations or provisions, you will go, and you'll drag those children with you. The army doesn't care about families. Not to mention the risks. What if you go out on patrol some day and don't come back? What happens to the children then? Better that they come with me now than suffer another bereavement and upheaval."

"It's clear to me you know nothing about military life or what your brother and my sister wanted for the children. All of life has risks. I could ask you the same question regarding your existence in whatever eastern city you come from. What if you were taken ill and died? What if you were struck down by a wagon on a busy street? If you had the children, what would become of them then? Taking them to live in the city won't guarantee they won't suffer bereavement. But I'd

51

rather have them here in a place they love and are familiar with than uproot them and take them away from the only life they've ever known."

The man was insufferable with his assumptions and patronizing tone. "I might know more about military life than you give me credit for. I know what it is like to have your father sent out on a patrol in the dead of winter only to freeze to death in a blizzard. I know what it is like to be dragged from pillar to post, leaving behind your home and your friends when some general in Washington decides to shake things up a bit. And I know what it is like for a grieving widow to live out her days on a meager pension that the government decided was all her husband was worth, though he gave his life to protect his country. So don't tell me I am acting out of ignorance. I know what is best for those children, and it isn't living by the bugle and the drum."

He stiffened. "We're through talking about this. The children are staying here. They are happy here, adjusting to their loss as well as can be expected, and I won't have them upset. You're welcome to visit them, but there will be no talk of them leaving here when you go."

Never had it occurred to her that anyone

would object to her taking the children, especially not this steely-eyed doctor. Despair and determination warred in her chest, and she found herself gripping her fingers into fists. Forcing herself to relax, Priscilla wandered over to the shelves, hoping that by stepping back, she could come at the problem from a new angle and make him see the error of his thinking.

Each jar was labeled, but she squinted, trying to make out the names. The penmanship was atrocious. She could just about make out the first letter of each word, but beyond that, nothing. Inside the jars resided stems, stalks, dried leaves, flower heads, all manner of plant material. "This is quite a collection. What do you do with all of them?"

Major Ryder joined her, taking down one of the jars and removing the lid. He breathed deeply, closing his eyes. Priscilla caught a whiff of a grassy, musky scent. He replaced the lid and the container. "They're all medicinal. I'm making a study of Indian herbal medicine. Over the past several years, I've collected hundreds of samples. This is angelica." He tapped the label.

"Your assistant needs some lessons in penmanship. I can't read any of these."

He frowned. "I don't have an assistant. I

wrote these."

An awkward silence followed. Pricilla found herself plucking at her cuff. She was saved having to find something to say by an eruption into the room. Shoes pounded the floorboards, and two tow-headed tornadoes skidded to a stop. Tessa hunched her thin shoulders and launched into speech. "Uncle Elliot, guess what? A Kickapoo band has been sighted coming up from their winter grounds. Dusty says on Saturday there's going to be an expedition to visit their camp and we can go if you say yes."

Timothy ignored both Tessa and his uncle, staring up at Priscilla. She swallowed hard. He looked so much like his father, her brother, that her heart constricted.

"Ten-hut!"

Priscilla blinked. In an instant the twins snapped to attention. The major did, too, snapping his boot heels together and putting on a stern expression.

"This is the second time today you've come pelting into the infirmary like buffalo calves. It's sloppy and undisciplined, and you've been trained better. I expect better." He clasped his hands behind his back and paced the floor in front of the twins. "I gave you leave to watch the training, and you were to return here the minute it was over."

He glanced at the pendulum clock on the far wall. "You are precisely eight minutes overdue. Would you care to explain your tardiness?"

Timothy's face flushed, and Tessa's lower lip stuck out. Finally, the boy said, "We stopped to talk to Dusty, sir. It won't happen again, sir."

The appalled feeling in Priscilla's chest grew. He was treating these children like raw recruits in need of a sergeant. The children, though standing at attention and facing forward, looked her over from the corners of their eyes, clearly curious. The major seemed to have forgotten her presence entirely. She cleared her throat, barely refraining from scooping the twins up and spiriting them away from their domineering uncle. Their situation was even worse than she'd feared.

"See that it doesn't. At ease, children. As you can see, we have a guest." Major Ryder tilted his head in her direction.

The kids relaxed, and Tessa shoved an unruly curl off her forehead. Her heart-shaped face lit up as she surveyed Priscilla from hair to hem. "Say, are you the lady who knocked Matthews off the roof?"

Elliot bit back a chuckle at the woman's

outraged expression. Trust Tessa to drop a cat among the pigeons. He hadn't missed the disapproval on Miss Hutchens's face when he'd ordered the twins to stand at attention, nor the pinched mouth when they'd called him sir. She clearly had a grudge against the military caused by losing her father — and fed, no doubt, by reading all sorts of claptrap printed in eastern newspapers and magazines.

Miss Hutchens's spine threatened to snap, she stood so stiffly. "I beg your pardon. I did no such thing. The poor man lost his footing and fell."

"But if he hadn't been trying to get a better look at you, you being so pretty and all, he wouldn't have lost his footing and tried to fly off the roof. Uncle Elliot said he broke his leg, and he'll be laid up for weeks." Tessa hitched her shawl up over her shoulders.

"Tessa, that's enough." Elliot frowned at her.

She pressed her lips together, but her expression said she had a lot more to say.

Though Tessa had brought up a point that should be addressed. "Tessa's right in one aspect. The men aren't used to having beautiful single women arrive at the fort. They'll be tripping over themselves to get a gander at you, to get close to you. If you aren't careful, you could give these impressionable young men the wrong idea, especially as you have made your feelings about the military life so plain to me. With the least bit of encouragement, you could incite these men to riot. It might be best if you kept your visit short and to stay away from the men as much as possible."

Miss Hutchens blinked, her pink lips parting as she sucked in a breath. "You think I'm beautiful?"

Elliot squashed his desire to smack his forehead. Out of everything he'd said, she picked out that to focus on? Just like a woman. "Ma'am, the truth is, the men would notice any woman, even one that looked like the south end of a northbound mule. I just don't want to have any more patients in my infirmary because you were parading around the post smiling and batting your eyelashes." Confounded woman didn't understand his point, even when he laid it out in front of her. Enough of this nonsense.

He drew the twins to stand before him, facing Priscilla. "Kids, this is Miss Hutchens, your aunt, your dad's sister. She's come for a *short* visit." *And she's not taking you when she goes.*

"Our aunt?" Their gazes locked on their

guest. Elliot didn't miss the glisten of tears on Miss Hutchens's lashes.

She knelt before the children and opened her arms, drawing them into her embrace. "I'm so glad to see you both. I came as soon as I could."

Neither child exactly melted into her arms. Timothy cast a get-me-out-of-this, plea-filled expression toward Elliot, and Tessa squirmed out of the hug as quickly as she could. They both edged back to stand one on either side of him. Priscilla rose slowly, trying and not succeeding in keeping the hurt from her face.

"I'm your Aunt Priscilla. Your father was my older brother. I'm so sorry for your loss."

They shrugged and nodded, and for the first time, Elliot realized the three of them, himself and the twins, weren't the only ones grieving. Priscilla had lost a brother. He felt a pang of guilt for thinking only of his own loss and the kids'. She might be a misguided easterner, but she was also a bereaved sibling who had traveled hundreds of miles to see her niece and nephew. The least he could do was be hospitable.

"Kids, why don't you go see what Samson's cooked up for supper and get washed up? Tell him I'll be a few minutes yet." They scampered out as if they'd been let

58

out of school early.

Priscilla took a handkerchief from her sleeve and dabbed at her eyes. "I'm sorry."

Her voice wobbled a bit, and for an instant she looked so much like Tessa in spite of her dark hair and eyes. He felt more of a heel than ever. "You'll have to excuse the children. They're not used to having family drop in out of nowhere. They'll warm up to you, and then you won't have a moment's peace for your whole visit."

She tucked the bit of lace and lawn back into her sleeve and nodded, lifting her chin as if embarrassed by her show of weakness. "You don't have to keep stressing the point that I'm only here for a short visit. I will leave when I'm good and ready, and that will be when the children can go with me."

"Then you're going to be here a good long time." Elliot regretted any softening toward her. She was made of steel and as tenacious as a bear trap. "Speaking of which, where did you plan to stay during your *visit*?"

Her pert little mouth opened and closed. "I assumed there would be lodging available."

"You assumed wrongly. The officers' quarters are full up. Even Lieutenant Dunn is bunking with the enlisted men tonight so his bride-to-be can have a bed for the night."

59

"Surely there's somewhere. The colonel's house?"

"Nope. Mrs. Colonel Bracken has her two spinster sisters staying with her, so her guest room is full up. You can't exactly bunk down in the barracks. You didn't give this little mission of mercy much thought, did you?"

"My only thought was to come to the children as quickly as I could. I had no idea that hospitality was so lacking with the US Cavalry, though I shouldn't be surprised. The army has been kicking me in the teeth my entire life." She turned and headed for the door.

"Where are you going?"

She stopped, gripping the doorjamb. "First to find some place to sleep for the night. Tomorrow, I intend to find the closest telegraph station."

"What for?"

"I must telegraph my employers to let them know I will be detained longer than I had anticipated. You say you won't give up the children, and I'm not leaving here without them. Your claim as their uncle is no stronger than mine as their aunt, and I intend to make you see reason."

"You're assuming you're the reasonable one in this conversation?" He smothered a smile.

Her head came up, and her eyes snapped fire. "Of course I am. Those children are not going to be left here to be barked at and treated like soldiers. They're going to grow up in a home with security and love. Security and love that your way of life can never provide."

"You know nothing about my way of life."

"I know it took my father and brother from me. I know that the army cares nothing for the families of the officers and enlisted men. But I care. I care about those children."

"You don't even know them. If you cared so much, why is this the first time they've ever met you?"

"Our family was estranged, thanks to the army. My brother chose the army over my mother and me."

"That's not the way I understood it. Chris told me his mother refused to speak to him when he told her he was going to continue in the army after the War. That she'd always hated the military and disowned him when he chose to follow in his father's footsteps."

"What happened between my mother and brother is none of your business."

"I think it is. Your family caused my sister much heartache, and now you want to barge in here and take her children away. Well, lady, I'll fight you tooth and nail. My sister and her husband wanted those children raised here, and I intend to follow their wishes."

A knock cut through their animosity. Private Simmons shouldered his way through the door carrying several bags.

"Major Ryder, Colonel Bracken sent me over with Miss Hutchens's belongings. He says you should bunk in with Sergeant Plover so Miss Hutchens can have your bed."

Elliot closed his eyes. Invite the enemy into his home? Give up his bed and bunk in with Plover, who snored like a drunken bull? And yet, when the commanding officer issued an order, he had no choice but to obey.

"Very well, Private."

He didn't miss the gleam of triumph in Priscilla's eyes. She may have won this battle, but she would not win the war.

Priscilla slipped into bed that night, trying hard not to think about it being his bed. His bed reluctantly given up for her use. She nestled her head on the feather pillow and stretched her toes, luxuriating in finally being able to relax after her long and trying day.

Nothing had gone according to her plans.

In her imaginings, she had been greeted with warmth and heralded as something of a heroine, coming to the rescue of her young niece and nephew, taking them away from the scene of their hardship and grief, surrounding them with love, providing them with a home.

Instead, she'd been met with distrust, distance, and refusal. And at the heart of them was Major Elliot Ryder. Good looks and educated manner aside, the man was a brute. Look how he treated the children like little soldiers. Making them stand at attention and follow military protocol. They might as well be prisoners.

Her heart ached for Timothy and Tessa. Timothy who studied everything and said little and looked so much like her brother. At dinner, his mannerisms had reminded her so strongly of Chris, she'd almost burst into tears.

And Tessa, little miss quicksilver. So talkative, in spite of the major's efforts to quell her. She seemed to be bursting with energy and drive, sitting still with great difficulty. At dinner, she'd picked at her food, staring at Priscilla over her fork. Several times the major had told her to get on with the business of eating before he removed her plate altogether.

Then there was Samson. A grizzle-haired black man who seemed to be half-servant, half-family retainer. He brought the food to the table then sat down and ate with the family. Priscilla had never shared a meal with a black man before, and she had to remind herself not to stare. Samson's manners were impeccable, and he even gently moved Tessa's elbow off the table a time or two. He and the major spoke about the injured man in the infirmary, almost as if Samson were a physician, too.

Then there was the major. Elliot. With his piercing gray eyes and broad shoulders. The man was determined to thwart her altruistic efforts. He was determined to keep the children here. And yet, she had to give him his due. He had given up his bed for her. And fed her. And given her access to the children.

Lord, I don't know what to do. I thought You wanted me to come get these children, to make a home for them and give them the family they need. I felt Your leading to come here so strongly. But now the major won't let me take the children? What should I do? My heart is breaking for Tessa and Timothy. They've lost so much, and they're in need of a woman's love. My claim to the children is as valid, as strong, as his. But how can I get him to see that letting me have the children is the best course?

A flinty look invaded his eyes the moment she mentioned taking custody of the children, a set to that jaw that bespoke a stubbornness she wasn't sure how to break.

Still, it was only her first day here. Perhaps, if she observed him closely, if she got to know the children better, and if she could logically and unemotionally present her case, surely then he would see the rightness of her plan and let the children go.

Give up his sister's children to a perfect stranger? Never! Elliot wriggled his shoulders, trying to find a comfortable spot on the straw-tick mattress. The bedding was so thin, the ropes crisscrossing the frame dug into his spine. Not to mention the blaring sounds coming from the other bunk. Sergeant Plover had no roommate for a reason. His snoring practically rattled the glass in the window.

Another sonorous blast rent the night air, and Elliot resisted the urge to throw a boot at the somnolent sergeant. He, a major, a post physician, had been rousted out of his comfortable bed. Though he could 'rank out' one of the other officers of lower rank, he couldn't bring himself to do it. Why turn out one of the lieutenants or captains, especially those with wives and kids? Any superior officer could pull rank and take the billet of any junior officer, and Elliot had seen men of equal rank pull out their calendars to calculate who had been in the service longer when it came to claiming officer housing. As a physician, he'd always had his own quarters near the infirmary, so he'd never "ranked out" another officer or been ranked out himself.

Until now.

Ranked out by that supercilious eastern miss who wanted to abscond with the twins.

And who smelled like roses.

He shook his head and rolled to his side. Where had that come from? Sure, she was pretty enough. Downright beautiful, really, but that shouldn't matter. If anything, it should put him further on his guard. He had more than enough reason to be wary of beautiful women.

He'd give her a week out here, with her fussy hair and stylish clothes. A week of frontier living would send her racing back to civilization.

Without the children.

CHAPTER THREE

Army women didn't lack for ingenuity, Priscilla would give them that much. Fern and Harry's wedding was set for two o' clock, and with the precision of a military drill, the women marshaled their forces and resources, creating a festive atmosphere for the nuptials seemingly out of thin air.

Mrs. Bracken was everywhere, ordering people around, but so nicely no one took umbrage.

"Private Zeller, move those tables together so we can spread them with a cloth." She pointed and motioned. "And drag the benches out of the barracks so folks will have a place to sit."

"You there, sweep this path. It looks as if an entire supply train barged through here."

"I wish it was later in the year. We'd have better flowers."

Priscilla had to hand it to Mrs. Bracken. She managed the soldiers as if *she* were the post commander.

Tablecloths snapped open and drifted down over the rough boards. Cutlery and table service appeared, as well as food from the officers' quarters and the soldiers' mess. Small bunches of wildflowers graced the tables, and Mrs. Bracken draped some pretty blue fabric along the porch railing of the commander's house where the ceremony was to take place.

"Your answers arrived, ma'am." The young man who had been manning the telegraph station in the colonel's office handed her two folded pieces of paper. He touched his hat and jogged away. She opened the telegrams. The first was from her boss.

PRAYING FOR SUCCESSFUL RESOLUTION AS SOON AS POSSIBLE. NEED YOU FOR WINTER CATALOG ILLUSTRATIONS. SEPT. 1ST AT THE LATEST. MR. CARTERSON.

Nodding to herself, she tucked that page away. Mr. Carterson was a dear man to work for. When she'd told him of her brother's death and the need to go get the children, he'd helped her with her travel arrangements and suggested she take a few weeks off after they arrived back in Cincinnati to get the children settled in their new home. And here he was extending her time off even more. A girl couldn't ask for a better boss.

The other telegram wasn't as encouraging.

CANNOT HOLD YOUR ROOM. FOUND NEW RENTER. MISS BISBY HOLDING YOUR POSSESSIONS. BAUMGARTNER.

Her landlady had found a new renter for her room. She supposed that was to be expected, but the thought of having nowhere to return to in the city was a daunting one, especially with the children in tow. But on the other hand, the idea was quite freeing. She could pursue her dream of settling into a house right away. The elderly lady who had roomed next to her at Baumgartner's Boardinghouse, Gertrude Bisby, would hold the few possessions she'd left behind.

Priscilla edged through the women decorating the commanding officer's front porch and headed to the room where Fern had taken refuge. Fern had sent word this morning asking if Priscilla would stand up with her at the wedding.

The bride turned toward the door as Priscilla edged inside. "Did you see Harry? How is he?" She bit her lower lip, eyes

69

entreating.

"I saw him as I came in, and he looks fine. Impatient. I thought he might wear a trench in the ground, he was pacing so much." She grinned. "He's with Major Ryder, who seems to be quite calm." And handsome in his dress uniform. Though his eyes had held a challenge when they happened to meet hers, sending a shiver through her. Arrogant man. She shoved him from her thoughts — which she seemed to be doing constantly since she'd met him — and concentrated on the bride.

Fern pressed her hands against her middle. "Do you think it's time to get dressed?" Her best dress, a blue calico sprigged with white flowers, lay draped across the bed. By Priscilla's standards the gown was rather plain, but Fern's eyes shone as she ran her hand over the cheerful fabric. "My mother and I sewed it. She said I could use it as a Sunday dress for the rest of the summer." She trailed her fingers over the cotton folds, her face alight as if she stroked the finest silk and lace.

"You're going to be a beautiful bride." Priscilla reached for the dress. "Let's get you into it, and then I'll fix your hair. Harry sent you these flowers." She held up the fistful of tiny blossoms. "I think they'd look lovely braided into your hair."

Dressing the bride took no time at all. She wore no hoops or elaborate underpinnings, just a simple chemise and petticoats. It was merely a matter of dropping the dress over her head and helping her button it up the back. Priscilla smoothed the lace collar, admiring the cameo Fern had pinned there. "Something old?"

"Yes. It was my grandmother's. And my shoes are my 'something new'." She stuck out her foot to admire her soot-black, kid leather boots. "And my dress is my 'something blue.' I guess that leaves the 'something borrowed.' " She frowned then shrugged. "Oh, well. I don't suppose there's any truth in these old sayings."

"Still, they can be kind of fun. I think I can take care of the 'something borrowed,' if you like." Priscilla drew the lace shawl she wore off her shoulders. "It was my mother's."

Fern exhaled, her fingers brushing the cobweb fabric. "Oh, Priscilla, it's beautiful. Are you sure? It looks so perfect with your dress."

Priscilla smoothed her hand over her gown, the amber satin rustling and sliding under her fingers. It was one of her favorite models of the season. One of the perquisites

71

of working for the catalog company was the deep discount she received on all their products. She'd known the minute she'd begun illustrating this dress for the spring catalog that she would buy it. "I'm very sure. The shawl is just the thing to add the finishing touch to your outfit."

By the time they had Fern's hair done — Priscilla wove the bright orange-yellow flowers into Fern's upswept curls — there remained little time before the ceremony. "There. You're the very picture of a beautiful bride."

Fern studied her reflection in the small mirror tacked to the wall. Pink cheeks, sparkling eyes, wide smile. She looked as happy as any girl should on her wedding day. A pang of something akin to envy pierced Priscilla, and she had to look away.

Picking up her bouquet from the bureau top, Fern examined Priscilla. "You look beautiful yourself. In a getup like that, you'd better take care. The men will be tripping over themselves to dance with you." She grinned. "If you're not careful, one of them will drag you off to the preacher and get a ring on your hand, lickety-split."

"Not likely." Priscilla tightened a couple of hairpins, checking her reflection in the mirror.

"Oh? Do you have a young man waiting for you back east?"

"No." Caring for her ailing mother and working for the catalog had taken up so much of Priscilla's time, she hadn't had the inclination or the energy for much of a social life. The occasional trip to the theater or a skating party or picnic with some of the young people from church, but no serious beau. "There's no one waiting for me at home."

"Good. Then no one will get his heart broken if someone out here sweeps you off your feet."

Before Priscilla could disabuse her mind of that notion, a knock sounded on the door. "Ladies? It's time."

She opened the door.

"I've been given the honor of giving away the bride." Commander Bracken, in full dress uniform, waited for them. He smiled. "Well, look at you two. It does my heart proud. I don't know that I'm fit to accompany two such beautiful young ladies, but I have a feeling if I don't get the bride out there soon, the groom will be breaking down the door." He offered the ladies his arms.

They stepped out the back door. "We'll go around this way and up the front steps.

Priscilla, you go ahead. Major Ryder's waiting to escort you. He'll be standing up with Lieutenant Dunn."

Her heart bumped hard once and settled into a steady, if slightly fast, rhythm. She and Major Ryder hadn't crossed swords that morning for the simple reason that she hadn't seen the man to speak to. Breakfast had been a quiet affair with just herself and the children, served by Samson. The twins had disappeared the moment the meal was over, and she hadn't seen them since. Yet another reason they would be better off with her. They seemed to be allowed to run wild here with little or no supervision. Who knew what they were up to? The major apparently had no qualms about letting them gallivant wherever their little hearts pleased.

There he was, waiting at the corner of the house. He looked her over from her upswept curls to the deep ruffle that covered her shoes, and she waited for his reaction. He seemed frozen for a moment, but then he gave her a polite smile. Bowing from the waist, he offered his arm.

"Ma'am." His eyes no longer challenged her. Instead, wariness had invaded their gray depths. Disappointment hitched down her spine. Though she hadn't dressed for the sole purpose of attracting his attention, she had expected some favorable response. After all, yesterday he had called her beautiful. Not that she was interested in him or really cared what he thought. But it was nice to be noticed.

She placed her hand in the crook of his elbow. Not even the wool of his tunic and the lace of her gloves could disguise the play of muscles under her fingers. He was certainly a fit man with a trim waist and athletic grace. With measured steps, he escorted her along the path and around to the front steps of the commander's house. Soldiers and women stood along the way, eager to see the bride coming behind. Priscilla caught some whispers and nods, and some of the soldiers elbowed each other in the ribs. At one point, she even heard a low whistle of approval as she passed. She kept a serene smile on her face and looked straight ahead. At least someone appreciated the care she'd taken with her dress and hair.

The band struck up a melody. She and Major Ryder gained the stairs, and at the top they parted to stand on either side of the chaplain and Harry. The lieutenant looked so shined and spit-polished it tugged at Priscilla's heart. He craned his neck, trying to catch a glimpse of Fern over the heads of the crowd.

The music changed, and a stir went through the crowd. Fern appeared on the colonel's arm, and Priscilla sucked in a breath. Fern's face shone with love and excitement, all trace of nerves gone. The sun glinted off her hair and teased the blossoms woven there. The gauzy shawl fluttered in the breeze.

Glancing back at Harry made Priscilla's heart hurt. He was so proud, so happy. A small ache started beneath her breastbone. What would it be like to have someone look like that at her, to be the center of one man's world to the exclusion of all else?

Her eyes flicked to Major Ryder's, and she blushed when she realized he wasn't looking at Fern. Effortlessly, he held her gaze, his expression somber, as if he were weighing her up. She finally tore her attention away and focused on the bride ascending the stairs.

The ceremony, though nothing like the elaborate affairs Priscilla had attended in the east, was beautiful and stirring, filled with love and promise. Its simplicity made its significance stand out. No bowers of blooms, no candles or organ music or fancy food. Just two people who loved each other above all else, pledging their lives and futures.

She found herself blinking rapidly, and she bit the inside of her lower lip to stay her tears. *Lord, please bless their union. Give them happiness in spite of the hardship I know they are going to face.*

When the preacher pronounced them man and wife and Harry took Fern into his embrace for the bridal kiss, the soldiers stomped, whistled, and threw their hats in the air. The kiss was ardent enough to draw sighs from the ladies present, Priscilla included. Though she barely knew Fern and Harry, she still found herself caught up in the romance of the moment, dabbing tears as the couple was introduced as husband and wife to the raucous approval of the soldiers.

Then the party began.

Major Ryder escorted her down the steps behind the bride and groom, his saber clanking on the stairs. When they reached the bottom, she found herself surrounded by a wall of blue.

"You'll have to wait until after the meal, boys." The major tightened his elbow against his side, pinning her hand more securely. "Mrs. Bracken has assigned the wedding party to sit at the colonel's table."

Scowls and grunts accompanied the shuffling of boots as they opened a path. Priscilla whispered, "What was that about?"

"They all want to sit with you during the meal." He frowned down at her.

She blinked. "All of them?"

"I told you to be careful. They're starved for female companionship. I told you not to encourage them."

"I haven't done anything wrong. I haven't done anything, period. I'm certainly not encouraging them."

"A woman like you doesn't have to *do* anything. The minute they caught sight of you in that rig, a fight started brewing."

"What's wrong with my dress?" She smoothed her hand down the buttons and across her skirt, trying to ignore a stab of disappointment. "It's the latest fashion, I assure you."

"Your dress is fine, and these men wouldn't know the latest fashion if they ran over it on the way to breakfast." His gruff voice rubbed her the wrong way. He led her to the chair beside Colonel Bracken. Pulling it out, he leaned down to whisper as she took her seat, "Truth is, you could wear a feed sack and the men here would still desire you."

Heat swirled in her cheeks. Did he include

himself in that number? Though what did it matter? Their ways lay far apart, and she would do well to remember that. No military man should dominate her thoughts and equilibrium like this.

"Where are the twins?" She sought a safer topic. "I haven't seen them since breakfast."

"Private Zeller has charge of them for the afternoon. Over there." He took his seat, careful to settle his saber, nodding to one of the tables loaded with soldiers. Two little blond heads flanked the young private. Tessa had abandoned her kepi, at least for the wedding, and her short golden curls tossed in the breeze.

"Why is Tessa's hair so short? It isn't even long enough to fashion into braids."

He tugged his gloves off and tucked them into his belt. "Indians are enamored of yellow hair, especially on little girls. Her parents kept her hair short to keep the Kickapoo from helping themselves to a lock or two."

She blinked. "They'd scalp a child?" Her hand went to her throat.

"No, they'd just cut off a curl or two to put in their medicine bag. Either that or they'd try to steal her to keep."

Priscilla straightened the cutlery beside her plate. Stealing children? More proof that this barbaric place was not where her niece and nephew should be brought up.

"And how is your patient this morning, the one that fell off the roof?"

"Samson is staying with him. I had a terrible time keeping the man in bed today. He wanted to attend the wedding, said if I wouldn't get him some crutches, he'd have his buddies carry him over on a litter."

She opened her napkin and spread it on her lap. "Samson seems to have a lot of responsibility in the infirmary." And with the twins.

"He's my right-hand man. He's a civilian I met during the War. If he was white, he'd be a doctor by now. I tried to get him to apply to a medical school, but he says he's too old for all of that. As it is, he's one of the best healers I've ever met. The twins adore him. They head his way for advice and sympathy when they think I'm not performing up to their expectations." He snapped open his napkin and gave her a wry smile. "Which seems to be whenever I say no to something they want to do."

The chaplain said grace, and dishes and bowls were passed. Colonel Bracken made the first toast, and then it was Major Ryder's turn. He stood, lifting his water glass, silhouetted against the pale, blue sky.

"Fern, I can't tell you how happy we are that you finally arrived and married Harry. He's been worthless for weeks waiting for you to get here." A smattering of laughter rippled through the assembly, and Harry grinned. He laced his fingers through Fern's and raised her hand to his lips.

The doctor continued, "You realize, I hope, that you've not only married a fine man, but you've married a lieutenant in the United States Cavalry. It takes a special woman to cast her lot in with this company. From everything Harry has told us about you — and he's gone on at some length" — another round of laughter, louder this time — "I'm certain you possess all the qualities he will need in a wife as he pursues his career here on the frontier. May God bless your marriage, and welcome to the regiment." He raised his glass to the bride, and everyone followed suit, cheering and standing up.

Everyone but Priscilla, who sipped from her glass, but couldn't help but wonder if Fern knew what she was getting into. What Elliot Ryder said was true. She was marrying not only Harry, but the regiment and the entire US Cavalry. And the cavalry would always have first claim on his heart.

Elliot helped Priscilla with her chair when the toasts were over, taking her arm and guiding her away from the tables. "You'd best hang back. Things will move pretty fast."

She arched her eyebrows over those expressive eyes, eyes the same amber color as her dress. "What will move fast?"

"Watch." He eyed the proceedings with pride. The men could really step-to when properly motivated. With precision and determination, groups of soldiers set to clearing and moving the tables and benches and chairs.

"They're eager to get to the dancing, and that can't start until they've made a space for it." Elliot stepped back, taking Priscilla with him as a pair of burly men strode by with a long table between them.

"A space for it? There's nothing but space right here." She waved toward the parade ground.

"We can't dance there." He smiled at her naivety. "No one is allowed on the parade ground except for drill, and only in uniform. And no civilian is allowed on the parade ground ever. Don't even cut the corner when you're walking around it. Keep to the path." Because there was no grass on the parade ground to mark its edges, the pathways had been lined with stones.

He pointed to a building across the fort. "That's the shops building. Blacksmith, bakery, saddler. You'll notice it's the only building that doesn't face the parade ground. That's because a lot of the workers there are civilians. It isn't fitting for them to look out on the parade ground or to be seen from it. The entrance to that building is in the back."

She shook her head, giving him a skeptical look. He reminded himself that she, too, was a civilian, and a jaded one at that. He couldn't expect her to understand military pride and protocol.

The band settled onto the barracks porch and began tuning up. A pale-haired whirlwind darted between blue legs and picnic accessories to skid to a stop in front of Priscilla. Tessa looked up into her face, and Priscilla used her handkerchief to wipe at a smudge on the girl's cheek — a gesture so like one Tessa's mother had done countless times, that Elliot's chest tightened at the memory. Gently, Priscilla smoothed Tessa's hair back, but the curls sprang forward once more. Elliot had often tried this last month to get Tess to stand still to have it brushed, but she'd wiggled and jerked away from him so much that any attempt to tame her hair usually ended in her tears and his frustration.

"Hello, Miss Tessa." Priscilla bent to put her eyes on the same level as the little girl's. "Are you having a good time?"

Tessa nodded. "You sure look pretty. What is that dress made of?" She reached out to touch Priscilla's skirt, and then glanced up at Elliot before tucking her hand behind her back.

Priscilla reached for Tessa's fingers. "It's called satin, and you can touch it. It's very smooth."

Her eyes rounded, and Elliot suppressed a smile. Tessa might be a little hoyden most of the time, but she was a woman in the making, as taken with pretty fripperies as any debutante.

"Are you going to dance?" Tessa directed the question to him, her head tilted to study him.

"So protocol dictates." He settled his hand on his saber.

"Does that mean yes?" She put her hands on her tiny hips, her mouth screwing up.

"Yes."

"With her?" She pointed to Priscilla.

"Most likely."

"Good." She darted away, mercurially fast.

Priscilla shook her head. "What was all that about?"

Elliot removed his gloves from his belt and tugged them on. "I imagine she thinks that if I dance with you, I'll fall hopelessly in love and beg you to marry me. She's gotten it into her head that I need a wife and that you will fill the bill nicely. I think she misses her mother very much, and if I would just get married, we could be a 'real' family." He grimaced to let Priscilla know he had no intention of following through on such faulty logic.

Her eyes widened. "I don't know about you needing a wife, but she's correct in her assumption that they need a woman to mother them. If you'd just let me take them home with me, they'd have a mother to look after them."

"I've already told you they aren't going anywhere. And I'm not marrying someone just to provide Tessa with a mother."

"Then you'd best disabuse Tessa of any notion that I would marry you or any other military man, because that is never going to happen." Her eyes snapped, and her cheeks flushed.

"I'm glad we understand one another, then."

"We do, indeed." She inclined her head to him, as if they had just finished a fencing match.

The band began to play, and Harry took Fern into his arms and swung her around the open, packed-dirt area, his eyes never leaving her face. His bride looked up at him, her face glowing. Elliot prayed they would always be as happy as they were right now.

Elliot's gaze shifted to Priscilla at his side. Her pert nose tilted up just a bit at the end, something he hadn't noticed before, and her foot tapped to the music. Her eyes had a dreamy quality to them, and her expression had softened as she watched the bride and groom. Too bad she couldn't be more like Fern, ready to stand by her officer and embrace the life he'd chosen.

The song ended, and the crowd applauded. Elliot reached for Priscilla's hand. "You and I, as the official witnesses, are expected to join them for the next."

He held out his arms, and she stepped into them. Well aware of the envious eyes of his fellow soldiers, he led her into the steps of the dance. Light as milkweed down, she followed his lead with practiced skill that made up for his rustiness. How long had it been since he'd held a woman in his arms this way? He'd been able to avoid post dances, always claiming work in the infirmary when the officers held a ball. As a consequence, he hadn't danced with anyone since Muriel, more than nine years ago. What a disaster that night had turned out to be.

His arms tightened, and he missed a step. Pivoting, he tried to cover his mistake. Priscilla looked up at him. He forced a smile and relaxed his hold. "Sorry. It's been a while."

"For me, too. I haven't danced for months. By rights both of us should still be in mourning, with Chris and Rebekah passing away so recently, but when my mother passed away last year, she made me promise her that when she died, I wouldn't wear black. She loathed black." Her eyes took on a somber look, one that matched the sadness he felt at the thought of Rebekah and Chris. His sister had loved dancing, exuberant and almost giddy at the mere mention of a party. She would've loved today's festivities.

Priscilla's hand rested in his light as a bird, and his palm on her waist grew warm against the smooth fabric of her dress. In time to the music he swung her around, pivoting, and her skirts belled out. Resisting the urge to draw her closer, he forced himself to remain detached and aloof. Difficult when her perfume filled his nostrils and her form filled his embrace. It really had been a long time since he'd had any feminine company.

The song came to an end, and they were surrounded once more. She thanked him for the dance and went into the arms of another. He edged back until he stood in the shade of the commander's house. To his left, the last table remained, set out with punch and the wedding cake. Beyond that were the wedding gifts, ready to be carried to the couple's new residence.

Every woman at the fort was pressed into dancing, from the commander's wife to the laundresses. The colonel whirled by with Mrs. Bracken, Major and Mrs. Crane, Fern with the sergeant-at-arms, and Priscilla with another soldier. Her face was bright and smiling up at her escort, her skirts swaying out as he swung her into a turn. By far the most eye-catching woman there.

After three more dances, she begged off and came to stand beside him in the shade. Her cheeks were pink with exertion.

"I told you that you would be much in demand." He was pleased she'd chosen to return to him, and annoyed that he was pleased. He shouldn't care, and he shouldn't be watching her like a Dutch uncle. She was nothing to him besides being the twins' aunt here for a short visit.

"They're all fine dancers, aren't they? And so enthusiastic. It sure is crowded out there." She dabbed at her throat with a lacy handkerchief.

"Most military men are good dancers. This party is a bit unusual. The enlisted men and officers don't often share social occasions, each group having their own gatherings, but this one was special. We use most any reason to celebrate and break up the monotony that can come with military service. You'll find there are plenty of dances and dinner parties and such to keep you busy until you leave our fair post."

She didn't rise to his bait at the jab about her soon departure, merely hooking a stray strand of hair off her cheek and tucking it behind her ear. "Fern looks so pretty. I had a hard time getting those flowers into her hair, but they look as if they will last for the duration of the party. I've never seen them before. I wonder what kind they are?"

"Mexican poppy. It is used to treat malarial chills, as well as kidney ailments, and cleansing the body after parturition." He recited the information, fresh in his mind from recently including it in his herbal journal. "However, the seeds are highly toxic, affecting the muscles, bowels, eyes, and liver, eventually causing death."

"I don't intend to ingest any, thank you." She gave him a startled glance.

Heat crept up his neck. "I'm sorry. One of my duties, and also a hobby of mine, as the post physician, is to make a catalog of the flora and fauna of the area surrounding the fort. I'm quite interested in herbal medicines, particularly those used by the Indians. As you saw when you visited the infirmary, I'm making quite a study of the topic, and sometimes I fear I can get carried away."

The smell of roses drifted off her skin as she snapped open her fan and created a stir of air to cool her cheeks. Her gaze followed the bridal couple as they danced by, faces rapt, eyes only for each other. "Do you think they'll be happy together?"

"Harry and Fern? I think so. She's got what it takes, and they're certainly in love."

"What it takes?"

"The right attitude and the strength to deal with situations as they arise. It's no easy life she's undertaking, but I think her love for Harry will see her through the hard times. No woman should marry a military man if she isn't willing to sacrifice a little."

"A little?" Her fan flicked faster, blowing the hair back from her temples in quick puffs. "A woman who marries a military man must be willing to sacrifice *everything*. Nothing really belongs to her. Not her home, not her yard, not even her husband. Everything is the property of the United States Army, and she is reminded of it daily. Her food is stamped US Army, her blankets bear their insignia, her husband's clothing, her trunks and boxes. All of it. At a moment's notice she can be called to uproot her family and move hundreds, if not thousands, of miles away. The living conditions are often primitive, supplies limited or non-existent, danger prevalent, and her husband constantly at risk. No woman should be asked to sacrifice like that." Her mouth set in a firm line, her eyes hard.

He blinked at her vehemence. "I hope you didn't share your opinions with the new bride."

"Of course not. She'll find out soon enough, I imagine. My mother certainly did, and I heard about it every day until she died."

That explained it. The woman must've indoctrinated her daughter well for her to be so adamant.

91

He tried to reason with Priscilla. "And yet, there are women who thrive in this life, who make the sacrifices they have to, meeting challenges with courage and ingenuity. They bring a softness and beauty with them that increases morale and civilizes the regiment. I'll agree that not everyone is cut out for the life of a military wife, but there are *some* who are suited beautifully to the challenge."

She bristled, her back straightening and the skin along her jaw tightening. He received no joy from being so blunt, but it was better to be truthful, however much it might hurt or annoy. He had no time for a woman who refused to stand by the man to whom she'd agreed to pledge her life. He, for one, had vowed never to lay himself open to that kind of treachery again.

A soldier approached and bowed. "Ma'am, if you've rested enough, it would be the pleasure of my life to share a dance with you."

Priscilla cast Elliot one last withering glare before snapping her fan closed and accepting the corporal's hand. "I'd be delighted, sir."

Before they'd taken the first steps of the reel, the band squawked to a dissonant halt. Heads swiveled, and Elliot stood away from the adobe wall of the building.

Easy as you please, an Indian strolled toward the fort from the river, unchallenged and unconcerned.

CHAPTER FOUR

Screams rent the air, and soldiers raced for their guns. Musical instruments clanged to the porch floor, and out of the corner of his eye, Elliot saw one of the women subsiding into a faint.

"Wait! Stop!" He shouted above the din, shouldering through the crowd, racing toward the figure striding toward him, his saber clanging at his side.

"Major Ryder, get back here," Major Crane commanded.

Though he clearly heard the order, he didn't turn around. Instead he halted, holding his hands wide.

The Indian stopped. Behind him, the prairie was empty, the scrub rustling in the breeze. Around him, the vegetation had been cut short to allow better visibility around the fort, and the Kickapoo stood halfway across this no-man's land.

Slowly, he raised the parfleche he carried,

the fringe rippling with the movement.

Boots pounded the ground, and Elliot found himself surrounded by soldiers, rifles all pointing at the Indian thirty yards away.

"Stop. Lower your guns. He means no harm."

Major Crane, his face a mask of fury, stomped close. "How can you know that?"

"I know this man. His name is Kennekuk. There's no need to fear. He's peaceful." Elliot was well aware of the major's hatred of Indians and his legendary temper, and had long sought to diffuse both . . . to no avail.

"There's no such thing as a peaceful Indian." The major's eyes narrowed, his hand gripping his pistol.

"Major Crane, this man is a friend. He's come to see me, and he's no danger to the fort."

"We'll see about that. Call him over here."

"Not until you lower your rifles and back away. He's not a fool."

Crane grunted. "He is if he thinks he can walk into the fort unchallenged." He whirled to the men. "Where were the pickets? How did he get this close with nobody noticing? The entire post could've been attacked, and not a soul was prepared?" His bellow made the kneeling men wince.

Elliot eased through the barricade of

95

soldiers and slowly closed the distance between himself and Kennekuk, who stood as if he were made of stone, bag dangling from his long arm.

The soldiers remained on alert, guns trained on Kennekuk. Elliot hoped none of them would get trigger happy and shoot him in the back as he approached his friend. When he reached Kennekuk, he turned and waved the men back. The soldiers withdrew to the buildings but kept their rifles ready, and the seasoned Kickapoo medicine man watched them with glittering dark eyes.

"Welcome." Elliot held out his hand, grasping Kennekuk's forearm and feeling the Indian's grip on his own. "I had heard your people had returned from the wintering grounds. I hadn't looked for you to come for a few weeks." He spoke a combination of English and a smattering of the Kickapoo he'd picked up.

"It was time. The wind has changed. The weather has changed. Though it appears Major Crane has not."

"I've tried." Elliot shrugged. "There is much bad blood between Crane and the Kickapoo. He won't forget the death of his brother."

"Nor will Chief Kishko forget the death of his son, but if we are to prevent more killing we must treat with one another, putting aside our anger." Deep seams lined Kennekuk's face, every crease testament to the hardship of war and the struggle for survival on the plains.

"Have your people wintered well?"

He nodded. "Some are no longer with us, and new ones have been born. It is the way of things. I brought you new medicines." He held up the bag once more.

"I'm eager to see what you have for me. Will you come to the hospital? There is a man there I would like you to see."

"Will Major Crane shoot me or try to keep me here?" He raised one eyebrow, twisting his mouth in a wry smile.

"I think you'll be safe, but just in case, how about if we don't go into the fort proper? We'll go around to the hospital."

"Will Sam-son be there?" As always, Kennekuk broke the name into two parts, as if the name was two separate words.

"He will be happy to see you, as I am. But the man I really wish you to look at has a broken leg." Elliot pointed to his thigh and made a motion with his hands as if breaking an imaginary stick in two.

"I will come. And the little ones? Are they still at the fort?"

"Oh yes. Tessa and Timothy are still here.

They'll be eager to see you, too. I should tell you, they live with me now. Their father and mother died of sickness this winter."

Sadness invaded Kennekuk's eyes, and he clasped Elliot's forearm once more. "I am sorry. For you and for the little ones. They should not have such sadness so young."

"Thank you, friend. It's been quite an adjustment for us all." He turned toward the adobe hospital on the northeast corner of the post behind the barracks. Kennekuk hesitated, eyeing the cluster of men and women gathered between the buildings.

"You were having a . . ." he frowned, searching for the word. "Party?"

"A wedding, actually."

The Indian's eyebrows rose. "Your wedding? You have found a wife?"

Elliot chuckled. "No. Not mine."

"You are too much alone. You need a wife. I had hoped you might find someone to share your lodge with this winter." They fell into step together, Kennekuk keeping his eyes focused on the hospital.

"You sound like Tessa. She's been pestering me to get married."

"The little one has much wisdom. You should listen."

"I'm not cut out for marriage."

"Perhaps you have not yet met the right

98

woman. Many a man flees from the idea of marriage until he meets the right woman. When he does, he cannot say the binding words fast enough."

The Indian's statement took Elliot right back to the moment he had first seen Muriel Upton. Red hair, glittering green eyes, porcelain skin so translucent it glowed. Laughing, vivacious, and so beautiful. And after six months of hard courting on his part, his affianced bride.

He'd been so young, a recently graduated medical student. The Civil War had broken out, and Elliot had enlisted the same day he put the engagement ring on her hand. And she'd promised to wait for him. After all, the war couldn't last long. In a few weeks, he'd be home again, and they would wed.

But the weeks had turned to months and then years. Attached to Sherman's troops, pushing ever deeper into the South, ever farther away from Muriel and home and all that he loved, he'd held onto her promise, treasured her letters, and dreamed of the day he could return to her. At first, the letters had come regularly, then sporadically, then not at all. He'd thought it was a result of disruption in the mail lines and how swiftly his unit was on the move.

He'd been in the midst of battle after

battle, treating the wounded, practicing the most urgent kind of medicine imaginable. Muriel had been his lodestone, the thought of her fresh loveliness the only thing that banished the cries of the wounded from his nightmares. If he had known at that time that she would give him back his ring, would he have been able to hang on to his reason in the midst of all that carnage?

The final straw had come when he'd returned home with the plan of staying in the army and making it his career. He'd already received his new posting and had come home to marry Muriel and bring her with him to the frontier.

She would have none of it. Hadn't his absence for years during the War been enough? How could he decide something like this without even talking to her about it? What on earth made him think she wanted to traipse off into the wilderness and live like a savage? She had intended to marry a doctor and live a comfortable existence.

Muriel gave him an ultimatum. He could have either her or the army, but he could not have both.

Elliot shrugged and sent a rueful grin toward Kennekuk. "Maybe some men do find the right woman, but it just doesn't work out. Let's go visit my patient." He'd never told anyone here about Muriel, and he had no intention of telling anyone ever. Rebekah had known, of course, but she considered he'd made a lucky escape. It was her opinion that Muriel had been all wrong for him, more interested in catching a socially acceptable husband, than in him as a man. She'd have made his life miserable here on the frontier.

They entered the hospital building, and Samson greeted them at the door. His white teeth flashed in his dark face as he gave Kennekuk a rare smile. "Good to see you again, Mr. Kennekuk."

Elliot led the way into the infirmary to where Matthews lay. The patient's leg hung suspended from a sturdy framework, held by ropes and weighted to keep a steady pull on the break. Samson had gone to the workshop the evening before, and with the help of one of the carpenters, had created the heavy, wooden brace to fit over the bed, much better than the quick rig they'd come up with yesterday to keep the leg straight as it healed.

Kennekuk walked over to the bed and bent over the sleeping patient. With his gnarled hand, he brushed the hair off the man's forehead, checking the temperature of his skin.

Matthews opened his eyes a slit, caught sight of Kennekuk, and half raised off the bed, his lids flying upward to expose startled eyes. "Gerrout!" He flailed at the Indian, making the mattress and pulley system creak and shudder.

"Easy, Soldier. He comes in peace." Elliot shook his head and pressed the man back onto the pillows.

Matthews flopped back, panting and clasping his chest. Great beads of sweat rolled off his temples, and he put one hand on his broken leg above the break, squeezing it hard. "Don't scare a man that way, sir. I thought the fort had been overrun. I thought he was bending over me to scalp me." His tongue darted out to moisten his dry lips.

Elliot sent an apology to Kennekuk with his eyes as he held a glass of water to Matthews's lips. "I'm sorry, Soldier. We thought you were asleep."

"Nearly scared me into eternity, Doc." Matthews muttered and let them reposition him in the bed.

But when Kennekuk stepped forward again, Matthews set his jaw. "Major Ryder, I don't want no red man touching me."

"He's a healer. He won't hurt you. In fact,

he's brought me some herbs that I might use in treating you."

"No. Get him away from me. And don't give me none of those herbs. He might've been sent in here by his tribe to poison folks. Get him out of here, I tell you." Matthews's face went red then white.

Kennekuk backed away from the bed. "Do not upset him. I will wait in the other room."

Elliot checked the ropes and splint, and then left Matthews in Samson's capable care. How would the Kickapoo and the whites ever live peaceably together if every encounter was met with violence and bigotry?

"Let's go to the hospital. I want to see Kennekuk." Tessa swung from the crossbar of a hitching post, her fingers laced around the dried, smooth wood. "We haven't seen him for a long time."

Timothy's eyebrows rose, and the corner of his mouth quirked up. He sent Priscilla a pleading look. "Please?"

"Kennekuk." Priscilla pressed her lips together. "Perhaps we should wait. The soldiers seem quite agitated right now." Several men in blue stood with their rifles ready, and Major Crane continued to pace and bellow at the pickets who had left their posts to join the party. It sounded as if they would be residing in the guardhouse for the next several days.

And yet, if she was truthful, she was curious to see a real live Indian up close.

"Are you sure it's safe?"

Tessa rolled her eyes, and Timothy gave her a pitying look.

"Of course it's safe. Kennekuk is our friend." Tessa blew a hank of curls off her forehead.

How could she resist these two? Tessa's exuberance and Timothy's quiet reserve both awakened a tenderness in Priscilla that she couldn't quell. And she had the impression Timothy rarely asked for anything. The arrival of the Indian had brought an abrupt ending to the party, and the cleanup was all but finished. Fern and Harry had disappeared into their one-room quarters after Fern had returned Priscilla's shawl with a smile and a squeeze of her hand as thanks.

"I suppose it would be all right. We need to head that way anyway." She offered her free hand to Timothy who, after a moment, took it. When she put out her hand to Tessa, she discovered the girl had already taken off toward the hospital, her feet clattering on the hard dirt.

Timothy and Priscilla followed her. A

fresh breeze rustled Priscilla's skirt and teased her hair. She carried her shawl folded over her arm, the temperature having risen considerably since sunup.

Tessa skipped, hopped, and did everything except walk sedately like a proper young lady, coming back to circle around them like the moon around the earth, impatient at their slower pace. "Where do you suppose Fern and Lieutenant Dunn went? As soon as Kennekuk showed up and the party fell apart, they disappeared. I thought Fern's dress was pretty and I wanted to tell her so, but I didn't get the chance before she left in such an all-fired hurry."

Priscilla's cheeks heated at the thought of where Fern and Harry had gone. Poor Fern. A single room in the officers' quarters for her bridal suite. What kind of honeymoon was that? Still, from the happy, anticipatory look on the bride's face, she didn't seem to mind the situation one bit.

Tessa neither waited for a reply to her question nor seemed to need or want one. "I guess I can tell her tomorrow. She's part of the regiment now, so we'll see her a lot. I wonder how Kennekuk's people weathered this winter. His tribe always goes down into Mexico for the winter. Did you hear we're going to visit the camp tomorrow? I love going to Kennekuk's camp. You're coming, too, aren't you? It's something you can tell your friends about when you go home. Uncle Elliot says you can't stay very long, so you might as well cram in as much stuff as you can while you're here."

Though the idea of seeing an honest to goodness Indian encampment intrigued and scared Priscilla in equal measure, the certainty with which Tessa accepted the notion of her going home stopped Priscilla in her tracks. Timothy kept walking a few paces, and his hand slipped from hers. Both twins halted to see what had happened.

"Hurry up, Aunt Priscilla. We don't want Kennekuk to leave before you get to meet him." Timothy took her hand again and tugged.

Tessa nodded and hopped-skipped a few steps. "Sometimes he brings us things. Last fall he brought me a rabbit-skin hood. And he gave Timothy that bag." She pointed at the leather pouch slung crossways on her brother's thin chest. Though she'd only known them a couple of days, Priscilla had the feeling that Timothy was rarely seen without it.

"Are you sure it will be safe, visiting the camp?" Everything she'd read in *Harper's* rushed through her mind, the atrocities, the savagery of the plains tribes. She'd felt safe since arriving at the fort, but she'd also assumed the Kickapoo would stay away.

Timothy frowned. "You're not one of *those* people, are you?"

"Those people?"

"Like Major Crane. He says the only good Indian is a dead Indian. You don't think that, do you?"

Tessa poked him in the shoulder. "Of course she isn't. That's ignorant. Uncle Elliot told us so. He says the Indians are just like anybody else, some are good and some are bad, and it's up to us to act fair and square, no matter what anyone else is doing. Aunt Priscilla isn't ignorant." She turned to Priscilla. "You aren't, are you?"

"No." She wasn't, was she?

"Good. I knew it. Fear and ignorance make people do silly things."

"Did Uncle Elliot tell you that, too?"

"Yep. Uncle Elliot says people often bring about the very things they're afraid of by being ignorant. Uncle Elliot says lying to Indians because you're afraid of what they might do makes them so mad, they often do the thing you were afraid of out of frustration. Like killing folks. He says we've lied to them enough. If we'd just be square with them, respect them as men, we could live in peace together."

Priscilla had the feeling that being with Tessa, she'd get a lot of "Uncle Elliot says." The twins clearly thought highly of their uncle, in spite of his treating them like soldiers instead of children. And she had to admit, there was the ring of truth in his words. The government hadn't treated Indians very well.

"C'mon." Tessa danced up the steps to the infirmary, and Priscilla and Timothy followed behind.

"Kennekuk!" Tessa obviously had no fear of the Indian standing in the surgery doorway. She launched herself at him. He opened his arms and scooped her up against his chest.

"Tessa." He hugged her and leaned her back in his arms so he could study her face. "You have grown some, but you are still the same little whirlwind."

Priscilla hung back in the doorway, wary yet curious. The Indian wore buckskin pants and a faded red shirt. Lines creased his face, and his black eyes glittered with warmth as he held the little girl. They touched foreheads, and he murmured something only Tessa could hear.

"Thank you. We miss them a lot."

The Indian's hand came out to cup

Timothy's head, drawing him close. "You still have your bag, I see."

Timothy nodded. "Want to see what I have in it?" He flipped the strap over his head and delved into the depths of the bag. "I have my knife." Holding up the small pocketknife, he clicked open the blade then snapped it shut.

Priscilla put her hand to her throat. What child of Timothy's age needed to carry a knife? He continued to rummage in the leather bag.

"And I have a canteen — though it's only a little one — and my flint and steel, and some jerky. I remembered what you said about always being ready to take care of myself if I got lost on the plains or something."

It was the longest speech she'd heard Timothy make, and the most enthusiastic.

"You have done well. You will be a great warrior someday. Just like your father."

A sound of protest erupted from Priscilla's throat before she could stop it. A great warrior. Not if she had anything to say about it.

Kennekuk looked at her for the first time, and her heart beat faster. A real, live Indian, with black eyes and mahogany skin.

"Kennekuk, this is our Aunt Priscilla. She's come for a visit." Tessa fingered the strings of beads hanging around the man's neck. "Aunt Priscilla, this is Kennekuk, a Kickapoo medicine man and our friend."

The Indian let the little girl slip down to stand beside him. He'd wiped all expression from his face, but he couldn't still his deep, glittering eyes.

Priscilla mustered her courage and her manners and stepped out of the doorway and into the hall. "How do you do? I'm pleased to meet you." She held out her hand. "From what little the children have told me, you are a great friend of theirs. I hope you will be my friend as well."

A spark lit the older man's eyes, and he took her hand between his. "The little ones are . . ." He appeared to be searching for the word. "It is good that you came to see them. Family is good when they are sad."

"I see you've met our visitor." Elliot stepped into the crowded hallway from the sick ward, wiping his hands on a towel.

Priscilla withdrew her hand from Kennekuk's grasp and clasped her fingers together at her waist. She had a feeling Elliot was evaluating her, studying her, looking for something. She hadn't a clue what, so she decided to ignore him.

Tessa tugged on Kennekuk's sleeve. "Did you bring us anything?"

"Tessa." Priscilla and Elliot said her name at the same time.

She looked slightly abashed, but glanced up hopefully at the medicine man.

"You know me well, little whirlwind. I brought you each a gift, and your uncle, too." He reached into his bag and pulled out a carved figure, placing it in Tessa's hand.

"Look, Uncle Elliot, it's me." She held up the piece. Priscilla gasped, intrigued by the fine workmanship. A tiny girl, hair blowing, skirts flowing, danced on one foot. The minute features were clearly those of Tessa.

"I thought of you in my winter lodge. You are always restless, always moving, like the wind through the brush." Kennekuk squeezed her shoulder.

Timothy stood patiently, and his face lit up when Kennekuk handed him a carved horse. Again the detail was exquisite. The boy recognized the animal immediately. "It's my pony, Sooty."

"For your uncle I have brought some herbs." He gave a small leather pouch to Elliot. "It is for coughing. Boil the root in water."

"What is it called?"

"The people call it Rattlesnake Master."

Elliot took a small notebook and pencil

from his pocket and jotted some notes. "Thank you. I will add it to my journal."

"I have something for Sam-son as well, but I will give that to him later." Kennekuk turned to Priscilla, removing one of the strings of beads from around his neck. "I did not know you would be here, but it would give me happiness if you would take this." He held out the beads.

She opened her mouth to protest, but Elliot caught her eye, giving a slight shake to his head.

"Thank you. They are beautiful." She took the beads, feeling the shiny, hard tubes as she slipped them over her neck. They lay on her chest, catching the light, amber cylinders drilled through and strung on a tough, fibrous thread.

"They go nice with your dress." Tessa tilted her head. "Like they belong."

Kennekuk studied Priscilla and then looked to Elliot. "I think the little one has spoken truth. You would do well to listen to her. Perhaps it is time to stop fleeing."

Priscilla had no idea what the man was talking about, nor did she know why Elliot had such a skeptical look on his face.

After Kennekuk took his leave, promising to see the children on the morrow when they visited the Kickapoo camp, they sat down to dinner prepared by Samson. Elliot observed his humble quarters, trying to compare them to what Priscilla, with her costly clothing and precise manners, must have come from. A table, a cookstove, open shelving, crates of medical supplies newly delivered but as yet unsorted piled in the corner. Not very glamorous.

He poked at the food on his plate, the exact same fare they'd eaten the night before. Canned peas, boiled beef, and hard bread. Priscilla said nothing, but Elliot could tell from her face, she wanted to.

His defenses went up. "It's healthy and filling."

She raised her eyebrows. "I didn't say anything."

"You didn't have to. I'm sure this isn't what you're used to."

"How would you know what I was used to?" She cut a piece of beef and put it in her mouth.

"You're from Cincinnati, right?"

She chewed, and chewed, swallowing and taking a drink of water to get the tough meat down. "That's right."

"Do they serve a lot of boiled beef in the city?"

"They serve a lot of things in the city."

She spoke deliberately, as if ready for a sparring match if that was what he wanted.

Tessa and Timothy watched them, no longer eating, and Elliot shifted in his chair. What was wrong with him? What was it about this woman that made him want to battle her? If he was honest with himself — something he tried to be — it was probably because he was afraid that if he didn't keep her on edge and wary of him, if he didn't antagonize her, he might give into the absurd urge he'd had all day to kiss her. And if that wasn't the most useless and dangerous thought he could have, he didn't know what was.

The lantern hanging over the center of the table cast a golden glow, racing along the dark glossy curls she'd swept up and back from her face, lighting the depths of her amber eyes, and shining off the string of beads Kennekuk had given her.

"Those are called hairpipe beads. Kennekuk must've traded with the Cheyenne for them."

Her hand came up to the necklace. "They're beautiful."

"I could tell you were going to refuse them. If you'd done that, Kennekuk would've been offended. One must never refuse a gift from a Kickapoo, even if you

114

don't want what he's offering."

Her arched brows rose. "It's not that I didn't want them. I just didn't want him to feel obligated to give me anything, especially if they had value to him. As he said, he had no idea I would be here."

Elliot stabbed his meat with his fork. "They did have value to him. They are not easy to make and not easy for a Kickapoo to get. But what gift is worth calling a gift if it isn't valuable to the giver?"

She looked so natural sitting at his table, helping Tessa cut up her food, reminding Timothy without words to use his napkin and not his sleeve. After less than two days, he could tell the kids were already warming up to her. He felt the need to give them all a gentle reminder. "All your friends back east will be curious when they see those."

Her lips pressed together for a moment, and the skin along her jaw tightened, but she didn't jab back.

He asked the question he'd been wanting to all day. "Did you get your telegram sent?"

"Yes. My boss said I didn't need to report back to work until September first, though I'm hoping I won't be away that long."

"September first? That's nearly three months from now." Three months was a long time. A lot could happen in that span.

She might give up and go home before then, or she might even discard some of her ridiculous notions about the army and accept the suit of some eager officer or enlisted man. Not him, of course, but she'd get offers, of that he had no doubt.

She lowered her lashes. "As I said, I'm hoping to be home before then. It depends on if I can wind up my business here in a timely manner."

Noting the interested expressions on the twins' faces, he bit back what he was going to say. "Are you looking forward to the excursion tomorrow?"

"Yes. Tessa said Kennekuk is a medicine man?"

Elliot nodded. "He's both a healer and a spiritual leader for his people. Often those two things are intertwined in the Kickapoo culture. He gathers herbs to treat illness, but he combines his treatment with prayers, chants, incantations, and ceremonies. He shares his knowledge of herbs and healing with me, and though I add my prayers for my patients' healing, I leave out the incantations and chants."

She smiled, and his heart kicked up a notch. Why weren't the children chattering like usual, especially Tessa, to provide some sort of distraction? If he wasn't careful, he'd say something stupid, like she had a lovely smile, or she smelled nice.

"Tomorrow, when we go to the village, you should wear something more appropriate to living out here. We won't be walking through a city park. Your fine satin will get ruined." He winced inwardly at the harsh tone in his voice and the flicker of pain in her eyes.

"I assure you I wasn't born yesterday. I don't customarily wear wedding attire on an outing. I'll don something less ornate." She crossed her knife and fork on her plate and placed her hands in her lap.

"I doubt you have anything suitable. Maybe you can borrow something from Fern." Elliot put down his fork. "We'd best get these two to bed. They have a big day tomorrow."

Priscilla rose, her dress rustling in a purely feminine way. "I can take care of them." She put her hand on Tessa's head to guide her toward their sleeping quarters.

"I'll help." He hefted Timothy out of his chair and tossed the boy over his shoulder. His nephew giggled and squirmed, twining his hands in Elliot's hair. Samson rose and began clearing the table.

Together Elliot and Priscilla got the twins ready for bed. Priscilla eyed the kids' room, his one-time storage room, which explained why there were crates stacked in the kitchen. He'd had to move his extra supplies out to move the children in. Now the room was crowded with two beds, two chests, and a washstand.

Elliot supervised Timothy at the washstand while observing Priscilla and Tessa. The little girl drew her nightgown from under the pillow, and Priscilla unbuttoned Tessa's pinafore and dress.

"This is my bed, and that's Timothy's. Uncle Elliot says in another year or so, we're going to need rooms of our own." Tessa squirmed into her nightgown. The hem stopped several inches above her ankles. Elliot frowned. When had she shot up? The thing had fit last week, hadn't it? He'd have to see about getting someone to sew a new one for her.

Timothy splashed a little water on his face, swiped it dry with his sleeve, and turned toward his bed.

"Oh no you don't, young man. Wet that cloth, apply some soap, and don't forget behind your ears and around the back of your neck."

"You say that every night." Timothy grinned and snatched the washcloth off the nail.

"I wouldn't have to if you would wash properly." He bent an assessing gaze on his nephew. "You'd go to bed filthy if I'd let you. Your turn, Miss Tessa." He rinsed the cloth and handed it to his niece. She scrubbed until her skin glowed pink.

"Will we leave for Kennekuk's camp early in the morning? I hope so, because I want to spend all day there." Her words came out jerky as she washed her cheeks.

"Midmorning, most likely. And we'll be there all day. Kennekuk says Chief Pekho-tah is planning on feeding us dinner and putting on a little show." He held back the covers for Timothy to slide into bed.

"A show?" Tessa stilled.

"They want to perform a fire dance for us, and they can't do that until after dark. So tomorrow will be a late night. You two had best get to sleep quickly." He smoothed the blankets over Timothy. "Prayers and then sleep."

Elliot braced himself for the most heart-warming and heart-wrenching part of his day, one he wouldn't miss and yet dreaded all the same. Tessa folded her hands under her chin and closed her eyes. Timothy did the same. Elliot's sister had told him about how Tessa had tried so hard to delay bed-time by praying for anyone and anything under the sun, until they'd finally had to put a stop to it. She got to pray for three things, Timothy got three, and then Rebekah and Chris would pray for the children. He'd witnessed it a few times before Chris and Rebekah died and thought it cute. Now he understood the burden of having two little lives to care for, to grow up in the knowledge of the Savior, to worry over and educate and discipline. Every night the feeling nearly overwhelmed him, forcing him to his knees in prayer.

"Dear Jesus," Tessa began, "bless Uncle Elliot, and help heal Mr. Matthews's leg, and thank You for the trip to the Indian camp tomorrow. Amen."

Timothy pressed the thumbs of his laced hands to the bridge of his nose, his eyes screwed shut. "Dear God, thanks that Kennekuk could visit, and thanks that Lieutenant Dunn finally got married so he can quit being so lonesome and sad for Miss Fern, and thanks for bringing Aunt Priscilla to visit. Could You please help her to like it here? Amen."

Elliot's eyes flew open, and his gaze collided with Priscilla's. He hadn't realized Timothy had warmed to her so quickly. Tessa had been an open book, but Timothy had been reserved and — Elliot had thought

— undecided about his aunt.

"Now you and Uncle Elliot have to pray." Tessa squinted through half-closed eyes at Priscilla. "That's what Mama and Daddy always did."

"You don't have to," Elliot rushed to re-assure Priscilla. "Not everyone is comfort-able praying in front of strangers."

"I'd like to. And anyway, you're not strangers. You're family — at least the twins are." Her cheeks looked a bit flushed, and her eyes had taken on a softness that drew him into their luminous depths. He swal-lowed and bowed his head.

"Dear Father, thank You for bringing me to Fort Bliss safely. I ask Your blessing on Tessa and Timothy. Give them peaceful sleep tonight. Watch over them and keep them. Draw them close to You. Amen."

Elliot reached out from where he sat on Timothy's bed and clasped Tessa's hand with one of his. Timothy took his other hand in their nightly ritual. "Heavenly Father, we thank You for the gift this day has been. Thank You for the marriage of Harry and Fern, and we ask Your blessing on their union. I thank You for Tessa and Timothy, and I pray that You will help me to be a good uncle to them." Tessa squeezed his hand. "Please watch over the kids. Bless our time tomorrow at the Indian camp. Help us to be salt and light. Amen."

He leaned over and kissed Tessa's forehead and patted Timothy's shoulder. "Good night. See you in the morning. If you need anything, you know where to find me."

Priscilla rose, too, and hovered beside the bed as if unsure. Timothy solved her problem by sitting up and holding his arms out.

She hugged him, her eyes closing for a moment as her cheek rested against his hair before she released him. Not to be left out, Tessa shot up off her pillow. "Me too."

"Of course." The little girl's thin arms went around her aunt's neck in a fierce embrace.

"G'nite, Aunt Priscilla."

As they walked out together, Elliot noticed Priscilla furtively wiping her cheek. "They get to you, don't they? Brave and sweet and exasperating and endearing." *Not unlike you.*

"I haven't been a part of bedtime prayers like that before. It makes me realize how much they lost when their parents died."

He fought the urge to take her into his arms, to rest his cheek on her hair and close his eyes, like she had when she'd hugged Timothy. He wasn't sure if it would be to comfort her or to draw comfort. His own lack of experience and confidence to raise his sister's children staggered him at times. How nice would it be to share that burden with someone who might understand his loss?

"I think they're adjusting well, but time will tell, I suppose." He shoved his hands into his pockets to keep from touching her.

"Poor little mites. It seems so unfair for them to be deprived of their parents so young."

"That's one of the first things you learn out here. Life isn't fair." Out here or any-where else. Life was just life. You took it as it came, resting in the knowledge that God was sovereign, and that He loved His children.

Her hand flew out in a wide arc. "How can you be so pragmatic about it? How can you wish them to continue in this life that is so harsh and takes so much from them? You're already stealing their childhood. Why should they have to give up even more than they've already lost?"

"Stealing their childhood?" All thought of comforting her fled.

"I saw that room. Military cots instead of beds? Footlockers with their names and the regiment stenciled on them? Do you force them to pass inspection every morning before breakfast? You treat them like little soldiers. And bless them if they don't try to act like soldiers. Even Tessa with that ridiculous forage cap she wears. She should have a proper sunbonnet. She should be able to grow her hair long like a normal girl and not be afraid of some Indian cutting it off or snatching her away. She should be learning to cook and sew. Instead she spends her days dogging soldiers, absorbing their manners, their language, and their biases. And then there's Timothy. He already speaks as if his future in the army is a foregone conclusion. He's known no other world, nor will he be exposed to any if he stays here with you. And the army will destroy him. He's so sensitive and gentle. The army will grind him up and spit him out. The way it does everyone."

Elliot blinked and grabbed her elbow, drawing her out onto the porch. "If we're going to cross swords, I'd prefer to do it outside where the children won't have to hear it." The night air swirled through the grass, and stars coated the sky.

"Now, what is this nonsense about me stealing the kids' childhood? I'll have you know, those beds and lockers came straight from their parents' house, arranged exactly as they had them in their room over in the officers' quarters. It's customary to stencil your name and regiment like that, in the event the army needs to send property to a new posting or to family back east. As to treating them like soldiers . . ." He spread his hands. "It's a method they understand and respond to. Perhaps it isn't the best, but I'm new to this parenting lark."

"It's distasteful. They're so recently bereaved, and so young . . ." Her voice cracked. "They need some coddling and comforting, something only a woman can provide." She crossed her arms, not in a judgmental way, but as if she needed some comforting and coddling herself.

He jammed his fingers through his hair. "I'm doing the best I can here. What do you want from me?"

"I want the children. I want you to let me take them back east and make a real home for them." Moonlight shone in her eyes and on her hair. Her tongue darted out to moisten her lips, and the moonlight glistened there, too. "I want you to let me mother them." She reached out and put her hand on his arm, tilting her head, appealing to him.

Elliot jerked back as if stung. He'd been softening toward her, letting her reveal all his inadequacies to be a parent to the twins, letting her draw him into her vulnerabilities with her pleas. Until she'd touched him. How like a woman to use her charms to bowl a man over. How like Muriel to turn enormous eyes, tears hovering on her lashes, at him. He steeled himself. "They're not leaving. I'm not turning my back on my promise to their mother."

Her lips parted, and she blinked away those treacherous teardrops. "Good night, Major Ryder." She went inside and shut the door of his own quarters firmly in his face.

CHAPTER FIVE

Priscilla allowed a young soldier to assist her into the wagon beside Fern, who glowed as a new bride should, and Mrs. Bracken, who oversaw the proceedings like a field marshal. Still stinging from her encounter with Major Ryder last night and again this morning, Priscilla scanned the assemblage for him.

Their argument at breakfast centered around whether the children should be allowed to ride their ponies on the expedition to the Kickapoo camp. The children and Elliot were in favor of the idea. Priscilla opposed. Though carried out in a civil tone in front of the twins, it was definitely an argument.

And she was firmly outranked in addition to being outnumbered.

Tessa and Timothy had run out of the house to the stables the minute they were excused from the table, laughing and chattering and ready to embrace their adventure. Elliot, after putting his foot down about their mode of transportation for the day, had disappeared into his surgery, leaving Priscilla to stew.

Fern nudged Priscilla's shoulder. "It seems we're back where we started, rattling around in this wagon. I'm glad the trip won't be as long today."

Harry brought his mount close to the wagon, and the newlyweds bent their heads together. Whatever he said left Fern blushing and smiling, her eyes following his lean form as he rode away to join his company. Mrs. Bracken smiled knowingly and patted Fern's knee, and it was Priscilla who felt left out.

A bugle sounded, and the chaos of milling horses and men around them sorted itself out into an orderly, double-wide column. The wagon Priscilla rode in took up position in the middle of the column, and with flags flying, they set off toward the river. The twins, as per Priscilla and Elliot's compromise, rode directly behind the wagon where she could keep an eye on them.

"Pekhotah's camp will be along the Rio Grande west of the fort." Mrs. Bracken took the jostling and jolting without showing any sign of discomfort. Her eyes were bright, as if embracing this adventure. Only Major Crane's wife wore a pinched, sour expression.

"And Pekhotah is the chief, the one in charge?" Fern asked.

"Yes, but not the way most easterners think," Mrs. Bracken answered. "The tribe will have several chiefs. They are the warriors who have lived a long time, or have been especially wise and brave, or both. They are more advisors than true rulers. The men of the tribe decide together what course to take, and with the Kickapoo, the women have some influence and input. It's a rather democratic society."

"Democratic." Mrs. Crane practically spat the word. "Heathen, that's what they are. Without conscience or morals. Thieving, murderous savages, every one of them."

Priscilla and Fern shared a look. The venom in the woman's words startled Priscilla. She herself was curious more than anything about the Kickapoo. She bore them no malice, but then again, she hadn't had anyone in her family killed by marauding Indians.

"Girls," Mrs. Bracken spoke to Priscilla and Fern, ignoring Mrs. Crane. "It isn't often we're invited like this into an Indian encampment. If these were Comanche or

Apache, we wouldn't be going. But we've had fairly good relations with this particular tribe of Kickapoo over the last few years. Major Ryder's friendship with the medicine man has been helpful. Last summer the major helped treat one of Pekhotah's infant sons who was ill, and since then, the chief has been willing to act peacefully toward the soldiers."

A quick check behind Priscilla showed the twins, eyes bright, heads high, trotting along on their shaggy ponies. Tessa wore her forage cap, and her legs stuck out under her skirt revealing quite a bit of her black stockings. She should be riding sidesaddle, not astride. Timothy caught Priscilla looking at him and raised his hand. Priscilla waved back.

Behind them, Elliot sat tall in his saddle, his long legs wrapped around the animal's barrel, his face shaded under the brim of his hat. Brass buttons gleamed, and sunlight reflected off the insignia on the front of his hat. His horse, a magnificent chestnut animal with white stockings and a white blaze, stalked the ground as if he owned it, tossing his head and snorting from time to time. Elliot seemed impervious to the beast's shenanigans. She'd heard the twins referring to the horse as Bill, which seemed an altogether too pedestrian name for such a steed.

Tessa's pony was a round little pinto named Wingfoot, another misnomer, for the stout beast had more plod than grace about him. Timothy's mount, black with a white star, rejoiced in the name Sooty, and picked up his feet with dainty precision, and seemed to be enjoying the whole enterprise immensely. Priscilla remembered her father taking her up before him on his horse when she was a small child. It was one of the few sharp memories she had of him, his arm around her, him leaning down to whisper in her ear, tickling her skin with his whiskers. He'd made her feel so safe.

And then he was just gone. Gone from her life. And everything had changed. She glanced back at the twins. They knew exactly how she felt, and it made her heart hurt for them all the more.

A ripple went through the procession as they approached the Indian camp. Lazy spirals of smoke drifted up just beyond a rise, and as they topped it, Priscilla took in the scene. At least forty odd shelters clustered along the river bank. They appeared to be made of poles and bark, round-topped little hovels. A band of ponies grazed at the far end of the camp, dogs barked, children ran, chasing each other and the dogs.

Colonel Bracken, Major Crane, Harry, and Elliot separated from the now-halted column and rode slowly toward the camp. Priscilla half-stood in the wagon to keep them in sight as they met a contingent of Kickapoo men that walked out from the camp.

"Everyone's just saying hello, letting each other know they mean no harm. It's an invited visit, for sure, but it's best to take things slowly." Mrs. Bracken kept a watchful eye on the proceedings.

Priscilla realized her heart was thumping, and she'd taken a death grip on the wagon side. Surely there wouldn't be trouble. She checked on the children. Tessa had broken formation and ridden a few paces away to be able to see better. One of the soldiers gently nudged her back into line with a wink and a smile.

The conversation must've gone well, for Harry waved his arm to the waiting soldiers, twenty in all, for them to come down. Priscilla exhaled and settled back on her seat.

As they entered the camp, she tried to take it all in at once. Who would've thought she would ever visit a real Kickapoo camp on the Texas plains? She drew her folio into her arms, eager to draw everything she saw so she would remember it forever.

Elliot pulled up alongside the wagon and dismounted in a fluid movement both graceful and masculine. His boots shone, and his piercing gray eyes swept over her. He'd said nothing about her dress today, but the twitch of his mustache when he sighted her full gray skirt and peach and gray striped waistcoat over a white shirred blouse told her he thought it unsuitable. But it was the most utilitarian garment she owned. Out of necessity she'd left her hoops at the fort, wearing three starched petticoats instead. She felt ungainly without the assistance of her hoops to hold out her skirt, but hoops in this instance would've been ridiculous. Moving to the end of the wagon, she gathered the fabric in one hand, reaching for the wagon side with the other.

"Here, let me." Elliot reached up to help her, his hands encompassing her waist. Her palms rested on his broad shoulders, and she felt the play of muscle under his woolen tunic. When her feet rested on the grass, she looked up into his face. This close, his lashes were even longer and thicker than she'd first thought, and his cheeks and chin bore the blue-black tone of a heavy beard. He smelled of sunshine and male and faintly of herbs. His eyes stared intently into hers, and she couldn't help but wonder if he liked what he saw. She'd been told that she was more than passably pretty, but she'd never cared that much before what others thought.

So why did she care what Elliot Ryder thought now? The man was impossibly stubborn and completely ignorant of how children should be raised, and . . . in his own way, very kind. She had a hard time reconciling those traits, but she had to be honest. He had shown the ability to be very caring.

"You and the kids stay where I can see you. There are some ceremonial things we have to complete that might seem boring and long to you and them, but it would be a grave insult to try to cut them short. I'll get you a place near me where you can see what's going on and not be in the way."

She nodded and only then did she realize she had failed to remove her hands from his shoulders. His hands still spanned her waist, and she could feel every finger through the layers of fabric. Confused, she stepped back and reached into the wagon for her tablet and charcoals.

Tessa charged into her legs. "Isn't it neat? Look at all the wickiups. I wish we could live in a wickiup."

Timothy couldn't stop turning at every sound and movement, clearly fascinated by everything he saw. "I wonder where Kennekuk is. He said he would show me how to carve a horse."

Dogs barked, men shouted, children laughed. The earthy smells of animal skins and warm sunshine and smoke swirled around her. She felt as if she had walked into an alien land. Her fingers went to the string of amber beads around her neck. A Kickapoo woman went past, and on her back in a blanket rode a darling little baby with eyes so black they glistened. Chubby cheeks indented with two perfect dimples, and four gleaming white teeth charmed Priscilla, as did the quiff of black hair standing atop the baby's crown.

"This way." Elliot took her elbow and guided her toward a campfire where sections of log had been set upright as seats. He settled the twins cross-legged on the ground in front of her and took a seat beside her. "You kids stay quiet and no squirming. The leader, Chief Pekhotah, is a great man, and he's going to address his guests. It would be very rude for you not to pay attention or to get all jumpy before he's done."

Priscilla folded her hands in her lap and turned her attention to the elderly man seated across from them. His dark hair had been parted in the middle and pulled back severely behind his ears. He wore a cloth headband, several ropes of beads around his neck, and a buttoned, long-sleeved shirt. His pants were covered by a long breech-clout of bright colored plaid. His face bore no expression, lips thin and flat, eyes half-lidded. To either side of him sat a row of Kickapoo men of various ages. Kennekuk squatted to Pekhotah's immediate right, and he nodded gravely to the children and to her. Elliot put a restraining hand on Tessa's shoulder when she waved to the medicine man.

"Those are the tribal chiefs, the leaders." Elliot adjusted his saber at his side. "Their chief wives will come to stand behind them during the welcome."

Pekhotah held up his hand and began to speak.

Priscilla understood no Kickapoo, so Elliot translated bits and pieces for her, keeping his voice low. "He is asking that we have peace together, his tribe and the white soldiers. They have come through a dark time of strife and only want to live in peace. He wants his children and his wives to be able to sleep well at night. He doesn't come as a wolf, but to talk plainly with us."

Pekhotah went on and on. Across the fire,

at the end of the row of Kickapoo sitting to the chief's left, a handsome, proud-featured young man sat with his hands on his knees. He wasn't looking at his chief or at the soldiers. Instead, he kept his eyes fixed on Priscilla. She tried not to look at him but found her gaze returning to his bold face again and again. Why did he stare? She wasn't the only woman from the fort in attendance today. Surely he'd seen white women before. And his look wasn't just curiosity. Her cheeks heated, and she wished she'd brought her fan along.

At last the chief finished speaking and lifted a red pouch from his side onto his lap.

"He's bringing out his peace pipe. He'll load it with tobacco or kinnikinnick — a tobacco made from red willow — and his chief wife will light it from the fire. Then he'll offer it to his soldiers and to a few of the officers."

"Will you smoke?"

"If it is offered to me, I cannot refuse, for it would be a deadly insult, but I'm sitting far enough away that it shouldn't come to me." He kept his voice low. "I've explained this to the children, that though I don't condone smoking tobacco, I could not be so rude as to insult my hosts by refusing in this instance."

She nodded her understanding, grateful for his explanations. Fear that she might do or say something that might offend their hosts in some way had stalked her ever since he'd first said she should stay by him.

As he predicted, the pipe made the rounds but didn't venture as far as where they sat. She let out a breath. "What happens now?"

"There will be some friendly competitions, wrestling, riding, shooting. Then a meal, then a ceremonial dance to end the evening."

"Should we have brought food? There's an awful lot of us to feed."

"Don't you worry. Colonel Bracken sent over a couple of steers yesterday, and Mrs. Bracken brought some other things along. Look, the colonel is presenting them now."

Tall and military in every aspect of his bearing, gray hair smooth and beard trimmed precisely, the colonel rose and motioned to a group of soldiers standing beside the wagon Priscilla had ridden in. The men unloaded a stack of blankets and several kegs.

"Flour, lard, some bags of rice, blankets, and trinkets. To say thank you for inviting us." Elliot rose and offered her his arm. "You kids can get up now. You did a great job sitting still. It would be all right for you to approach Kennekuk now. I know he wants to introduce you to his family. But remember, especially you, Tess, stay where I can see you. Don't go into any of the wickiups without me, and don't wander off."

Women and children who had been hanging back during the ceremony mingled with the women from the fort. Priscilla noticed the Kickapoo women did not approach any of the soldiers alone.

"Kickapoo women are expected to be chaste and circumspect. A trait I admire in their culture. None of the unmarried women will talk to a man unless a member of her family is present. They watch over their women closely." Elliot nodded to a young warrior who strode by — the same young man who had stared at her throughout the welcome ceremony. Priscilla felt the man's bold stare again, and her hand tightened on Elliot's elbow.

He glanced down at her, his eyebrows raised.

"Do you know him?" she whispered, looking over her shoulder at the retreating Indian.

"Not by name. I've seen him a few times, why?"

She shrugged. "No reason."

Kennekuk approached, the twins holding his hands, faces alight.

Elliot grasped his forearm. "My friend."

"Guess what, Uncle Elliot? We met Kennekuk's wife and his children, and then we met his *other* wife. Did you know he had two?" Tessa's eyes went round. "I didn't know someone could have two wives at the same time."

"Tessa." Priscilla bent a look at the little girl.

"It is . . . fine." Kennekuk winked at Tessa. "It is good for our peoples to know each other. Yes, I have two wives. They are sisters, and they have been with me for many years. My children are nearly grown now, and soon, they will marry and have children of their own. Perhaps that is why I like these two so much. They remind me of my children when they were small."

"I brought you some new herbs." Elliot patted a pouch on his black belt. "Is there somewhere we can go to talk about them?"

"Come."

Elliot turned to Priscilla. "If you and the children would like, you can go with Fern and Harry to watch the contests. Kennekuk and I will be some time, I'm afraid, and you would be bored. When we get to talking of medicaments and herbs, we can go on for longer than Chief Pekhotah."

"Of course. We'll be fine," Priscilla assured him, though she felt anything but certain. However, her curiosity warred with uneasiness. *Stop being silly. Nothing bad is going to happen. There are twenty soldiers here, and everyone is being friendly.*

She and the kids hurried to catch up with Fern and Harry as they walked through the camp toward where the horses grazed on the sparse brush. Fern held onto Harry's arm, and he beamed down on her. Priscilla wouldn't have begrudged them ignoring everyone else, but they graciously included herself and the twins in their conversation.

"Thank you for letting us tag along with you."

"Isn't it exciting? I have so much to write home about already." Fern tucked a stray curl back under her sunbonnet. "And Harry assures me there will be much more before the day is out."

"They're really putting on a show for us." Harry's accent bespoke his New England upbringing. "Our families will never have encountered anything like this."

Wrestling matches were first. By far the ones that drew the most cheers were the bouts between a Kickapoo and a soldier.

They circled one another, grappled, threw, and tussled. A winner would be declared, and it would start all over. Priscilla found a place to sit and opened her sketchbook. Rather than draw the men wrestling, she drew portraits of some of the Kickapoo women and children. Before long, several youngsters had gathered around her, watching her, laughing and pointing at the drawings of their own faces and chattering. One by one they sat for her, and when she'd finished their sketch, she gave them the picture.

When only one man was left standing in the wrestling ring — the same young man who had stared so boldly at Priscilla earlier — he was declared the overall winner. He grinned, his teeth a white slash in his sweat-slicked face. He stared boldly at Priscilla, his hands on his hips, his bare chest heaving from his exertion.

Uneasiness scampered up her spine, and she looked away, thankful when the call went out for riders to assemble for the horse races. Priscilla herded the children ahead of her, barely able to concentrate on their chatter as the Kickapoo man's unnerving stare followed her every move.

Where was Elliot? She would feel so much better if he were at her side.

The races were much more to her liking than the wrestling. And the horsemanship of the Kickapoo warriors was excellent. Several rode with not so much as a blanket on their mounts, their long legs wrapped tightly around their horses' girths, leaning over their necks, whooping and shouting. Hooves thrashed the ground, throwing up great clouds of sandy earth. Bays, chestnuts, pintos, and grays flashed by in each race.

More than just racing horses, there were also feats of strength and marksmanship. Targets were set up along a route, and Indians, galloping their horses headlong, threw lances and shot arrows with bone-chilling accuracy. They showed off all manner of weaponry from war clubs to axes.

Match races were set up, and several of the soldiers took part. Tessa and Timothy cheered loudly when Corporal Rhodes won his race. Kennekuk and Elliot finally joined the spectators, and the twins recounted everything they'd missed. Priscilla found the tension in her shoulders easing now that Elliot had returned to their group.

Chief Pekhotah raised his hand and spoke a few words. Elliot translated for Priscilla. "He says there has been a challenge raised, since the results of the races are an even tie between the Kickapoo and the soldiers. He wants the best horse and horseman from the fort to face their champion."

Harry shrugged. "Guess that means you, Major."

"Me?" Elliot frowned. "No, thank you. I think I'll pass."

"Your Bill is the fastest animal we've got."

"Yeah, Uncle Elliot. Race him. You'll beat him all hollow." Tessa hopped up and down, her forage cap sliding over her eyes.

"Looks like the colonel agrees." Harry nodded toward Colonel Bracken, who was walking toward them. "I'll go get your mount."

Elliot's lips compressed, and his eyes clouded. "I should've anticipated this."

"Don't you want to race?" Priscilla shaded her eyes.

He sighed and lowered his voice as his commanding officer drew near. "I'd rather not show all my cards. I do have a fast horse, and if the Kickapoo know how fast he is, they're much more likely to try to steal him sometime when I'm out on a patrol."

"I thought things were peaceful between the fort and the tribe?"

He smoothed his mustache. "They are at the moment, but that doesn't mean they always will be. And no Kickapoo worth his salt would pass up on a chance to own a horse like Bill."

Kennekuk grinned and nodded. "Yes, that is true."

Colonel Bracken drew near and said, "Major Ryder, it would seem you're being called to action. They want a match race, and you're the obvious choice."

Elliot drew a deep breath, glanced at Kennekuk, then at Priscilla. "Yes, sir." He removed his hat and began unbuttoning his tunic. Beneath the brass buttons and blue wool, he wore a simple white shirt and suspenders. The suspenders bit into his shoulders, wrinkling the fabric and emphasizing his masculine build. Priscilla took the possessions he handed her, including his sword, folding his tunic over her arm and pressing it to her waist.

"Take good care of these." Elliot removed his watch from his pocket and placed it in her hand.

She wanted to protest, but she bit her lip. Elliot didn't want to race. He had valid reasons for not wanting to, and yet, here was his commanding officer telling him he had to. Yet another example of how futile it was to try to reason with the great machine that was the US Army.

The Kickapoo champion stalked by with his horse, and Priscilla's breath hitched. It was the man who had won the wrestling match. The man who had stared at her. He stopped, taking in their group, the children, Priscilla holding Elliot's clothing. His brows came down, his face twisted in a scowl, and he turned abruptly away, headed toward the starting line. His horse, a rangy pinto, sidled and snorted, tossing his head as if eager for the challenge awaiting him. The animal wore no tack, not so much as a saddle blanket.

"Unsaddle my horse." Elliot tucked his shirt in more securely. "All that gear will just slow us down."

"You sure?" Harry moved to the stirrup and flipped it over the saddle to reach the girth.

Elliot ignored the hands clasped to help him mount and grabbed a handful of mane. With an agile leap, he swung astride the tall animal and lifted his reins. Looking down into Priscilla's face, he smiled. "You look worried."

She shrugged, clutching his belongings, trying to quell the uneasiness plaguing her.

Gathering up his reins, he asked, "Wish me well?"

She shaded her eyes, trying to ignore how handsome and . . . vital . . . he looked with the sun glinting off his black hair, his gray eyes alight with anticipation. "Be safe . . . and go fast."

The course was a wide horseshoe out onto the floodplain and had been marked with tasseled lances pierced into the earth. All along the way, young Kickapoo boys sat atop their ponies, ready to cheer the racers as they sped by.

Priscilla's heart fluttered as the two riders lined up. A pistol shot started them off. Elliot's chestnut leaped from the line alongside the pinto, and with shouts of encouragement from the onlookers, they thundered away.

For almost the entire circuit, they were in view, and there was hardly a pace between them. Both men bent low over their mounts' necks, urging them on. Harry, standing next to Priscilla, scooped Tessa up in his arms so she could see, and Kennekuk appeared at their side to do the same for Timothy.

Tessa yelled and cheered, but Priscilla found she couldn't make a sound. A knot had lodged in her throat, and she clenched her fingers around the pocket watch until they ached, hugging his possessions to her breast. Her own involvement surprised her. Why should she care who won a simple horse race? And yet she did care. She wanted Elliot to win.

147

As the two riders came toward the finish line, neither horse seemed able to put a nose out in front. Elliot had his hands high on Bill's neck, pumping, his face lost in the horse's streaming mane. His opponent raced only inches away. At the last minute, Elliot's horse seemed to falter in stride, and the pinto swept by, half a length ahead.

Priscilla let out a breath she didn't know she'd held, lightheaded and trembling. She tried to swallow, but her mouth was dry.

"He didn't win." Tessa couldn't hide the incredulity in her tone.

"It was a good race. Close until the very end." Harry let her slide to the ground.

Priscilla took Tessa's hand, lest she disappear into the crowd. "Don't wander off, Tessa. Uncle Elliot will come to us."

Corporal Rhodes hurried forward to take the reins from Elliot, who had dismounted and held out his hand to his opponent. The Kickapoo took it, grasping him by the forearm. Whatever he said startled Elliot, who looked over in Priscilla's direction and shook his head. They spoke for a few more minutes before parting, and Elliot came toward her.

His hair was in disarray, and sweat glistened at his temples. As he drew near, he shrugged. "You can't win them all." He wiped his forehead and winked at Priscilla. His smile made her narrow her eyes.

She stepped close to whisper. "Did you lose that race on purpose?"

Again he shrugged. "What do you think?" Mischief lurked in his eyes, and the idea of sharing a secret with him made her pulse erratic.

Before she could answer, Tessa hugged Elliot hard around the thighs. "I thought you were the best, even if you didn't win."

He gently removed her cap and bent down to drop a kiss on her head. "Thank you, sweetling."

The adoration in Tessa's eyes as she looked up at her uncle squeezed Priscilla's heart. They shared a touching bond, and for the first time, Priscilla realized that it might hurt the children to be separated from him. And yet, sometimes one had to make hard decisions if they were in the best interest of the children. A proper home, proper schooling, safety and security. That's what the children needed. And love. She could provide them with all the love they could ever need, if she only got the chance.

Elliot reached out and tweaked Timothy's nose. "Are you having a good time, Tim?"

Timothy nodded, his flaxen hair tousled, and the freckles standing out on his nose.

"There's so much to see. I wish I'd brought my notebook. I don't want to forget anything."

"By the way, Priscilla, the man I rode against, his name is Niganithat. It means He Who Flies First." Elliot's eyes danced with some inner amusement. "He's sent me over with a proposition."

Priscilla glanced over to where a group of Kickapoo men stood, her skin tightening when she saw Niganithat staring at her. "I'm not interested in any propositions from him. He makes me uncomfortable."

"Ah, but I'm honor-bound to deliver his message. He says you are very beautiful, and when I made it clear to him that you are not my woman and the mother of my children, he offered for your hand in marriage."

Her mouth fell open and all the air rushed out of her lungs. Fern, who had overheard, gasped and giggled.

"That's ridiculous. He doesn't even know me. He can't be serious." Priscilla handed Elliot his hat and tunic, waiting for him to don both before returning his sidearm, belt, and saber.

"Oh, but he is. He has made a most generous offer. He's willing to trade his horse for you." Though Elliot tried to keep a straight face, his mustache twitched, and the dimple in his cheek appeared. "It's a very good horse, as you saw. Very fast." Finally, he could hold his laughter no longer. "If you could see your face."

Heat charged up her neck and into her cheeks. Of all the farcical situations. And Elliot laughing at her like a . . . a . . . baboon. "This is absurd. Please give him my regrets." Head high, she pitched his pocket watch at him, picked up her skirts, and marched away.

By the time dusk fell, Priscilla had had enough of the Indian camp. Niganithat had hovered a dozen yards away from her for most of the day, and he'd upped his offer — using Kennekuk as his messenger this time — to his best horse *and* three dogs. She kept her attention focused on the twins and deliberately away from her would-be suitor.

Dinner was . . . anticlimactic. She had expected something exotic, but what she got was standard military fare. Roasted turnips, boiled beef, and hardtack biscuits. The one surprise was roasted pumpkin.

"They grew the pumpkins over the winter down in Mexico." Elliot forked a bite of the orange vegetable into his mouth. "They're already planting their gardens here. Corn, squash, pumpkins, beans."

Priscilla tasted the pumpkin. It was a far cry from pumpkin pie, but she smiled and swallowed, stabbing another piece on her plate.

"We'll make a frontierswoman out of you yet." He set aside his plate and gathered Tessa onto his lap. "You getting sleepy? You've had a big day."

Tessa nodded, resting her head against his shoulder. Timothy sat cross-legged at his feet, carving on a knot of wood, his face a mask of concentration.

"Be careful with that knife, Timothy," Priscilla couldn't help but caution.

"He's fine. His dad first started him with carving, and Kennekuk has given him some pointers," Elliot said, scanning the faces across the bonfire.

This gave Priscilla pause. She hadn't known her brother carved wood. Of course, she hadn't seen him in some years, not since he left to join the army when she was eleven. Along the way he'd acquired a wife and two children, but he had never returned home. Her sense of isolation grew when Timothy tucked his knife and carving into his bag and leaned back against Elliot's legs. With her parents both gone and her brother, too, these children were her only family. She *had* to convince Elliot to let her create a home for them.

Elliot watched Priscilla in the firelight. He had to admit, she'd reacted well to her encounter with the Kickapoo. Unlike Mrs. Crane, who all day had complained and glared and predicted disaster, Priscilla had been cordial, curious, and interested in the goings on. She'd smiled at the Kickapoo women who had wanted to touch her dress, had cheered the contests and games, and not once made a disparaging remark.

He didn't miss the watchful eye she kept on the children, especially Tessa, who seemed to fascinate their hosts with her blond curls and china-blue eyes. Several of the warriors had asked for a piece of her hair, in spite of the short haircut, but Elliot had declined. They'd use it as a talisman, and it might give them the idea that they possessed part of her spirit.

Niganithat scowled from across the fire. He clapped his hands on his knees and rose, stalking toward them, his face intense. Priscilla stiffened and shot Elliot an imploring glance. He had to hand it to her, she'd stood up fairly well under the repeated offers, but it was all beginning to wear a bit thin.

Elliot shifted Tessa to Priscilla's lap and

153

rose. "I should've told him you were my woman. That would've ended it." As he said the words, his heart jolted. His woman. He supposed she was, in a way. She was under his care, after all. That must be why it sounded all right to his ears. He moved to stand slightly in front of Priscilla and the kids as Niganithat advanced on them.

"I will give you the horse and *five* dogs. Five good dogs." Niganithat pointed to the row of canines tethered by his wickiup.

Drawing a deep breath, Elliot pretended to consider the notion so as not to give offense by rejecting him too quickly. At last, he shook his head. "I'm sorry, but the answer is still no."

Niganithat threw his hands up, rolling his eyes. "No woman is worth six dogs." He stalked away, every line of his body indignant.

"What did he say?" Priscilla tugged on his sleeve. He translated, and the outraged look on her face made him laugh.

She sputtered and fussed. "That's barbaric. A horse and five dogs?"

"Five *good* dogs," Elliot reminded her. "But not six." He laughed again when she turned her shoulder to him. But he didn't miss the twitch of her lips or the light in her eyes. She had a good sense of humor. He couldn't imagine what Mrs. Crane's response to such an offer would've been.

As night fell, the drums started, and several young Kickapoo men rose and began to dance and chant. One, in a magnificent owl-feather headdress, stomped the ground harder than the rest, raising his fists to the night sky and shouting. Around and around the fire they went, the leader getting closer and closer to the spectators with each round. Several of the men wore bells tied just below their knees, chiming and jangling with each stomp. Others, clad only in leggings and breech-clouts, had oiled their bodies with animal grease, and glistened in the firelight.

Tessa stiffened on Priscilla's lap, and Timothy pressed back hard against Elliot's legs. Priscilla's eyes were round and her face pale as the lead warrior shook his fists, the cords of his neck standing out as he released an eerie howl. Her arms went around her niece, tucking Tessa's head under her chin and shielding her.

Dusty squatted beside Elliot. "That's Wahpecatqua. I recognize him from a little skirmish we had up in the Sierra Blancos. He was trading with some Comancheros when we happened up on them."

Elliot rose and stepped away from the fire

into the shadows. "Are you sure?"

"I'm sure. They had a couple of Mexican women, probably kidnapped for slave trade. We broke up the meeting, but they got away."

Comancheros. Men who traded with the Comanche and Kickapoo and other plains tribes. The trouble was, they traded blankets and guns and whiskey for Mexican slaves kidnapped from their villages and dragged north.

Harry came over to join them. "Major," he addressed Elliot by his rank, something he only did when other soldiers were present. "Some of the women are getting scared. This was supposed to be a friendly dance, and it's getting rather serious, don't you think?"

Elliot stroked his mustache. "I agree. I think now would be a good time to head back to the fort. I'd just as soon have the women and children where it's safe."

"Agreed." Harry checked his sidearm.

"Corporal Rhodes," Elliot said. "Go get the horses and wagon ready, and I'll have a word with the colonel and see if I can't get Kennekuk's attention and let him know we're leaving."

Harry waited until the solder had saluted and gone. "Things sure change when you're a family man, don't they? I've only been married a day, and already, I'm making choices based on what's best for my wife. I wouldn't mind hanging around to see if we can learn some more about what the relationship between this tribe and the Comancheros might be, but not if it puts my wife at risk."

Elliot nodded. He'd experienced the same change in thinking when he'd inherited the twins. And for now, he had not just the children to think about, but a pretty eastern visitor who had already captured the attention of one warrior.

CHAPTER SIX

"What do you children do all day if there's no school?" Priscilla sat between the twins on the porch steps. She stifled a yawn. Her sleep had been troubled with images of the dancing silhouettes against the leaping campfire and the throbbing of the drums. The uneasiness that had stalked her all day last week as they visited the Indian camp continued to rumble behind her breastbone. The breeze kicked up a dust devil, swirling it across the parade ground, scattering sand and grit until it blew itself out in the cactus and creosote bushes beyond the commander's house.

"Depends." Tessa plucked a long blade of dry grass and broke it into little pieces as she talked. "Uncle Elliot has chores for us to do. I have to sweep up the kitchen, and Timothy has to fill the water buckets and the wood box. Those are the ones we have to do every day. Then there are the special chores that come up." The sunshine bounced off her curls and picked out the freckles on her pert little nose. "And we help Samson when he asks."

Timothy nodded. "And we play with the other kids. There aren't many at the fort right now, and most of them are bigger than us or way smaller."

"And none of them like horses as much as us. Sometimes the big kids tease us and tell us we smell like the stables. I don't like them much. I'd rather play with Timothy." Tessa wrinkled her little nose.

"I like best when we get to help out at the shops." Timothy put his elbows on his knees and propped his cheeks on his fists. Sweat dampened the hair at his temples into sharp points that clung to his skin. The temperature had soared, making the distance shimmer and the close-up broil.

"The shops?" She fixed his collar, smoothing it down.

"Sure." He pointed to the building on the northeast corner of the square. The only one that didn't open out onto the hard-baked parade ground.

"That's right. Your uncle pointed them out to me. What are they again?"

"Blacksmith, bakery, saddler, carpenter's shop. Sometimes the baker lets us punch down the dough for the bread. He makes so much bread you can hardly believe it. Each of the barracks has their own kitchen and mess hall, but the baker makes the bread for all the troops. I like the bakery the best. It smells good."

Tessa, never one to be outdone, shook her head. "I like it when the blacksmith or the carpenter lets us straighten out bent nails. Sometimes we use the vise and sometimes we use a hammer."

"And sometimes he puts a little gunpowder on the anvil and hits it with a hammer. Bang!" Timothy scrunched his shoulders. "That's fun."

Priscilla shook her head. Though the twins had a measure of supervision, she couldn't say much about the quality. They seemed to have free run of the place. "Is there anywhere at the fort where you can't go?"

"Sure," Timothy nodded. "We can't go into the barracks or into the guardhouse or into the commissary or the commander's house. Not unless we're invited. But the shops are different. They're run by civilians." The way he said the word made her wonder if he thought civilians inferior.

Tessa nodded. "They just work here. They're not part of the regiment. Not like us."

Smoothing her dark green skirt over her knees, Priscilla pondered whether to talk about their parents. They both seemed to have accepted being orphaned with surprising maturity. Or had they dealt with their grief at all? She hadn't known them before, nor had she seen them in the days and weeks immediately following Chris and Rebekah's deaths. She decided to address the issue obliquely. "What did you do with your time before you came to live with your uncle?"

"When Papa came home, after retreat each night, he'd play with us. We'd help him clean his equipment, his saddle and bridle and such, and he'd let us watch while he cleaned his guns. But he never let us touch those. Papa said we were too little yet, but someday he'd teach us both to shoot because everybody out here needs to know how to shoot a gun." Timothy pointed his index finger as if he held a pistol and snapped off a few imaginary shots. "When his equipment was all up to regulation, then we'd play checkers or tag or guessing games or charades. Papa was good at charades."

The more she heard of her brother and his parenting, the larger her loss became. How she wished she'd known him and been part of his life before it was too late.

Tessa stuck her boots out in front of her. They were scuffed, and a couple of buttons had fallen off, but she waggled them happily. "We went to school last fall, but the teacher left at Christmastime. After that Mama made us do some lessons, and we always helped with the housework. You have to keep your quarters neat in the army. You never know when there might be an inspection. But we had fun, too. Mama was a good cook, and she grew flowers. She had a little garden behind our quarters where she grew vegetables and flowers. Mrs. Crane has the garden now, but she didn't plant anything in it. She said she would rather get her vegetables from the locals, and growing flowers is a waste of time. It's all gone to weeds now."

Resentment prickled Priscilla's skin. How sad to think of Rebekah's garden lying fallow. "What else did you do with your mama?"

"We rode a lot. I miss riding." Tessa threw the last piece of her grass stem to the ground. "We can't ride unless a grown-up goes with us. Mama was a good rider, and she'd take us almost every afternoon."

"Uncle Elliot is too busy to take us. He has to be an officer and a doctor, and he can't get much time off. Corporal Rhodes takes us sometimes, but he's got a lot to do being in charge of the officers' stables," Timothy said. "It's all right though. Duty first."

Elliot's first duty should be toward these children. They were running wild out here on the plains. "So you mostly fend for yourselves during the daytime?"

Timothy shrugged. "There's always something to do."

"Well, you know what I would like to do?"

"What?" they asked in unison.

"I'd like to go for a ride."

Tessa tilted her head. "Can you ride? You didn't ride over to the Kickapoo camp. You went in a wagon."

She tousled the little girl's curls. "I can ride, and I'd love to take you and Timothy out. Do you think your Corporal Rhodes could find a horse for me?"

They popped to their feet. Timothy took off at a run for the stables before skidding to a halt half a dozen strides later. "Are you a *good* rider?"

She smiled. "Tell Corporal Rhodes I want a dependable mount but not a plug. I'm no Kickapoo warrior, but I can ride well enough, I imagine. I'm going to change into proper clothes, and Tessa and I will meet you at the stables."

A half an hour later she and Tessa entered
the officers' stables, a square layout with
barns on three sides and a stackyard fenced
off in the center. Glossy rumps, chestnut,
black, bay, and a couple of grays, stood in
long lines, tethered in the shade of the barn
roofs.

"Our ponies are over here." Tessa tugged
on her hand.

Timothy stood with Corporal Rhodes. His
pony, Sooty, wore a saddle and bridle and
dozed in the afternoon sunshine. Another
soldier led Wingfoot out and tied him to a
hitching rail. "You want me to saddle him
up for you Miss Tessa, or do you want to do
it yourself?"

"I'll do it, thanks."

Corporal Rhodes winked at Priscilla and
without being overt, helped Tessa hoist the
saddle onto her rotund little mount and get
the cinch tight. As he worked, he addressed
Priscilla.

"Ma'am, Timothy tells me you'd like to
go for a ride. I've borrowed Mrs. Bracken's
sidesaddle for you, and I've put you up on
the horse your sister-in-law rode when she
took the children out. A bit of spirit, but
biddable. He'll give you a nice ride." He
waved to a black-pointed bay with a deep
chest and a long barrel.

Priscilla lifted the hem of her blue velvet riding habit and went to make friends.

"His name is Applejack," the corporal called after her.

"Hello, Applejack." She let him sniff her palm, running her other hand under the crest of his mane. Even through her gloves she could feel the warmth of his hide. He whiffed and nickered, shaking his head and rattling his bridle bit.

"I'll help you, ma'am." Corporal Rhodes bent and laced his fingers together, tossing her aboard with a quick, easy jerk.

She hooked her right leg into the fixed horn and stuck her left foot into the stirrup. Gathering her reins, she turned her mount. "Is there anything I should know?"

Rhodes shaded his eyes and watched her walk her mount. "There are a couple of patrols out for the day, exercising the horses and working on field drills. If you see them, stay out of the way. Stay within sight of the fort at all times. The kids know where they can go. And if you see anything that worries you, beat it back here like your hair's on fire. Other than that, have a great time. It's good for the kids you're here. They've been missing their folks, and they miss riding out."

Once they left the stable area, Priscilla

pulled up. "Where shall we go?"

"Let's go down to the river. I like it when Wingfoot splashes the water." Tessa shook up her reins and booted her pony in the ribs. The pinto took off, and Sooty, with Timothy bending over his neck, followed close behind.

Priscilla nudged her horse with her heel and lifted the reins. Applejack loped along and quickly overtook the smaller ponies. They galloped toward the dusty trees that flanked the Rio Grande. Adobe houses and stick corrals clustered together along the way, housing the residents of the town of El Paso. Priscilla had yet to venture into the town, having kept Colonel Bracken's caution in mind.

The gray-green smudge of trees grew larger, separating itself into individual trees. The wind rustled through the leaves, and Priscilla anticipated cooler air beneath their shading branches. As the horses headed southeast, Priscilla checked over her shoulder to make sure she could still see the flag flying above Fort Bliss.

They passed through a grove of brushy trees, and Priscilla inhaled deeply. "Are these what I think they are?" Small green fruit clustered at the ends of the dusty green-leafed branches.

"It's an orange grove. Mama brought us through here right before she got sick, and all the trees were covered with little white blossoms. It smelled heavenly." Tessa used her little quirt to poke at the fruit. "In a few months, we'll have oranges and watermelons and tomatoes to eat. Uncle Elliot will buy them from the local farmers."

"I love watermelon." Timothy grinned. "And I can spit the seeds almost as far as Uncle Elliot."

"You can, can you?" Priscilla laughed at his proud statement.

On the other side of the grove, the bank sloped down to the water.

Tessa pulled Wingfoot up at the edge of the river. "This is the ford." She pointed across the water with her little quirt to a cluster of adobe buildings. "That's Paso del Norte. The Pass of the North."

Timothy loosened his reins, and Sooty ducked his black head down to drink. "That's Mexico. When bandits and Indians do bad things in Texas, they race to get across the river into Mexico because our troopers can't chase them there. It makes the men mad."

Something caught Priscilla's eye, and she glanced quickly to her right. Barely visible through the hanging tree limbs, a lean figure sat atop his horse twenty yards upstream. Not a soldier, not a resident of El Paso. An Indian.

She recognized the pinto horse first and then knew the rider. Niganithat. The Kickapoo who had wanted to marry her. What was he doing here?

Her mouth went dry, and she looked behind her, suddenly aware that she couldn't see the fort flag. Her heart thudded against her ribs, and she tried to keep her tone calm so as not to alarm the children. "We'd best be getting back."

"So soon?"

"Let's make it a race."

"But Applejack will win. His legs are the longest," Tessa pointed out.

"Then I'll give you a head start."

"Can we go round the long way? Over the irrigation trench? First one to the ditch wins?" Timothy asked.

"Sure, you two lead the way. Ready? Set? Go!"

The twins booted their startled ponies, letting out shrieks as Sooty and Wingfoot took off up the bank. Priscilla held Applejack to a slow lope, keeping the children in sight, checking over her shoulder to see if Niganithat followed. No sign of him. As the ponies burst through the orange grove out onto the sandy plain, she loosened the reins and let the horse run. The fort came into view, and she relaxed. It was a coincidence, the Kickapoo being at the river at the same time. And he wouldn't come this close to the fort.

She exulted in the feel of the wind against her face, the thud of hoofbeats, the warm, muscled animal beneath her. Freedom poured through her like it had never done before. No longer hemmed in by bridle path etiquette or the censoring eyes of city matrons, the wide open plain infused her with a recklessness she barely recognized.

The twins stuck to their mounts like little sand burrs, and the small horses bobbed side by side. When they reached the ditch, their ponies scrambled down the slope, splashed through the water, and heaved up the far side. Priscilla guided Applejack toward the ditch, but instead of plowing through it, he gathered himself and leapt! Her heart shot into her throat, and she grabbed his mane. Landing gracefully on the far side, the gelding swished his tail. Priscilla couldn't quell her laughter. Her hair had tumbled out of its pins and lay on her shoulders. She must look like she'd been picked up by a dust devil. Turning in a wide circle, she laughed and eased Applejack to a snorting, head-tossing stop.

The twins turned their horses back and stopped near her, their eyes wide.

"You jumped." Tessa's jaw was slack. "I didn't know you could do that, not in a sidesaddle."

Priscilla laughed. "Just because one dresses and rides like a lady doesn't mean she can't have some fun."

She shaded her eyes. "What's that dust rising over there?"

"Probably the mounted drill. Can we go watch?" Tessa sent her a hopeful look.

"All right. For a little while, but we have to stay out of the way, remember?"

Timothy led the way, and he stopped atop a small outcrop of crumbly rock. Below, nearly two-dozen horses walked in formation. The unmistakable tones of a bugle rang out, carried on the wind.

"That's the call to fight as skirmishers." Timothy pointed. "That's when they dismount and advance on foot." Half the riders dismounted, rifles ready. They knelt in a row, aiming their gun barrels at an imaginary enemy.

Priscilla and the twins continued to watch the men drill, the children educating Priscilla and amazing her with their knowledge.

"That's charge." Tessa clapped her hands

as the men below lined up, drew their swords, and rode as one across the prairie.

Applejack snorted and stomped. Priscilla held him in. "I think he wants to be down there with them."

"He's a warhorse. He knows the bugle calls as well as the men do." Timothy lifted his reins. "Where shall we go now?"

"I want to go to the cemetery." Tessa pushed her curls back and resettled her forage cap.

Timothy frowned. "Why?"

"I just want to." She shrugged and looked at the horizon.

"They aren't there."

"I know that. I'm not stupid." Her pink tongue poked out.

"Then why do you want to go there? There's nothing there but markers." Clouds had invaded his clear blue eyes.

Priscilla put her hand on Timothy's shoulder. "You don't have to go if you don't want to. But if Tessa wants to, that's all right, too. And I'd like to pay my respects."

"That's what I want to do." Tessa turned Wingfoot toward the fort. "I want to pay my respects."

Timothy seemed to wrestle within himself. As if coming to a determination, his lips set and his shoulders straightened. "I'll go."

Letting the twins lead the way, Priscilla followed. These poor children. They knew bugle calls and cavalry formations, but they had hardly any formal education. They could ride as if they'd been born in the saddle, but they had no one to show them the gentler, more civilized side of life. Here at this fort, there was no organized school, no regular church services. They were hundreds of miles from the closest museum or theater. Everything they were missing out on weighed heavily on her heart.

And the only thing standing between them and the life she wanted to give them was their uncle.

The children turned their ponies north. On a bare patch of ground, someone had constructed a low, adobe wall. Inside, a couple of scraggly trees struggled to survive. Mexican poppy plants poked up through the cracked dirt.

They dismounted and tied their horses to the wooden pickets at the gate.

Timothy swung the iron grille open. "Most of these graves are soldiers who died of the cholera or the typhoid. Mama and Papa are down here."

At the end of the row, two wooden headstones stood out as newer than the rest. The twins stood at the foot of the graves, and

Priscilla put her arms around their shoulders.

Captain Christopher W. Hutchens and Rebekah R. Ryder Hutchens and the dates carved into simple slabs of cottonwood. How long before these markers looked like the others in the row, weathered, warped? How long before Elliot was reassigned and left Fort Bliss? The army never left a regiment in a posting for too long. How long before there was no one to visit the graves, no one who knew the story of Chris and Rebekah? A hard lump formed in her throat. Grief for the brother she had barely known, the sister-in-law who had left her children much too soon, and for the twins, who had lost so much, welled in her chest until it became a physical ache.

What if her mother hadn't let bitterness cut her off from her son? What if Priscilla had been able to have a normal relationship with her brother, to get to know his family before it was too late?

What if Christopher hadn't chosen the army as a career? If he had come home from the War and gotten a regular job, married and settled down in Cincinnati?

What if . . . ? Regret tinged the sunshine.

"Is it all right to talk to them?" Tessa reached up and clasped Priscilla's hand.

"Of course, sweetheart."

Timothy shrugged off Priscilla's arm. "I'm going to go keep a lookout. Call me when you're ready to go." He strode away to the far side of the burial ground and leaned against the fence, facing the southeast, his back to the graves.

Her heart broke for him. She hadn't missed the shine of tears in his eyes. His movements were so rigid she knew he was fighting for control. Poor little boy, thinking he had to act like a man.

"What's wrong with him?" Tessa's brow wrinkled. "What is he mad at?"

"Everybody grieves differently, Tess. Timothy's grief is more private than yours or mine. He just needs a little time. You go ahead and say what you want to say to your folks. Timothy will be all right."

Tessa stared after her twin for a moment and then sighed. "I sure miss you, Mama and Papa. We live with Uncle Elliot now in his quarters. He's doing a good job taking care of us, but he has lots of help. Samson cooks for us, so we don't starve. Uncle Elliot can't cook a lick. And Aunt Priscilla came. She came all the way from Cincinnati, which is a big city in Ohio. She's staying with us for the summer. She has pretty clothes, and she doesn't know *anything* about the army. But she can ride, maybe even as good as you, Mama. And she dances really well. I think Uncle Elliot likes her, but he doesn't want to. They're fighting about something, but me and Timothy don't know what it is. They won't tell us. But it has something to do with us kids, because Mrs. Crane said when they figured out what they were going to do with us, it would be a blessing and a load off their minds."

Priscilla pressed her lips together. Mrs. Crane said far too much and stuck her nose into far more than was her business. It bothered her that the children had picked up on the tension between herself and Elliot. Here she'd come to make sure the children had security and love, and she was causing them doubt and anxiety.

"That's all, I guess. Except I miss you, and I wish you were here. Uncle Elliot is nice, but it isn't the same." Tessa scrubbed the heel of her hand under her nose. Sadness infused her voice and her expression, weighing down her pixie features.

Squeezing her shoulder, Priscilla handed her a clean hankie while blinking away the sting of her own tears. "That was very nice, Tessa. I'm sure your mother and father are proud of you. And I don't want you and

Timothy to worry about anything concerning your uncle Elliot and me. We both love you and want what's best for you and your brother."

She handed the crumpled hankie back. "Should I go get Timothy?"

"Sure."

"Can we race our ponies one more time before we have to head back?"

"Absolutely."

Tessa scampered off, shedding her sorrow, living in the moment, like a child should.

Priscilla stared at the grave markers. "Chris, Rebekah, I do love your children, and I will find a way to do what is best for them. I promise."

Elliot had to admit, having Priscilla Hutchens here wasn't all bad. In the week since they'd visited the Kickapoo camp, she'd made his life considerably easier. He didn't worry about where the twins were or what they were up to nearly as much. After a bit of initial — and understandable — reserve, they'd taken to her like soldiers to good grub.

He bent over his journal, describing the medicinal uses of mug-wort. Samson moved quietly around the surgery, cleaning and organizing. With only Matthews in the ward, things had been rather quiet.

Chatter and giggling preceded Tessa's eruption into the room. "Guess what, Uncle Elliot? Aunt Priscilla's a really good rider. Mrs. Bracken loaned her a sidesaddle, and Aunt Priscilla rode as good as Mama. Applejack just sailed over the gully like a bird. I bet he went nearly as fast as Bill."

By the time Tessa had to stop and draw a breath, Priscilla and Timothy had caught up to her. Priscilla wore a dark blue riding habit and carried a crop in her hand. Her hair lay in glorious disorder on her shoulders, all glossy and brown, and flags of color flew in her cheeks.

"We had a wonderful time. Next time I will put my hair in a net." She flipped her hair over her shoulders in a gesture so feminine, Elliot sucked in a breath.

He wiped his ink pen and set it down. "I didn't know you could ride."

She removed her tan, leather gloves. "It's one of the few things I remember about my father — your grandfather, children. He taught me to ride when I was very young. I kept it up, even after . . ." She folded the gloves into one another, matching the fingers precisely. "Though I mostly rode in the city parks. I had a favorite horse from the livery stable nearby that I used to rent for an hour at a time. Sometimes I'd be invited to friends' houses in the country and we'd ride. I loved that."

Her eyes sparkled, and Elliot found himself mesmerized, their gazes locked. An invisible thread stretched between them, a connection that wrapped tendrils around him and yet didn't feel at all constricting. Samson cleared his throat, and Elliot broke the stare.

"Children, how's 'bout we go find something to eat? I made some molasses cookies that should be cooled off by now." Samson held out his hands. Tessa and Timothy beamed.

Left alone with Priscilla, Elliot offered her a chair. "Please, sit."

He smiled as she eased onto the chair slowly.

She laughed. "I know, I'm moving kind of gingerly. It's been a while since I was in a saddle." She adjusted her skirts into precise folds. "But it felt so good to race against the wind and blow away some of the cobwebs."

"I know how you feel. Where'd you go, and who went with you?"

"Just the twins and myself. We went through an orchard and saw the Rio Grande." A furrow appeared between her brows. "I saw that man again, Niganithat?

He was in the trees by the river." She pressed her lips together. "He didn't approach us, but it made me uneasy all the same. I challenged the children to a race so we could get closer to the fort quickly. Then we rode out to watch the soldiers practice maneuvers."

Elliot frowned. "Niganithat was that close to El Paso? That's unusual. Was he alone?"

"As far as I could tell. I didn't linger at the river." She shrugged and tapped her toe with her crop. "Tessa asked if we could go to the cemetery, so we went there." A shadow passed over her face. "It's so barren. I don't think I've ever been to a cemetery that had no grass."

"I'd like to plant some flowers on Chris and Rebekah's graves, but it's so arid here, they would die without someone toting water to them every day. You say Tessa asked to see the graves? They haven't been out there since the funeral."

"Yes. Timothy didn't say much, but then again, he rarely does." She studied her fingers in her lap. "Tessa talked the whole time. It's so strange. Chris was my brother, and I knew almost nothing about him the past fifteen years. He was barely grown the last time I saw him. I never met his wife. I don't even know what she looked like."

"That's easy." He opened the belly drawer on his desk and withdrew a flat, velvet-covered case. He opened the hasp and handed it to her. Two faces looked out from the matched oval frames inside. "That's Chris and Rebekah. Chris had that taken just after the War ended. And that was Rebekah on her eighteenth birthday, about a month before she married Chris."

Priscilla studied his sister's picture for a long time. "You and your sister have the same eyes."

He nodded. "A family trait. From our father. But Rebekah was fair where I'm dark. And she was small, delicate but not fragile. Chris used to tell her she was as tough as an old boot."

Her dark brows rose. "An old boot? How flattering."

"He meant it as a compliment. I've never met anyone more capable than Rebekah, in spite of her diminutive size. Not even giving birth to twins daunted her. I was thrilled when Chris was assigned to this regiment. Having my sister living just across the parade ground was a rare blessing. I miss her every day. And Chris, too. He was a good friend and a good father. They left some awfully big shoes to fill." Elliot flipped through his journal. "Some days I wonder

180

how I'm going to raise the twins all alone. I'm glad I have Samson and Dusty and the rest of the fort to help out. Even you, for a little while."

"For a little while. I take it that means you haven't yet changed your mind about letting me take the children home with me?"

"That's right. They stay with me."

"In spite of the fact that you have no one to look after them during the day, no consistent mother figure to nurture and care for them? You've said yourself you can't do it alone, but Samson and Corporal Rhodes, and a bunch of men are no substitute for a mother's love. Can't you see that? They need a proper home." She knotted her folded gloves, making the leather creak.

He snapped the book closed. "If I am struggling to do right by the children with the aid of two hundred men, how do you propose to do better by them all alone, even if you are in a city? You say they need a mother figure, but what about a father figure?"

"I'm not ruling out the possibility of marriage in the future."

"To some eastern dandy?" The idea bothered him more than he wanted to admit.

"Just because a man lives on the east side of the Mississippi River, that doesn't make him a dandy. There are plenty of fine, manly, decent men who live and work in the east." Her lips pressed together and she eyed him disapprovingly. "Anyway, I can't see that it is any of your concern."

"It isn't. If you were taking the twins to live with you, it would be, but since they aren't going anywhere, who you marry has nothing to do with me."

The strident call of a bugle caught his attention. He rose. "It's time for Assembly." He loosened the muscles in his jaw. On every topic they got along fine, except when it came to the children. She wouldn't leave off pestering him about them, and he would never give them up. The sooner she realized that, the better.

Why didn't he realize she couldn't just forget about the children's well-being? Every day she spent with them only strengthened the bonds of her love and her resolve to make a home for them. A home far away from the caprices and dangers of military life. She followed him out of the surgery and into the evening's waning sunshine. Tessa and Timothy tumbled down the steps of the doctor's quarters next door.

"It's almost time for Retreat. Come watch, Aunt Priscilla. You haven't seen it yet. Every

time we ask, you say you're too busy helping Samson with supper. But he's got it all
ready, so you can come with us." Tessa
bounced on the balls of her feet. The sunbonnet Priscilla had finally cajoled her into
wearing hung by its strings down her back,
flopping with each hop.

"Come watch." Elliot took her elbow. "It
will do you good."

"Do me good? How so?"

"Maybe you need a dose of patriotism and
pageantry to show you we're not all cretins
and barbarians."

"I never said *all* of you were."

He laughed, but his tone held little mirth.
"Only the stubborn doctor who won't give
you your way?" He held his hands out to
the children. "Come on, kids. Your aunt
must be tired from her ride." Leaning down,
he whispered loudly enough for Priscilla to
hear, "She is a little cranky. Saddle-sore,
you think? Maybe it's best if she stays here."

Priscilla's mouth tightened. "I am not
cranky. I'd be delighted to attend Retreat
with you."

Elliot straightened and grinned, obviously
happy to have baited her into going.

She turned away. How could he be so
impossibly unmoving on the one thing that
mattered to her more than anything else,

and yet so engaging and fascinating in every other way? The children raced ahead, around the corner of the barracks.

The parade ground teemed with soldiers, brass buttons gleaming in the lowering sun, gold braid and trim set off against a sea of blue. Elliot led her along the path in front of the barracks to join the women along the west side of the parade ground in front of the commander's house. The regimental band took up positions on the closest barracks's porch.

Elliot brought her to stand beside Fern, released her elbow, and bowed. "Please, wait here with the other ladies. I'll return after Retreat has been blown."

He marched away, leaving her standing on the crushed gravel.

"I understand you went for a ride today," Mrs. Bracken said, watching the soldiers assemble on the porches. "Mrs. Crane stopped by and told me. She says you're quite the horsewoman. That certainly comes in handy out here."

"Thank you for the loan of your sidesaddle. We had a very nice time." Though how Mrs. Crane knew about their ride or her abilities on a horse mystified Priscilla. Did the woman use smoke signals?

Harry strode by and winked at Fern in

passing. She blushed, smiling.

Mrs. Crane snorted. "Enjoy it while you can, this newly wedded bliss. The mundane sets in soon enough. That is if he doesn't get killed by an Indian first."

"Beulah, don't rub the icing off the gingerbread," Mrs. Bracken scolded. "Let them be happy. I for one don't believe in this nonsense about the romance going out of a marriage over time. Why, the colonel is one of the most romantic men I know, and we've been married for more than twenty years."

Priscilla caught Fern's eye and quickly turned away. Laughter built up in her throat, and she squashed it down. Fern clutched her arm, shaking with giggles. Colonel Bracken? The idea of that gray, plain, ordinary army man being romantic? Absurd. And yet, who really knew what went on between a husband and wife in the privacy of their own home? Perhaps he read poetry to her or serenaded her with love songs? She turned a laugh into a cough, training her attention on the proceedings before her.

Mrs. Crane, not to be squashed, bit back. "I understand we're getting a new supply officer. He's a captain. I guess that means you'll be ranked out, Fern. Where will you go? There are no more rooms in the officers' quarters."

Fern's brow puckered. "I hadn't heard."

A satisfied smile curved Mrs. Crane's mouth. "I guess that's what happens when you're the wife of the lowest-ranking officer at a post."

"Priscilla," Mrs. Bracken took charge of the conversation. "Are you familiar with the evening routine? I don't remember seeing you at Retreat thus far in your visit?"

"This is my first time, but the children have been trying to educate me. This part is Assembly and Adjutant's Call?"

"Yes, and Retreat follows. The regiment will assemble before the barracks, and then the officers will march the companies out onto the parade ground. They take position according to the order of battle. When everyone is in place, the officers will report to the colonel, since he's the senior officer present. Then Retreat will take place."

The thump of so many boots striking the ground in unison as the men marched thudded in Priscilla's ears. So much blue fabric, so much braid and brass. As the music rose above the sound, something stirred in Priscilla. Her back straightened, and she found herself in like company among the women. Children stilled, and overhead the flag snapped on its tall, slender pole.

Several officers gathered in front of the barracks, and without meaning to, her eyes picked out Elliot. His campaign hat sat at a slight angle on his dark hair, and his tall frame stood steeple-straight. He stared ahead, his saber at his side, his boots gleaming. No doubt about it, he was all male, exuding masculinity and intelligence in equal measure, and he looked good in a uniform. In spite of herself, she found him very appealing. Too bad he was military — and stubborn. If he'd been a civilian, he'd have set her heart to racing and her imagination to spinning fantasies of romance and a future.

The music ended.

"Attention!" Nearly one hundred soldiers snapped upright, staring straight ahead, eyes on Colonel Bracken, who stood at attention before them. The men saluted, and he returned the brisk gesture. Arms slapped to their sides, and they all turned as one to address the colors. The plaintive tones of a lone bugle filled the air. Two men tugged on the flag rope, and the Stars and Stripes drifted down.

In spite of her antagonism toward all things military, Priscilla couldn't stop the shiver that raced up her arms to the top of her head. There was something rather . . .

haunting . . . majestic . . . moving? about the lowering of the colors. So many young men, all facing the flag, all paying tribute to the nation they served.

A lump formed in her throat, but she forced it down. *There's nothing romantic about the army, Priscilla Hutchens, and you'd do well to remember that. The army demands everything you have, and even then, it isn't enough. They can march and salute and bugle till kingdom come, and nothing will change. When the army says go, they'll go, regardless of family or home or anything else.*

Fern, standing so straight beside her, sniffed and slipped a handkerchief from her sleeve to dab at her eyes. "It's so . . . soul stirring, isn't it? I'm so proud of Harry, I could burst."

Priscilla said nothing. Why ruin Fern's happiness? She'd find out soon enough what it meant to be a military wife. Though Priscilla didn't care for Mrs. Crane, she could appreciate the woman's realistic approach to the hardships of being a military wife.

When the colors were properly folded, orders were shouted, and a concussive blast and belch of smoke emitted from the cannon at the base of the flagpole. The shockwave hit Priscilla in the chest, making it feel hollowed out. The acrid smell of burnt gunpowder drifted on the evening breeze.

Tessa and Timothy, knowing what was coming, had placed their hands over their ears. The minute the cannon blast drifted away, Tessa began to hop on her toes.

"Company, dismissed!" The shout rang out, and the men marched off the parade ground. As soon as their boots hit the graveled path, the men broke ranks. Tessa and Timothy scampered down the path, disappearing into the forest of blue-clad legs, and emerging on the gravel path that bisected the parade ground and led to the flagpole. They ran, laughing, with a handful of other children and placed their hands on the barrel of the cannon. The soldiers tending the artillery piece grinned and tousled heads, joking with the youngsters.

Among the women, one young woman, obviously pregnant, smiled. "Every evening it's the same. They race out there to touch the cannon, still warm from the firing." She pressed her hand against her side under her ribs. "Won't be long until this little soldier is born. I imagine he or she will be doing the same before I know it."

Mrs. Bracken beside her smiled indulgently. "Another child of the regiment. They say once you're born into the army, your heart belongs to it for life, no matter how far you roam."

Priscilla's heart rebelled. That might be true of some, but her heart belonged to herself, born into a regiment or not. And it would never belong to the army.

CHAPTER SEVEN

"But I don't like practicing my writing. Uncle Elliot doesn't make me work this hard." Tessa plunked her elbow on the table and propped her cheek on her fist. "Why doesn't Timothy have to practice?"

Priscilla wiped the table clear of supper crumbs. "Because he didn't play the wag this afternoon like you did. He finished his copy work, and now he is free to do what he wants. It's a tough lesson, but one you would do well to learn early. Work first, play after. Remember what you told me? Duty first?"

"I don't like schoolwork, especially penmanship." The little girl rolled the pencil back and forth on her empty paper.

"Perhaps you haven't gone about it in the right way." Shaking out the dishcloth at the door, Priscilla hung it on the rail behind the wash tub. "Maybe we can find a way to make it a little more fun. Timothy, will you go get my brown case from the shelf in there?" She pointed to the room where she was staying, unable to say "my room." Even though she'd been using it for more than two weeks, it was still clearly Elliot's room.

Timothy returned with her art case. She opened the hasp and spread the box until both sides lay flat on the tabletop. Rows of oil pastels, bottles of inks, ranks of pencils, each tucked into the space designed for it. On the other side, pads of paper and loose sheets, some blank, some not.

Her eyes traveled over the pages of ladies gowns, shoes, hats, and accessories, each one familiar through having created it. She was surprised that she didn't miss her job at Carterson's more. Working for the catalog company had been such a big part of her life, a real coup, and her bosses had been pleased with her work and credited her with an increase in their sales. And yet, over the past couple of weeks, she'd barely thought about her office or what might be happening in the company. The children had consumed all of her time and thoughts.

Of course, when she went back, she'd have to see about doing more work from home rather than going in to the office each day.

That is, if she could pry the children away from Elliot.

"What are those?" Tessa crowded at her elbow. Timothy pulled a chair up opposite her and sat up on his knees, leaning far over the table on his palms.

"They're pictures of clothes and things that you can purchase. My job back home is as an illustrator for Carterson Ladies' Emporium Catalog. I draw the pictures for the products they sell."

Tessa's eyes grew round, and she snatched her finger back before she touched one of the colored pages. "Look at that dress."

"It's a silk ball gown. That kind of fabric is called brocade, and it's delightfully rich feeling. The gown comes in that deep purple, a royal blue, or pale yellow. I used the purple for the illustration because I could show the fern leaf design on the fabric best in purple. It's a dress for dancing in." She could almost hear the music. How fun would it be to don that beautiful dress and dance the evening away in the arms of a handsome suitor? But when she closed her eyes, it was Elliot's face that appeared in her mind's eye. Her eyelids flew open, and she returned her attention to the picture.

Tessa screwed up her nose and shook her head. "That would never work for a dance. Look. The back drags the ground. It would snag and get all dirty."

"It's not meant for walking around in the sand. A lady who wore this dress would arrive at the ball in a carriage and go right to the ballroom where the floor would be as smooth as glass. And if necessary, the train can be adjusted by tucking it up under the bustle." She tapped the back of the gown.

"Bustles are silly, too. As silly as hoops. They get in the way of running and riding." Tessa dismissed the dress. "I wish I could wear pants like Timothy, but Uncle Elliot said no, just like mama did."

"I'm glad to see he draws the line somewhere. You'll change your mind someday about dresses and dressing up. There's a magical feeling when you put on a pretty dress and fix your hair and step out onto the dance floor for your very first grown-up dance. When some handsome young man takes you into his arms and leads you into a waltz or reel, you'll be glad you're not dressed in pants." Memories of her own first dance, of the thrill and excitement and anticipation, swept over her. She glanced up to find Elliot standing in the doorway listening. Heat charged into her cheeks, and she couldn't break his stare. Those gray eyes searched hers until she was afraid he might be able to read her thoughts.

Tessa nudged her elbow. "I thought you

said you could make penmanship fun."

"Oh, of course." Flustered, she tapped her papers together, able at last to tear her gaze away. "Pull up your chair. You can do this, too, Timothy." She ran her fingers down the row of oil pastels and chose a red one. "Let's put a little variety into the work to keep things interesting. You can choose a color."

"Blue. I like blue." Tessa pointed to a pale, robin's egg blue stick.

"Can I have yellow?" Timothy asked.

Priscilla gave them their choices and took a piece of blank paper, keenly aware of Elliot still standing in the doorway.

"Tessa, my first teacher taught us to treat writing like drawing. Instead of copying letters or writing words, I draw the shapes of the letters. Like I would draw a circle or a triangle, I can make an *O* or an *A*." She drew the letters in red on the top of her page. "Even though you don't care for penmanship, it is important to be able to write, to form the letters correctly, so you can communicate efficiently. And it's good to discipline yourself to do some things you don't like to do. We'd all like to play every day, but that wouldn't be good for us. God created us to work, and if we all decided to just play, nothing would get done."

"I s'pose." Tessa plunked down and made a row of blue *A*'s.

"That doesn't mean we can't have some fun while we work though." Priscilla leaned over and drew an *O* on her paper, then with a few quick strokes, changed the *O* to a cat's face. "What can you make out of an *O*?"

"Do mine." Timothy wrote a yellow *O* and passed his paper to Priscilla. She turned it into a wide-eyed owl.

Elliot pushed himself off the doorjamb and took a seat at the head of the table. He drew the stack of Priscilla's drawings toward himself and began leafing through them. After a while, he joined in the penmanship-art lesson, though everyone, including Elliot, laughed at his horrible scrawl and unrecognizable figures. Timothy proved quite adept at drawing, showing some raw talent that excited Priscilla with possibilities. Tessa seemed more interested in what everyone else was doing than in working too much herself, but with some cajoling, she managed to fill her page with letters and drawings.

The time flew, and before Priscilla realized it, a bugle sounded Taps out on the parade ground. Nine o'clock already. Time for lights out in the barracks. And past bedtime for the children. Together, Priscilla and Elliot got the twins into their nightclothes, heard their prayers, and tucked them in. At the last moment, Tessa lurched up out of bed and caught Priscilla in a tight hug around the neck.

"You were right. Penmanship can be fun. Thank you for showing us your drawings and letting us use your art stuff." She placed a kiss on Priscilla's cheek that made her eyes sting.

"You're welcome, Tess. It was my pleasure. Sleep tight, sweetie."

Returning to the kitchen, she began gathering her pencils and pastels. Elliot joined her and put his hand atop hers. She went still, the touch of his hand sending a shiver up her arm that had nothing to do with being cold.

"Wait. I want to talk to you about something." He removed his hand and motioned to her chair.

Her heart leapt. Perhaps he'd changed his mind about the children.

Taking up one of her drawings, this one of a row of fancy hats adorned with feathers and flowers and ribbons, he said, "I had no idea you were an artist. These are quite well done."

"Thank you. Though I've not had any formal training, I've always been able to draw, and when I finished school, I answered an advertisement in the paper looking for a copy artist. I had to work to support my mother and myself. When she passed away a year ago, I had only myself."

"And your father died while in the service?"

"Yes. He perished in a blizzard while he and his men were out on a patrol. My mother took Chris and me with her to Cincinnati, where she was from. Then Chris enlisted and broke my mother's heart. She refused to talk about my father or my brother after that. She died a bitter woman who believed she had been wronged by the army and the men in her life." A knot sat in Priscilla's middle. Her mother had been an angry, sad woman, difficult to live with, and yet pitiable at the same time.

"That can't have been easy for you, living with all that bitterness."

"It wasn't, for a long time. But one Sunday my pastor spoke of the sin of bitterness. He likened being bitter against someone to drinking poison and then waiting for the other person to get sick. I realized at that time that I needed to ask for God's forgiveness for being bitter at my life's circumstances."

"So you're no longer bitter about the

army?" His eyebrows rose.

"Oh, I'm not bitter. But I'm not stupid either. Knowing what I know about how the army treats families, I would be a fool to put myself in that position, or to allow those I love to be put in that position either. That's why I know it is in the best interest of the children to remove them. A military man will always choose his career over his family, and I never want to be second in my husband's heart."

Elliot's lips pressed together, and he stroked his mustache. "I see. I didn't actually mean to talk about that right now."

"What did you want to talk about?"

"I wanted to offer you a job."

She sat back, blinking. "A job? Taking care of the children?"

"No, though I do appreciate all you're doing for them, especially the lessons. I know their education has been a bit hit or miss, what with the fort not currently having a schoolteacher. No, I have a job in mind that is nearer to your own vocation." He spread the drawings out before him. "As I believe I mentioned, I'm compiling an herbal journal documenting the medicinal properties of various plants, particularly those used in Indian healing. And as you've reason to know," he paused and squinted at a page of his own drawings and squiggles, "that while I believe I am a decent doctor, no one could ever accuse me of being an artist."

She grinned. His return smile filled her middle with warmth and made her heart beat faster.

"I need illustrations to accompany my entries so readers can identify the plants by sight. I've been at a loss as to how to accomplish this, but seeing these drawings of yours, I think you just might be the answer to my prayers."

Again his smile did strange things to her heart. Her hand went to her throat, and she moistened her lips. The answer to his prayers? She blew out a slow breath.

"We could work on it in the evenings, after the children go to bed. I wouldn't expect you to spend time away from them to illustrate for me. I've made pressings of every herb and flower I plan to use, so you wouldn't be expected to go out into the fields. Everything is over in my office. I can get Samson or one of the soldiers to stay here after the kids go to bed, so we can work over at the infirmary." He leaned forward, his gray eyes alight. Passion for his project infused his voice. "It would be a collaborative effort, and I'd make sure, when the book was printed, that you got credit."

"How many illustrations might you need?" She only had eight more weeks until she had to be back in Cincinnati for her job. By that time, if she hadn't convinced Elliot to let her take the twins, she'd have to see about what the law could do for her.

"It's quite a large book, with more than one hundred entries."

"I see." The idea of creating again appealed to her, as did the idea of spending more time with Elliot — for the sole purpose of having more time to persuade him around to her way of thinking, of course. She gathered pencils and pastels, fitting them into her case. "I'd like to give it a try. I could do as much as I can now, and perhaps, when it's time for me to leave, I can take the rest of the pressings and your notes with me and return the illustrations to you or send them to your publisher when I finish them."

He had been shuffling through papers, tapping them together, but his movements stilled. "You're still planning on leaving in August?"

"I can't stay here indefinitely."

"No, I suppose not." He pulled one page that refused to align itself from the stack, glanced at it, and then held it up to study more carefully. "What's this?" He turned the page.

She reached for it, but he pulled it just out of her grasp.

"This is no catalog illustration."

"No, it's a house."

"That's you on the front porch." He laid the paper flat on the table where the overhead lamp could shine more fully on it.

She didn't need to look at it. From the rose-covered trellis to the gingerbread trim to the hanging baskets of flowers on the wraparound porch, she knew every line and detail.

"Who is that with you?" He pointed to the lean, dark, mustachioed man on the porch swing next to her in the drawing.

"Nobody." Why wouldn't he let it go before she died of embarrassment? The man on the porch swing had dark hair and a dark mustache — in fact, he could be mistaken for Elliot except the man wasn't in uniform.

"Looks like somebody to me."

"I drew that a long time ago. It's the home I'm going to build someday. Where I would live with my husband and family." She shrugged, feeling as if a private part of her heart had been laid bare. She took the paper and placed it on the bottom of the stack. "Of course, I wouldn't draw it that way now."

His eyebrows rose. "Why not?"

"Instead of a husband, I would draw the twins on the porch swing with me."

CHAPTER EIGHT

"I don't know how you can be so cheerful. You're living in a hallway." Priscilla edged around the corner of the bed to sit at Fern's tiny table. Only a thin curtain blocked off the Dunn's living space from the rest of the officers' quarters. "And one man still has to walk through it to get to his room. You'd think the army could at least provide adequate quarters for their officers, especially the ones with families."

Fern laughed. "I guess the army has a different idea of what the word *adequate* means. We won't be stuck here for long anyway. When Major Crane's transfer is approved, there will be another shuffle, and we'll have our own room again. Harry said we could either camp here in the hallway for a while, or we could use one of the Sibley tents. If this doesn't work out, we can still opt for the tent."

"Is Major Crane transferring?" Priscilla

sipped her tea. "I hope wherever it is, Mrs. Crane is happy, because she's clearly not happy here. She never seems to have anything nice to say. I've never met such a sour woman who delighted in spreading her vinegar so much."

"Harry says she is still bitter because her brother-in-law was killed by Indians almost a year ago. Major Crane was on the patrol that found him, riddled with arrows. Somewhere northwest of here. He was stationed over in New Mexico, and Apaches got him."

Priscilla bit her lower lip, ashamed of herself. "I didn't know. How horrible for them. No wonder they're so nasty about the Indians. When we visited the Kickapoo camp, you could almost feel the hatred and fear coming off Mrs. Crane in waves. I'm surprised she went at all."

"Harry was surprised, too. Whenever I'm around Mrs. Crane, I remind myself of her loss. Otherwise, I'm afraid I would say something . . . uncharitable." Fern lowered her voice when she made that admission.

"Oh, Fern, you're a better woman that I am. I'm afraid I would say something way beyond uncharitable. It might even be downright rude. And I don't think I would be as cheerful as you are about existing in this cramped hallway, temporary or not.

Though given the choice, I'd have opted for here over a tent, too." She shivered. "I can't imagine making a home in one of them."

Fern nodded over her teacup. "I know, though I guess I could if I had to. I mean, as long as I have Harry, I can live anywhere."

A knock sounded on the hallway wall beyond the curtain. "Missus Dunn? Miz Hutchens?"

Fern reached out and opened the curtain, the metal curtain rings clacking together. "Yes? Samson. Come in."

He swept his hat from his head. "Ma'am, Major Ryder sent me to fetch Miss Hutchens, and he asks if you can watch the twins. Miz Dugan has started her laboring, and the major would like Miss Hutchens to he'p him with the delivery."

"Me?" Priscilla's cup rattled in the saucer. "I've never helped with a childbirth before in my life."

Samson bobbed his grizzled head. "Yes, ma'am. Miz Dugan is one of the laundresses, and she ain't married. She said she didn't want one of those hoity-toity officers' wives to help out, not when they've been lookin' down on her for having a baby born on the wrong side o' the blanket, so to speak." He shrugged and rolled his eyes. "I don't b'leve she was meaning you, Missus

Dunn. You ain't been here long enough for her to know you."

"What about one of the other laundresses?" A knot formed in Priscilla's chest under her heart. "Can't they help?"

"Miz Dugan ain't on the best of terms with them either. It's you or one of the orderlies. She won't have a colored man like me help either." He shrugged again, as if the social strata of the fort's women was more than he could comprehend. It was more than Priscilla wanted to cogitate at the moment either.

"Very well. I don't know what good I can do, but I'll try. Fern, the children are at the river fishing with a couple of the enlisted men. They're supposed to be back before Stable Call." She paused, realizing she'd begun to tell time by the bugles instead of the clock. "I don't know how long we'll be. Samson will give the children dinner and see them to bed after supper." The last was directed at Samson, who smiled and turned his hat round and round in his work-roughened hands.

"Yes, ma'am. I'll see to the young'uns. There's only a couple of patients in the infirmary, and they ain't serious sick."

Fern moved a pitcher and bowl off a trunk pushed up hard against the bed and opened it. "You'll want this." She withdrew an apron. "You don't want to risk spoiling your pretty dress."

"Thank you." What was she getting herself into? She slipped her head through the loop and tied the apron strings behind her as she followed Samson out into the sunshine. The late afternoon sun beat down on the earth without mercy, and the incessant breeze scudded sand and dust, piling it in the lea of buildings.

"Miz Dugan's shack is over there in Suds Row. Behind the warehouse."

"Suds Row?"

"That's where the laundresses live. Miz Dugan's place is the second from this end." He pointed and then headed the other direction, back to the infirmary.

Priscilla drew a deep breath and walked toward the row of single-room adobe dwellings. The smells of smoke, starch, and hot water encompassed her. Women bent over washtubs, stoked fires under boiling kettles, and pegged out wet clothing to line dry in the sunshine. Most wore their hair up in kerchiefs and had their sleeves rolled up to reveal tanned, muscular forearms. One woman had her skirts tucked up into her waistband, showing laddered stockings and bedraggled petticoats. A pair of toddlers napped on a blanket in the shade of one of the houses.

The adobe house Samson had indicated had no one in the front yard, no fire under the kettle. She knocked on the rough wooden door. Elliot opened it, wiping his hands on a towel.

"Thanks for coming. I need someone, but Maybelle was adamant it couldn't be one of the officers' wives."

"That's right," came a strident voice from the bed in the corner. "I won't have one of them plaster saints in here spreading their piety and pretendin' to care about me, all the while lookin' down on me and my kid." She arched her back and fisted her hands in the sheets, emitting a low groan as a contraction took her. When she could breathe again, she fixed a hard glare on Priscilla. "So if you've a mind to preach at me, missy, you can just turn right around and go back wherever you came from. I don't need you or your opinions on having babies without bein' married."

For a moment Priscilla was tempted to do just that, but then she caught the thread of fear in the woman's voice, the panic lurking in her eyes. Compassion spread through her, but she had a feeling Maybelle Dugan wouldn't respond well to compassion at the moment. At least not the kind of compassion people easily recognized. Priscilla's spine stiffened.

"I assure you, my only thought is to assist Major Ryder in bringing your baby safely into the world. I have no desire to preach to you, though if I did it would be about rudeness, not moral character."

To her surprise, Maybelle Dugan threw her head back and laughed. "This one's got some sand, Doc. She'll do me just fine." Another contraction gripped her, reddening her face and seizing every muscle.

Elliot bent over her, placing his hand high on the mound of her pregnancy and consulting his pocket watch. "Breathe, Maybelle. Your baby needs air."

Maybelle gulped in a breath, and Priscilla found herself doing the same. Strange quivers attacked the backs of Priscilla's knees, and a swirly, lightheaded feeling took up residence behind her eyes. She grabbed a chair back to steady herself. She was really going to help with a childbirth.

"Priscilla, fetch me a couple of buckets of fresh water. Start a fire out in the yard under the boiler and pour the water in there. Maybelle, things are progressing nicely, but your contractions are inconsistent. It will likely be a few hours before you're holding your baby in your arms." Elliot unbuttoned his tunic and shrugged it off as Priscilla gathered two pails from beside the door.

Priscilla stepped outside and nearly collided with a woman on the stoop.

"How's she doing?" The woman set two buckets of water on the dirt. One bucket steamed gently. "I'll trade you. I figured the doc would need some fresh water."

"Thank you. That's very thoughtful of you."

The woman shrugged. Her hair straggled from beneath her kerchief, and she shoved it back under the cloth. "I been where Maybelle's at. She can use all the help she can git. My name's Gilda, by the way." She stuck out her hand, red and large knuckled.

"I'm Priscilla. Thank you for the water."

"I know who you are. Seems like every one of my laundry customers is talking about the doctor's pretty lady. They're placin' bets on how soon you two will marry."

"Oh, no, I'm not marrying the major. I'm only here for a visit, to see my niece and nephew." Priscilla rushed to disabuse the woman's mind.

"Hmph. There's been plenty of gals come out here to visit relations, and I ain't seen a one of them return unmarried. The doc has his eye on you, that's for sure. Why else would he give up his bed and let you stay? Word is, you two are working late over to the surgery nearly every night." Her eyebrows rose, and she lifted the hem of her apron up to fan herself. "Some folks say it's an odd place to do one's courtin', but then again, officers are odd people, ain't they?" She elbowed Priscilla and gave her a wink.

She turned and left before Priscilla could answer, scooping up the empty buckets and calling back over her shoulder, "I'll bring you some more water and get yer fire started. I'll tend to it, too. If you need anything else, just step outside and wave. I'll be working next door at my washtub till dark, just like every day."

Hefting the full buckets, Priscilla reentered the cabin. "What should I do?" She kept her voice low as she eased aside a pile of dishes to set the buckets on the table, felt it wobble, and transferred the pails to the floor instead. The cabin was in a sorry state, badly in need of tidying. She was hard-pressed to find a place free of clutter.

"That was fast." Elliot lifted one of the buckets and filled a tin basin. He lowered his tone, too.

"Someone named Gilda brought it. She's coming back with more, and she said she'll tend the fire outside."

"Good. Wet one of those clothes and bathe Maybelle's face. Try to keep her relaxed. If she can relax through the pains, it will go easier for her."

"Stop yer whispering. I can't abide whispering." Maybelle tossed her head on the pillow, frowning.

"Maybelle, I have to go answer Officers' Call and check in at the infirmary, but I'll be back. Nothing's going to happen in the next little while. Priscilla will stay with you, and I'll return as soon as I can."

"Yer leaving?" Maybelle struggled to sit upright.

"Only for a bit. I have complete confidence in Priscilla here. She'll take good care of you. But you have to behave yourself. You're going to relax and do what she tells you, right? And no giving her the harsh side of your tongue?"

Maybelle scowled, but nodded, giving her reluctant promise.

Priscilla followed him to the door. Once outside, she latched onto his sleeve. "What are you doing? I don't have the vaguest notion of what I'm supposed to do here. I've never even seen a baby born, much less delivered one."

"You won't have to deliver a baby. For

now all you have to do is to be her friend. That's what she really needs at the moment. Think about what you would want and need in her circumstances."

"I'd want and need a doctor." She wanted to close her eyes and wish this entire situation away.

He chuckled and patted her hand. "Keep her as comfortable as you can, talk to her, be there for her. Have you a timepiece?" When she shook her head, he handed her his watch, warm from his hand. "Keep track of the contractions, and if they get to be about five minutes apart and steady, send someone for me. I have a few things to see to, but I should be back in plenty of time. Fern's taking care of the twins, right?"

"Yes, they're being seen to, but, Elliot . . ."

He winked at her, smiling. "You'll be fine. Just relax and breathe through the contractions." His step was altogether too jaunty as he walked away from her.

Returning to Maybelle, Priscilla tried to mask the panic clawing up her windpipe. "How are you doing?"

"How'my doing? I hurt. That's how I'm doing." Sweat dotted her brow, and her hair stuck to her forehead and neck.

Wringing out a cloth, Priscilla wiped Maybelle's brow. "What else can I do for you?

What would you like?"

"You can trade places. I'd like that a lot."
A ghost of a smile quirked the corner of her
mouth.

Priscilla laughed, startled. "Well, aside
from that, how about if I brush and braid
your hair? It might be more comfortable to
have it corralled." She found Maybelle's
hairbrush and a ribbon and assisted her in
sitting up.

With long, rhythmic strokes, she brought
some order to the riot of red curls. She
paused each time a contraction came,
reminding Maybelle to take some deep
breaths.

"This nightgown is damp with sweat. How
about we get you into something dry?"

Maybelle shook her head. "I only have the
one nightgown."

Shame trickled through Priscilla as she
thought of the stack of nightclothes in her
trunk. "Wait right here." She headed to the
door.

"And just where else would I be going?"

"You're right, that was silly. I'll only be a
minute."

"Fine, go. Everyone else leaves me."

Priscilla flagged a passing soldier and sent
him to find Fern. She dispatched Fern on
her errand, and in less than twenty minutes,

her friend returned with a valise.

"Sit up again, Maybelle. Let's get you out of that gown."

"Yer daft. I told you I only have the one."

"Now you have more than one." Priscilla shook out the folds of one of her own nightgowns.

"I don't need yer charity," Maybelle snapped.

Remembering what Elliot had said, she ignored Maybelle's rudeness. "I'm not offering charity. I'm offering friendship. You'll feel better in a clean gown. If you want to lie there in your own sweat, then fine, but you're cutting off your nose to spite your face."

"Friendship. Why would the likes of you want to be friends with me?" Suspicion laced her tone, but she began unbuttoning the front of her gown.

"The way you're acting, I have no idea."

Which set Maybelle to laughing. "Yup, you've got sand. I like you."

They got Maybelle changed and tucked back into bed. Priscilla stuck her head outside and Gilda came over, agreeing to take the nightgown and wash it.

The contractions came harder and faster, and Priscilla watched the timepiece, coaching Maybelle through the pains and praying

Elliot would return soon. In between, she chatted about the twins and the antics they got up to. Each time she stopped talking, Maybelle would ask her to go on. "It gives me something to think about. Makes me not so afraid."

I wish it would work that way for me.

Elliot fidgeted through the officers' meeting, ducked into the infirmary and checked on his patients there, all the while wondering how Priscilla was getting on. He was proud of her, tackling this challenge. From her pale face and trembling hands, he knew she had to be scared to death. And Maybelle was no easy soul to deal with. She could be as abrasive as a mule's bray, and as ornery as a buffalo.

By the time he had fulfilled his duties for the day, it was almost three hours since he'd left Maybelle's side. But the army was adamant. Official duties came before aiding civilians, and though Maybelle was an employee of the army, she was still, technically, a civilian. The major in him understood. The doctor in him struggled with the idea.

He knocked and entered the cabin, stopping in the doorway, amazed at the transformation. Where once squalor had reigned, now order prevailed. No more dirty dishes, no more baskets of unfolded laundry, no more crumpled blankets on the bed. Priscilla had worked wonders. Maybelle even looked better with her hair combed and braided and, if he wasn't mistaken, wearing a different nightgown.

Judging by their expressions, he'd be hard-pressed to decide which one was happier to see him. Maybelle's brow bore deep furrows as she concentrated on her labor. Elliot unbuttoned his tunic and laid it across a chair back. While he rolled up his sleeves, he asked, "How far apart are they?"

"Almost five minutes, but a few are closer. I was just about to send someone for you." Priscilla wiped Maybelle's forehead and neck. "You're doing well, Maybelle. Take a couple of deep breaths."

Elliot washed his hands and checked his patient.

"Nice work, Maybelle. I think you're about ready to have this baby."

An hour later, Elliot cut and tied the cord and handed Priscilla the squalling red bundle of baby. Priscilla took the child, wrapping it in a cloth and crooning. Elliot didn't miss the tender expression in her eyes, an almost maternal look that smacked him in the chest.

To distract himself, he told Maybelle,

"You have a girl. She'll go about six and a half pounds, I think. Got your red hair, too."

"Got my lungs, from the sound of her." Maybelle lay back, exhausted.

"Priscilla, wash her quickly in warm water, make sure you get all the creases, and then get her bundled up. We don't want her to get a chill. I'll finish up here with Maybelle, and then you can introduce her to her daughter."

The baby cried all through her first bath then quieted as she was wrapped close and cuddled. Maybelle held out her arms and took her baby. Priscilla began cleaning up, and Elliot rolled down his sleeves. "What will you name her?"

"I'll be calling her Brigit, after me ma."

"Brigit Dugan. That's a fine name. Is there someone you want to tell about her birth?"

Maybelle's brown eyes flicked upward, and her mouth twisted in a wry grimace. "Yer meaning her pa? No, that scoundrel deserted last winter. I've no notion where he is, nor do I want to. Me and Brigit will do just fine on our own."

"I know you think that, Maybelle, but you're going to have to accept some help, at least for the next few days. You had a pretty routine labor and birth, but I don't want you out of that bed for at least forty-eight hours."

"And who's going to do my washing? If I don't wash, I don't get paid. And those other women will pinch my best customers."

"Forty-eight hours, Maybelle, or I'll bung you into the hospital. Let Gilda and the others help you out. They won't pinch your customers while you're laid up. I'll see to it. I'll go talk to her now."

When he returned, Gilda in tow, Maybelle was sleeping. Priscilla stood in the middle of the room, holding the baby, swaying gently. The knot of hair at her nape had loosened a bit, softening her profile in the lamplight. Her apron was crumpled and stained, and her eyes were tired, but she looked so beautiful, it gave him pause. Muriel had been a beautiful woman, too, but there the similarities ended. He couldn't imagine the fastidious and fragile Muriel putting up with the rigors of being a doctor's wife, much less that of the army. She hadn't been one to endure being put upon. Priscilla seemed to spend her days doing for others, the twins, Fern, Maybelle and her baby . . . even himself. She'd mended his clothes, cleaned his house, helped prepare his meals, and taken on the illustrating of the herbal journal, all without complaint. The only thing she asked of him was the one thing he couldn't give her.

Gilda shouldered by him and took the baby. "Don't you two worry. I'll see to her and the little one. She's a stubborn woman, but she's no fool. Get on home now and have a good meal. I'll give Maybelle some soup when she wakes up."

Elliot donned his tunic, picked up his medical bag — packed and closed up by Priscilla — and took her elbow. They stepped outside to a sky filled with stars. She took a deep breath, leaning on him a little bit. "I'm so tired, I didn't even realize it was night. I hope the twins behaved for Fern and Samson."

"You did well. I'm proud of you."

"You don't know how many times I wanted to run right out that door and not stop until I had my head hidden under my pillow. It was scary and beautiful, and I was so afraid I'd do something wrong or that she'd have that baby before you got back."

"That makes you all the more brave. Even though you've never helped with a birthing before, there were several times when you anticipated what I would need. I didn't even have to ask for something and you'd be right there with it. You would make a great nurse.

We work well together." And they did. Whether it was getting the children tucked into bed, sorting and organizing the herbal journal, or bringing a baby into the world, they made a great team.

Which opened his imagination up to all sorts of possibilities. But that way lay disaster as he had cause to know. Never again would he risk placing his heart in someone else's care. Not even someone who seemed to fit into his life as well as Priscilla.

CHAPTER NINE

A week later, Priscilla gathered her art case and checked in on the twins one last time. They lay on their cots, lashes curving on cheeks flushed with sleep. Tessa had had a rough day. Reluctant to come inside to do chores midmorning, squirming and scowling by turns as she stood on a chair while Priscilla pinned newspaper pattern pieces on her for a new dress Priscilla was making for her, and then lesson time, which ended in a stormy bout of tears. The day had been a series of emotional episodes that had worn everyone out.

Priscilla had finally taken the little girl on her lap and held her, stroking her hair and rocking while Timothy looked on with worried eyes.

"What's wrong, Tessa?"

"I . . . miss . . . mama . . ." she'd finally sobbed out.

Priscilla's heart had broken right in two.

Blinking hard to stem her own tears, she crooned softly and squeezed Tessa. "I know, sweetheart. I'm so sorry. It's all right to miss her. And it's all right to cry about it every now and again."

"It was that mean old Mrs. Crane who started it." Timothy smacked his fist into his hand. "Even before the funeral was over, she and Major Crane moved into the quarters where we used to live with Mama and Pa. They bought a lot of the furniture from Uncle Elliot, since he didn't really have room for much of it. This morning she told Tessa Mama's furniture was mostly hideous, and she was painting the sideboard and dining room table white. Mama spent hours scraping the paint off that table when she first got it, and then she sanded it and stained it. I know the table belongs to Mrs. Crane now, and she can do what she wants with it, but she didn't have to be so mean about it. She said Mama had been a fool to spend so much time on a worthless piece of junk that she'd have to leave behind when the regiment moved on."

It was a long speech for Timothy, accompanied by reddened cheeks and fierce eyes. Timothy was hard to rile, but when he got mad, his wrath burned white-hot.

Priscilla considered her words carefully,

though her chest was tight and her anger rising. "I'll agree Mrs. Crane's words were not well chosen, but perhaps she was being more tactless than cruel. Perhaps she didn't realize what she was saying or how hurtful it could be."

"She's meaner than a bilious snake." Tessa swiped at her cheeks. Priscilla hid her smile at this description, dug her handkerchief out of her sleeve, and mopped at the little girl's tears.

"That's no reason for us to be unkind." Guilt pricked her. She'd thought . . . and said . . . unkind things about Mrs. Crane on more than one occasion, and here she was lecturing the children. "Let's not dwell on Mrs. Crane. Tessa is missing her mama. I'm sorry I didn't get to know her, but she must've been a special lady to have two such wonderful children. I'd love to hear about her. What do you remember best?"

Both children had joined in, telling her all about their mother and father and revealing how much they had loved being an army family. Often their descriptions included their uncle Elliot, and she realized how much a part of their lives he had been, even before their parents passed away. Tessa finally calmed down, and dinner had been peaceful.

Now, Priscilla straightened the blanket over Timothy and brushed a curl off Tessa's brow. How quickly this pair had climbed into her heart. If Elliot wouldn't budge and let her take them with her when she left, how would she bear it?

Elliot. He filled far too many of her thoughts these days. She should be concentrating on the children, but he kept intruding on her mind. She rarely saw him before the noon meal, since he slept over at the barracks and had duties to see to regarding Sick Call, inspections of the food, water, and living conditions of the men, officers' meetings, even cavalry drill and target practice upon occasion. He spent a great deal of time in the infirmary treating everything from digestive upsets to broken bones to burns. Each day, as the time for the noon meal approached, Priscilla found herself listening for his footsteps on the porch, smoothing her hair and dress, reminding herself how silly she was being.

And now, as she closed the door and headed to the surgery, she had to remind herself again. Elliot was married to the army. The cavalry was as much a part of his makeup as his medical degree or his interest in herbs. She had one goal here: gain custody of the children. It was silly to be

distracted by her attraction to a military man.

Lamplight burned from a wall sconce in the entryway of the infirmary. She peeked into the ward on her right. No Elliot. An orderly sat on a straight-backed chair, dozing between two occupied cots. One of the civilian blacksmiths had burned his hand rather badly at his forge, requiring him to stay in the post hospital. The other cot was taken by a young man who had gotten careless around the colonel's horse. Unfortunately, the animal had lashed out and kicked the soldier in the head. He had yet to regain consciousness, and Elliot had been worried about him at lunch, and still worried at supper.

She crossed the hall and tapped on the surgery door before entering, careful to leave the door open behind her.

Elliot turned from his desk. Two large glass lamps shed light on the work surface, made brighter by reflectors behind them. He had removed his blue tunic and rolled up the sleeves of his white shirt. His hair, normally smooth or even flattened by his hat, bore signs of his having run his fingers through it — something he often did while filling out paperwork. A lock of dark hair fell over his forehead.

"Good evening." Priscilla clutched her art case to her middle as she crossed the room, resisting the urge to brush his hair back.

He stood. "The twins finally fall asleep?"

"Yes. After the emotional day Tessa had, I'm not surprised." Priscilla set her case on the desk. She breathed deeply of the herbal, medicinal scent in the room. Long after she was gone from here, she would associate those smells with the surgery . . . and Elliot.

Elliot had opened the windows, and the simple cotton curtains fluttered in the evening breeze.

"I'm glad you were with her today." He resumed his seat, propping his cheek on his fist, his elbow resting on his papers. "She's such a volatile little thing, and when she cries, I haven't the faintest notion what to do. It seems, with girls, that whatever you tried the last time is exactly the wrong thing to do the next. That verse in Proverbs is correct. 'There be three things which are too wonderful for me, yea, four which I know not: The way of an eagle in the air; the way of a serpent upon a rock; the way of a ship in the midst of the sea; and the way of a man with a maid.' Women, no matter the age, are a complete mystery to men."

His eyes, so light between dark lashes, shone with teasing, and his mustache twitched.

"I refuse to let you bait me." She opened her case. "I thought we had work to do."

"We do." Straightening, he reached for several thin sheets of tissue paper. "Here are the next set of samples." The papers rustled as he peeled back the first one revealing a pressed plant.

"What is that?"

Elliot consulted a paper tag, holding it to the lamplight and squinting.

"Is your handwriting so bad that *you* can't even make it out?" She raised her eyebrows.

"And I refuse to let you bait me. This is boneset. I acquired this sample when I was stationed up in Kansas at Fort Larned. They have a big slough north and east of the fort that has a trove of new samples. Boneset grows in wet soil, flowers in August and September, has barely any scent, and a bitter taste. This is just the top of the plant. They can grow from two to five feet, but only the leaves and flowers are used as medicine."

Priscilla studied the flattened plant, gauging how to draw it. "What is it used for?"

"Lots of things, actually. It's a stimulant, a tonic, a diaphoretic, an emetic, an aperient, even an antispasmodic. It depends on the strength of the dose and the temperature at which it is given. This one is easy to identify in the field because the stem appears to pierce through the leaves. The Latin for boneset is *Eupartorium perfoliatum.* The main drawback to this as a medicine is the bitter taste. I mix it with honey, ginger, and anise and use it as a cough syrup for children sometimes." His passion for his work infused his voice and expression, and as had happened over and over, Priscilla found herself drawn to both the subject and the physician.

She drew a quick sketch of how she thought the plant must look, prepressed, and leaned back so he could study the drawing. "That's very good, very close. The leaves are flatter, and you can see the veining. And the top resembles Queen Anne's Lace. The flowers tightly bunched."

She drew another version beside it. "Like this?" His head came close once more, and she found herself studying his profile, the bluish-black hint of beard, the strong jawline and straight nose, the intelligent brow and dark lashes. She caught the faint smell of peppermint and smiled. Often after supper, he chewed on a toothpick he'd soaked in peppermint oil. Another scent she would forever link with him.

"That's perfect. You've caught on quickly.

Your artistic ability really was an answer to my prayers."

His praise made her heart glow. They worked well together, and the herbal journal was coming together nicely.

"I imagine your employers miss your talents." He drew his notebook closer and picked up his pencil. "The kids will miss the art lessons when you leave."

The glow was doused as quickly as a candle in a bucket of water. "Why do you do that?"

"Do what?" His brows came together, and he stroked his mustache.

"Keep reminding me that I'll be leaving here. I know I will. I don't need you to tell me." The pale green chalk snapped in her fingers. "And that you intend me to leave here alone."

"As you said before, you can't stay here forever."

His reasonable tone made his words hurt all the more. Her lips grew stiff as she fought to keep her composure. She wanted to fly apart like Tessa had today, to cry and kick and fuss against the injustice of his actions.

"I don't intend to stay forever. I didn't think I'd be staying even this long, and I wouldn't have if you weren't so mule stubborn. Why can't you see that the children would be better off with me, living where it's civilized, where they can put down roots and have stability and a home?"

He rubbed his hands down his face and sighed. "I'm not going to argue with you about this."

"You're leaving me no choice." Her hands fisted in her lap.

"What do you mean?"

"I shall be forced to take the matter to court if we can't come to some reasonable agreement." Though she hadn't the foggiest notion of how to go about such a thing, nor what her chances of winning such a lawsuit might be. Consulting a lawyer would be the first step, she supposed, but she couldn't do that until she returned to the city, and that would mean leaving the children here.

All warmth and amusement evaporated from his eyes. They glittered like ice. "You'd sue me for custody?"

"If I had to." She raised her chin, refusing to back down, though she knew he might call her bluff.

"In spite of their parents' wishes?"

"How do I know what their wishes were? You've produced no will. No one can corroborate your claim that they intended you to have the children."

"And you can't produce proof that they wanted you to have the children either. And I have the benefit of having been a part of the children's lives up to now, which is more than you can claim. You never laid eyes on them until after they were orphaned. How do you think a judge will like that? If you take this to court, I'll be forced to fight you every step of the way. I won't abandon those children. When I give my word, I keep it."

Frustration made her eyes sting and water, but after his comment about women crying, she refused to give in to the urge. "As do I, so mark my words. I will do what is best for the children." She hated that her voice wobbled, and she blinked furiously.

"Excuse me, sir?"

They whirled toward the door. The orderly hovered, shifting his weight from foot to foot, and heat rushed up her cheeks as she realized how loud their voices had become. Mortified to be caught quarreling, she looked away and used the cuff of her sleeve to dab her eyes.

"What is it, Hopkins?" Elliot acted as if nothing untoward had occurred.

"You said you wanted to know right away if there was any change. It's Stephens, sir. He's moving and mumbling as if he might come out of it."

Elliot bounded to his feet and headed to the ward. The orderly followed, and after a moment, Priscilla did, too. Perhaps there was something she could do to help.

"Hold him, Hopkins." Elliot bent over the young man who thrashed on his cot. His head, swathed in bandages, swung from side to side, and a gut-splitting groan erupted from his pale lips. Elliot glanced up, caught sight of her, and jerked his chin toward the surgery. "Priscilla, get me the laudanum. It's on the dispensary shelf, listed alphabetically."

She dashed back into the surgery and consulted the wall of glass vials and containers. Thankful for the time she'd spent studying Elliot's handwriting, she found the bottle she was looking for and hurried back to his side.

He didn't bother with a spoon, uncorking the brown flask and holding Stephen's rigid jaw, forcing his mouth open. "Here, Soldier. Swallow this. It will help with the pain." He raised the bottle to the lamplight to check how much had been taken, passed it back to Priscilla without looking at her, and used his thumb to raise first one, then the other of the man's eyelids. Through it all, Hopkins, the orderly, all but lay across the injured man's legs to keep him from bucking off the bed.

After a few moments, Stephens relaxed. His breathing became deeper, and the rigid cords in his neck loosened. One by one his fingers eased their grip on the sheets. Priscilla swallowed and replaced the stopper on the laudanum.

Elliot held up Stephens's wrist, watching the rise and fall of his chest, then lifted the lamp from the wall. He turned the patient's head and peered into his ear. "I was afraid of this. His brain is bleeding into his head, but there's nowhere for the blood to go. The swelling is literally crushing his brain. I'm going to have to use the trephine and relieve the pressure." He set the lantern on the side table.

Hopkins's eyes grew round, and his face went white. "Sir? You're going to cut his head open?" He swayed.

"Get hold of yourself, man. I'll need your help, and Samson's, too. Priscilla, go to the house and send Samson to me. There's no time to lose."

The orderly slapped his hand over his mouth and rushed for the door. The unmistakable sound of someone losing his supper reached their ears.

"I don't think Hopkins is going to be much help. Why is he an orderly anyway?"

Priscilla headed toward the door.

"I don't get trained orderlies. I get whoever is next on the duty roster. That's why Samson is so vital to me." Elliot shook his head.

"Perhaps we should send Hopkins to stay at the house with the twins. I can help you and Samson."

He eyed her with uncertainty. "Are you sure? It isn't going to be like anything you've done before."

"I've a strong stomach." She gave a laugh, though it was more nerves than humor. "At least stronger than Hopkins'."

Coming to a decision, he moved briskly into the surgery, speaking over his shoulder. "Hopkins, send Samson to me and stay in my quarters with the children. Priscilla, come with me. We need to ready the surgery."

Priscilla marveled at his knowledge and efficiency. Within moments every lamp in the surgery had been lit, instruments laid out, and medicines selected. She scrubbed the leather surface of the operating table with carbolic acid and a scrub brush, and laid it with a clean sheet as per his instructions. Samson appeared, and together, he and Elliot transferred the patient to the surgery.

"I need you to stand here alongside him. Very slowly drip this liquid onto this folded cloth over his nose and mouth so he breathes in the fumes." Elliot demonstrated with the still-capped bottle. "The trick is to keep from inhaling it yourself, as it will make you faint or even knock you out. I'll leave the windows open, and if you feel faint or dizzy, run over and take a few breaths of fresh air to clear your head."

Priscilla took the cloth and bottle and moved to the side of the table. Her hands shook, but she steadied them. The patient, Stephens, didn't look to be more than nineteen or twenty, his face ashen, his breath shallow. He wasn't unconscious, but his eyes had a glazed, drugged look.

"If you can, try not to look at what we're doing." Elliot washed his hands, drying them on a rough towel. He buttoned himself into a white coat to protect his clothing. "It won't be pretty, so best you don't see it."

Samson had quietly been unwrapping Stephens's head and shaving a patch of hair from the surgical site.

"Go ahead, Priscilla. I want him good and deep before I start."

She uncapped the bottle, and fearing to spill too much, eased a drop onto the cloth.

"Several to begin with, then slowly. I'll let

you know if you need to speed it up or slow it down." Elliot didn't even glance at her, his focus on the patient.

A sickly-sweet, cloying odor drifted up from the bottle and stuck in the back of Priscilla's throat. Narrowing her concentration to the clear liquid drops, she ignored the murmurs between Elliot and Samson and the clinking of instruments.

Stephens didn't stir, but something alerted Priscilla. At the same moment, Elliot's hands stilled.

"He's breathing very queerly."

"Stop the anesthetic." Elliot checked Stephens's pupils then placed first his hand then his ear on the young man's chest. For a long time, he listened. Samson came around the table and checked under the man's jaw for a pulse, and then lifted a small mirror from the instrument tray, holding it under Stephens's nose.

"Nothing?" Elliot asked.

Samson shook his wooly head, the lines deepening in his wise, old face.

"No, no, no. C'mon." Elliot checked for a pulse again, lifting Stephens's arms and pumping them. "Breathe, kid. You're too young to die." He fisted his hand and pounded the man's chest. "Beat."

For several minutes he worked over the

body, imploring it by word and action to live. At last Samson touched Elliot's shoulder. "It's no use. He's gone now."

Elliot's shoulders slumped. The coat bore streaks of fresh blood, as did his hands, and the sight sent a swoopy, empty feeling flying up Priscilla's spine. Mechanically, she screwed the cap on the chloroform and set it on the bench behind her.

"Don't you be taking it too hard." Samson drew a sheet off a shelf and covered the soldier completely. "You had no choice about this surgery. That boy was going to die if you didn't at least try."

Elliot nodded, his eyes staring into some distance only he could see. He walked blindly over to the wash basin and sank his hands into the water. It swirled pink. Plucking up the towel, he left the surgery. The front door closed behind him.

"Where's he going?" Priscilla leaned against the counter, as stunned by Elliot's departure as by how quickly someone could be alive then dead.

"He always takes it hard when he loses a patient. Especially the ones that were probly gonna die anyway. He don't like to feel helpless." Samson began to clean up. "Why don't you go after him? I'll tend to things here. He always feels better if he can talk things out."

"Where will he go?"

"Not far. You'll find him easy enough."

Priscilla stepped outside, breathing deeply of the cool night air. The rope on the flagpole slapped gently in the breeze, and lamplight shone in the windows of the barracks. A thousand stars, flung against the indigo sky, drew her attention up.

"Samson sent you along, I suppose?"

She turned. Elliot leaned his shoulder against the corner of the infirmary. Moonlight created shadows that hid his face, but his voice was weary. He had his hands jammed in his pockets. His balled up coat lay on the steps.

"He thought you might want to talk." When she drew close, she could see the anguish in his gray eyes. Her heart constricted, and she put her hand on his arm. "I'm so sorry."

He shuddered at her touch, raising his hands and dragging them down his face. "I can't help but think if only I had the right medicines, the right instruments and training, I could save so many more. So often, I feel like I'm fighting with my hands tied." He pounded his fist against the wall. "I might as well have never studied medicine if I can't save one boy from dying."

"You did everything you could. Samson said there wasn't much hope even before the surgery. It was a nasty wound that probably should've killed him outright. Think of all the people here you've helped. Matthews is walking again with the help of a crutch, and soon he won't need that. The blacksmith will be back at his forge thanks to your expert care. Not to mention Maybelle's baby or Mrs. Bracken's cough. And lots of people have told me how hard you worked when the fever hit this spring."

He gave a bitter laugh. "Not hard enough to prevent Chris and Rebekah from dying and leaving the twins without parents."

She grabbed his elbow, her temper rising. "Nobody blames you for that, least of all the twins. Enough of this wallowing. You're a good doctor who cares deeply for his patients. You of all people must know that you cannot save everyone." She tipped her chin up to stare at the night sky. "Life and death are in the hands of the Creator, and aren't we blessed because of it? Imagine what a mess we would make of things if we were the ones in charge."

He blinked, and this time his laugh held a tinge of mirth. "You're quite the little firebrand, aren't you?"

"Well, if you're going to be so silly, someone has to snap you out of it. You're an excellent physician, and this post would be considerably worse off if you weren't here. You lost a patient, in spite of your best efforts. Take it on the chin and keep going."

He grasped her elbows. "Whoa, pull in your horns. All right, I admit it. I do tend to get down on myself. Samson's taken me to task about it before, but I think I like hearing it from you better."

"Why?" She tried not to feel the warmth of his fingers on her arms. Heat spiraled along her skin, and she swallowed.

"You're prettier than Samson." He smiled, his teeth gleaming white. "And you're tougher than I thought you'd be."

"Tougher? I don't know if a lady likes to be called tough." She teased him, relieved that his gloom seemed to have lifted a bit, but breathless at the same time. When he put himself out to be charming, he was nearly irresistible. And standing this close to him, in the moonlight, after sharing such an emotional time, was playing havoc with her senses.

He turned her around. "There, now I can see you better with the moonlight shining on your face. Maybe *tough* isn't the right word. I should've said *strong*. You're stronger than I thought you'd be. I can't think of another woman on this post who would travel all this way by herself, be prepared to take on twins to raise all on her own, rides like a Comanche warrior, and thinks nothing of helping out with childbirth or surgery." He trailed the backs of his fingers down her cheek sending sensations darting through her, making her tremble. "When I first saw you, I thought you were some hothouse pansy with your fancy clothes and fine disdain for all things army. I thought you wouldn't last a week out here. But you fit in just fine."

Her breath deserted her at the warm light in his eyes. Striving for calm, she forced a laugh. "We do what we have to do. And taking on the twins is a labor of love."

"And what would you call helping me?" He tilted his head and closed the distance between them.

Dangerous.

She couldn't form a single word. Was he going to kiss her? Did she want him to? Her eyelids fluttered as her heart banged against her ribs.

His lips hovered just inches from hers, and his breath washed her cheek with the faint smell of peppermint. Her mouth went dry, and her lips parted. This was madness.

She'd die if he kissed her. She'd die if he didn't.

The clear tones of the bugle reached out to them, breaking the spell, and she stepped back, banging her elbow against the side of the building. The impact drove home just how close they had come to crossing a line they could never get back over. What had she been thinking? They were adversaries. She must have been out of her mind.

"I should go." Surely the darkness would hide the heat in her face, though she couldn't quite quell the wobble in her voice.

His hands returned to his pockets, a strange expression on his face. Was that a tinge of regret? What for? For almost kissing her, or for not going through with it?

She took a few paces back, relieved and yet frustrated. "Good night."

"Sleep well, Priscilla." His voice sounded tight.

Later, in bed, she pressed the heels of her hands to her eyes, mortified. A match between them would never work out. He was career military. And didn't she have reason to know firsthand how the army destroyed families?

You're a fool, Priscilla Hutchens, and you'd do best to remember why you came out here in the first place, no matter how charming and appealing Elliot Ryder is.

CHAPTER TEN

"You look so beautiful." Tessa's eyes grew round as Priscilla stepped out of the bedroom. "You're going to be the prettiest lady at the dance."

Brushing her palms down her snug bodice, Priscilla pressed her lips together. "Do you think so? It's not too much?" Why she was asking advice from a child, she didn't know, but she needed some reassurance. The wine-colored brocade satin caught the fading light from the window. Elliot would be here soon, and in spite of all the warnings she'd given herself, she couldn't help the flutter in her heart.

"I bet all the soldiers will be tripping over themselves to dance with you. You will remember to tell us all about it in the morning, right?" Tessa, sweet in her pinafore and for once without the battered forage cap, twirled one golden curl around her finger. Her hair had grown out a bit from the blunt chop she'd worn when Priscilla first arrived nearly six weeks ago. "Mama always told us about the parties the next day."

"I'll remember. And I have something for you. Come sit here and I'll fetch it."

She returned with her hand mirror, hairbrush, and a length of blue satin ribbon. "I saw this in the sutler's store and thought of you. Look, it's embroidered with daisies." She'd been in the process of slowly introducing more feminine articles into Tessa's daily life, and after the initial resistance, the little girl had warmed up to the idea. She no longer fought wearing a pinafore and petticoat, though she grumbled about them at first when she was going to ride her pony. However, seeing Priscilla ride sidesaddle in a complete riding habit had convinced Tessa that she could be adventurous and feminine.

"Will you do my hair like yours?" Tessa held the ribbon, running it between her fingers.

"I wish I could, but yours isn't quite long enough. I'll try something with the ribbon, and if you don't like it, you can take it out." She drew the brush through Tessa's curls, loving the silky, smooth texture, light as gossamer and a clear, golden yellow. Her own hair was heavy, dark brown. She'd spent an hour holding her curling iron over the lamp glass crimping and curling, pinning up each section until the back of her head was a mass of curls. Turning her head to look in the mirror, she checked that everything was still in place. Her silver combs shone, and jutting upward, three burgundy ostrich feathers sent out downy fronds.

Gently pulling Tessa's hair up and back, she tied the ribbon into a sweet bow headband. "There, you look beautiful."

Tessa turned her head this way and that checking out the new hairstyle. "I like it." Her lips split in a wide grin that looked so much like Priscilla's memories of Christopher, it took her breath away. Christopher must've been so proud of his daughter.

"Don't you think I look nice, Timothy?" Tessa asked.

The boy glanced up from his carving, hardly giving his sister a moment's notice. "You look all right, I guess. For a girl."

Tessa stuck out her tongue, but Timothy didn't see. He was busy working on a small block of wood, creating a pile of shavings.

"Be sure you clean up after yourself, Timothy. I'm tired of finding sawdust on the table. And don't you mind him, Tessa. You look very nice." Priscilla patted Tessa's narrow shoulder.

"You both look nice. Better than nice, I'd

say. You two look lovely as a poem." Elliot's mellow voice rippled across Priscilla's skin. Her eyes met his, but she couldn't say a word.

"Boy, Uncle Elliot, you look spiffy." Tessa bounded off her chair and wrapped her arms around his waist. "I can see my reflection in your boots, they're so shiny."

Priscilla gripped the back of a chair for support. She'd never seen Elliot looking so fine. His brass buttons gleamed. Every bit of metal on his sword and scabbard shone, and those boots. The gloss of the knee-high black boots threw the light back. He wore a yellow sash at his waist, tied at the side and hanging to the knees. The sash matched exactly the golden stripe down the side of his pants, as well as the braid and insignias on his shoulders and collar.

He'd had his hair cut and trimmed his mustache, and his gray eyes were alight with interest. "I can see I'll have to get my request for a dance in early. Once the men catch sight of you in that rig, they'll be lined up out the door to lead you out onto the floor."

Happiness caught her by surprise. She'd dressed for a purpose, though she hadn't been willing to admit it even to herself until this moment. The dress, the hair, the feathers, all of it had been selected hoping for a word, a glance, some sign of his approval. Turning away, she tried to hide her pleasure.

"Now, children, Samson is going to give you your supper, and then he'll read to you for a bit. After that it's bedtime and no arguing. You be good." She picked up her lace gloves and her fan. Taking Elliot's offered arm, she fortified herself for the evening's entertainment. They walked outside, and she found herself unable to concentrate on the beautiful night sky. Her attention focused on the strength of the arm under her hand, and the easy, confident way he moved. So masculine and assured. She couldn't think of a single intelligent thing to say.

Elliot seemed to have no difficulty conversing. "A work detail spent the entire day shifting supplies out of one warehouse and stacking it in the other to make enough room for the dance. And Mrs. Bracken was urging them on every step of the way. They'd no sooner get something moved than she was sweeping and decorating and ordering people about. I'm pretty sure she's the real commander of this post. We all, Colonel Bracken included, dance to her piping." Elliot placed his hand over Priscilla's in the crook of his elbow, and she had to force herself to pay attention to his words.

"That's not really true. She is a model of efficiency, and she has a fine way of getting people to do things, but the colonel calls the tune. You know she has little say in the majority of things that affect her life." Priscilla caught the tang of shaving soap and carbolic and herbs that was uniquely Elliot and breathed it in deeply, trying to memorize the scent.

"Such as?"

"Where she will live and for how long. None of you has any idea how long you will be posted here at Fort Bliss. Tomorrow orders may come for you to march to Arizona Territory or Utah or even to Georgia or Washington for that matter. And Mrs. Bracken has no say in that at all."

Elliot was silent for a moment. "That's true, Mrs. Bracken has no say in where she will live, but she does have a say in *how* she will live. She's a living, breathing example of being content, no matter what her circumstances. You know she's from a well-to-do family back east? She's lived in a mansion, and she's lived in a tent, and she's been content in both."

Priscilla couldn't miss the slight chiding in his tone, or was it her own conscience telling her Elliot was right? She thrust that notion away and changed the subject.

"There's quite a crowd." Light blazed from every window of the long, adobe warehouse. From every corner of the fort, soldiers and ladies converged on the impromptu ballroom.

"Most times, the officers and enlisted men have separate entertainments, but this time Colonel Bracken has invited all the corporals and sergeants as well as all the civilian contractors and their wives. With all the officers, there will be about fifty people I should think."

"And the privates are in charge of standing guard while the officers dine and dance?"

Elliot shrugged. "You have to start in the service somewhere, and Mrs. Bracken won't forget them. She's no doubt already got sandwiches and cake set aside for those who didn't get an invitation."

They met Fern and Harry at the door. Fern wore the same dress she'd worn for her wedding. She'd tucked her hair into a crocheted hairnet and looked sweet and demure. Priscilla suddenly felt overdressed and gaudy.

"Oh, Priscilla, that's a lovely gown." Fern eyed the black lace cap sleeves, the pointed polonaise, and the full, sweeping skirt cunningly draped to fall almost straight in the front and swathing back and up into a reasonable bustle. Or it had seemed reasonable until she realized, stepping into the warehouse-turned-ballroom, that none of the other ladies was wearing one.

Mrs. Bracken and Mrs. Crane wore silk, but both dresses were several years out of fashion, and Mrs. Crane's black dress showed signs of having been altered more than once. Most of the ladies wore calico or poplin or lawn. They'd dressed up by adding a bit of lace at the throat or a brooch or necklace and taking more care with their hair.

A blush started at her neckline and crept hot inch by hot inch to her carefully coiffed hairline. Would they think her pretentious? Or snobbish? Or just stupid to have brought such an ornate gown to a frontier fort? Probably all of those things. But this was the wardrobe she had. She would only be here a few more weeks at the most, and it didn't make sense to revamp to more serviceable attire. And she'd need these clothes when she returned to the east.

Elliot must've sensed her embarrassment, for he squeezed her hand at his elbow. "I'm the envy of every man in the room. I told you you'd cause a stir. Let's go give our greetings to the colonel and Mrs. Bracken, and then I'm claiming the first dance." He led her to the colonel's receiving line.

"My, my, you've done fine for yourself, Major Ryder. Miss Hutchens, you look a picture." Colonel Bracken bent over her hand, clicking his heels together as he bowed. "Doesn't she look lovely, my dear?"

"Beautiful. You'll be the belle of the ball. Your dress is perfection." Mrs. Bracken's cheeks glowed with pleasure, and she clasped Priscilla's hand warmly. "You're so stylish, it puts me to shame. It's been so long since I've been back east, I hardly know what the current fashion is." But her eyes bore no malice or judgment, and her smile made Priscilla feel better.

"Nonsense, my dear." The colonel patted her hand. "You are as beautiful as the day we first met, and you make everything you wear look lovely." The colonel winked. Mrs. Bracken blushed at his compliment and tapped his arm. Their clear affection for one another warmed Priscilla's heart. Evidently some couples could be happily married even after long years of service to the military.

Mrs. Crane, standing next in the receiving line, scoured Priscilla from head to toe with an appraising glare, her persimmon pucker in full force. "That dress is completely impractical. What possessed you to bring it along? You'd be better off in some home-spun or cotton. I declare, girls these days don't have the sense God gave a baby chicken." She turned her attention to Fern. "You, at least, seem to have grasped perfectly the meaning of plain and sensible dress. If you take off that lace collar, you could wear that dress to wash clothes or pick beans."

Willing to bite her tongue when the vitriol was directed her way, Priscilla could not be silent when sideswipe insults were delivered to sweet, kind Fern, who had never done anything to harm Mrs. Crane. Squeezing Fern's hand, Priscilla smiled sweetly. "I disagree about Fern's dress. She's as pretty as can be, and I'm sure she wouldn't dream of wearing her wedding dress into the garden to pick beans. As far as my dress is concerned, you're probably right. Of course, as the *much* older woman here, you would have more experience in these matters."

Fern, whose lips had whitened at first, now coughed into her handkerchief, smothering laughter. Both Elliot and Harry took their elbows and led them quickly away from the mottle-faced Mrs. Crane who blinked and sputtered and uttered several "Well, I never's."

"You girls are incorrigible." Elliot shook

255

his head as he tried to hide his smile.

"I know she lost her brother-in-law and all, but I wouldn't think that was enough to make her so sour." Harry tugged at his white gloves.

"I think it's more than that." Elliot pulled on his own dress gloves. "I surmise she's allowed discontent to move in and take root. If you let that happen, pretty soon, nothing makes you happy. Especially not the happiness of other people."

The band sorted itself out and played a military air. Elliot bent to whisper to Priscilla. "There will be a Grand March where the couples will pair off and promenade. I'd be pleased if you'd accompany me." He crooked his elbow.

She tucked her hand into his arm, her heart knocking against her ribs. With another musical flourish, the band began to play a march. "We step out by rank, so we'll go right after the colonel and Mrs. Bracken and Major and Mrs. Crane."

They fell into line and matched their steps. Around the perimeter of the room, those soldiers without partners stood at attention. The Brackens stopped at the end of the room and turned, and the couples marched by, arm in arm, the men stopping to salute and the ladies to curtsey.

There was something so formal and courtly about the proceedings, unlike any dance Priscilla had been to before. The men in uniform, the sabers, the protocol. Knowing how remote they were here on the Texas desert, and yet how linked they were to other military men in this great country, gave her a sense of belonging. Pride welled in her heart at these brave men . . . and women. Fern, so obviously adoring of her new husband, Mrs. Bracken, calm and accepting of her lot as an army wife, Mrs. Dillon, the new quartermaster's wife, who had just moved to the fort, but was already making plans to organize a new term of school as soon as her grown daughter arrived to teach.

Then there was Mrs. Crane, who seemed to despise all things military, just as Priscilla's mother had. Whose discontent had turned her face into a hard mask and her tongue to a prickly pear patch.

Obviously some women could make a go of it, and some couldn't. As Priscilla curtseyed deeply to the colonel, her skirt rustling around her, she glanced at the serene and wise face of Mrs. Bracken and wondered. What would it be like to be counted among these military wives? To be as loyal to an army husband as Mrs. Bracken? Could she

be that brave and unselfish?

Or was she cut from the same cloth as her mother? When the going got tough, would she fold and run?

Elliot turned her to the right to follow the Cranes around the room, nodding to the soldiers lined along the wall. Priscilla didn't miss the soldiers' admiring glances and smiles. With so many men present and so few women, she had a feeling her feet were going to be sore tomorrow.

At the end of the brief parade, the band changed tunes. "Pair up for the Virginia Reel."

Priscilla took her place opposite Elliot, halfway down the line. As she performed the familiar steps, allowing Elliot to swing her around, lead her down and around and under the outstretched arms of the lead couple, happiness filled her. For the first time in a long time, she was actually happy.

And at a military dance, of all places.

Elliot sucked in a breath as Priscilla smiled up at him. Her eyes shone, and her cheeks glowed. For the first time since he'd met her, she seemed . . . at ease? As if a knot inside her had finally come untangled. His hands met hers in the dance, and he wished they weren't wearing gloves. He'd love to

feel her skin against his, to lace his fingers with hers and press their palms together.

As it was, the scent of her perfume had wrapped itself around his senses and pulled him into her warmth. He hadn't felt this heady since . . . the party celebrating his engagement to Muriel.

His thoughts faltered, and he had to concentrate on the dance steps. Always before, thoughts of Muriel had come accompanied by a stab of pain and humiliation. Now the only feeling he could identify was relief. Relief to have escaped. Imagine if he'd married her before heading off to war, only to come home and find her unwilling to follow him in his career choice?

Muriel hadn't been content with him. When he thought about it, Muriel hadn't been content with much. Even before he left for battle, she'd been pushing him about getting a big house, about perhaps moving to a larger city to set up a practice that would be more lucrative than a small town in Wisconsin, about purchasing a new carriage. The list had gone on and on. And he, like a fool, had thought that once they were married, she'd settle in and be happy with the life he could provide for her.

The dance ended, and Priscilla curtseyed to him. He bowed and took her hand, only to be crowded around with blue uniformed soldiers seeking the next dance. She was whisked away from him, and he found himself standing along the wall with the other single men.

"Major, can I ask you a question?"

He turned to Matthews, who leaned on his crutches. "Something about your leg? Is it giving you trouble?"

"No, sir, it's not about the leg. It's coming along fine. I'll be glad when this splint comes off." Matthews tugged at his collar. "I wanted to ask you about Miss Hutchens. Are you courting her, sir?"

Elliot stilled. "Why do you ask?"

"Well, sir, if you aren't, I was figuring on throwing my hat into the ring, so to speak. She's a fine looking woman. Any man would be proud to have her on his arm."

Any man would. In spite of his vow to himself after the Muriel debacle, Elliot had found himself thinking upon those same lines, thinking about his pretty visitor in more than just a casual way. But he wasn't courting her. Priscilla would never accept his suit, even if he was inclined to make it. Not after everything she'd said about the army and army life. No, he wasn't courting her. But the thought of anyone else courting her didn't sit well either.

"She's headed back east in a few weeks."

Matthews shrugged. "Lots of women have come out here intending to go back east and have stayed on to get married. Wasn't it General Sherman who called frontier forts a marriage bureau of sorts because of all the female visitors getting hitched?"

Harry joined them and nudged Elliot. "We'll be lucky to get one more dance apiece with those girls. Look at how the men are cutting in on each other, especially with Priscilla."

Elliot had been looking. She could hardly dance more than a few steps before being swept into the arms of another. A green, seething feeling bubbled in his gut. To see her so happy and carefree, smiling and laughing up into the faces of her partners. He wanted to be the recipient of those smiles.

Major Crane strode toward them and frowned at Corporal Matthews until the corporal saluted and then stumped away on his crutches. "Gentlemen. The colonel wanted me to tell you that you've both been selected for the next patrol. You'll be pulling out first thing in the morning."

Patrol. Elliot trained his attention on the major. "How long?"

"Expect to be gone three to four weeks.

First, you'll accompany a wagon train along the California trail and then curl north and circle back. The colonel wants to know what we can expect in the way of Indian activity this summer, and he's hoping to keep up the patrol pressure, show a little bit of force in numbers, so the tribes will think twice before getting frisky. They've already attacked one supply train coming out of Santa Fe. Two dead and six wounded."

"Do they know who's responsible?"

Crane scowled. "Of course they do. It's the Kickapoo. And don't start spouting about how only a few renegades are responsible. Pekhotah knows who among his tribe is on the warpath. He's harboring killers, and you know it, for all he talks about wanting to live in peace. We should hunt down every last one of those savages and rid the plains. Until we do, no one will be safe."

"Not every Kickapoo is evil. They're doing the best they can in the face of an impossible situation. They've been chased off their lands by whites and Indians alike until they've nowhere left to go. I don't condone the killing. You know that. But killing them all in kind isn't the answer either."

Crane's face reddened. "And just what is the answer? More palavering over a peace pipe, making promises we all know neither side will keep? Mark my words. It's going to come down to total extermination or subjugation before this is through. And not you or those Indian-loving, bleeding hearts in Washington will change it."

Elliot bit his tongue, knowing arguing with Major Crane on Indian issues always ended the same.

"How many men in the patrol?" Elliot's mind drifted to the things he would need to pack, the medical supplies and sample vials and jars for collecting new botanical specimens. He hadn't been on a foray since last fall. The campfires, the riding, the scouting, the camaraderie. Even the danger. He'd missed it. The post physician only went out on patrol with a sizeable troop. Smaller parties didn't merit a doctor along.

"Thirty. You'll be the ranking officer, but Lieutenant Dunn will lead the men. You're along in a medical capacity only. There will be an officers' meeting at 0500 hours. The quartermaster has prepared your supply packs."

"Why weren't we told about this sooner?" Elliot stepped back as a couple waltzed closely by.

"You didn't need to know sooner." Major Crane looked down his nose before turning away.

Typical army reasoning. You went where you were told when you were told, trusting the higher-ups to know what they were doing. Elliot was well used to it now.

Harry swallowed. "My first command away from the post. All I can say is I'm glad you're going along. I hope you don't mind if I ask for advice from time to time."

"You'll do fine."

"Fern's not going to like me being gone for nearly a month."

Elliot nodded, and then it struck him.

The twins.

Since taking on the children, he hadn't been away from the fort. Who would look after them?

Priscilla.

Relief at having someone to take care of them in his absence washed over him. Samson was fine for short bouts of childcare, but he was old, and he had his duties at the infirmary to see to, especially in Elliot's absence. But now Priscilla was here, someone of their own to watch over them.

Harry rested his hand on the hilt of his sword. "I think it's time I cut in and danced with my wife again. I don't want her forgetting what I look like while I'm gone." He gave Elliot a nod and entered the fray on the dance floor.

Elliot bided his time, knowing how the men had looked forward to this Officers' Ball. If he monopolized Priscilla, he'd hear about it later from those who felt slighted. Time enough to broach the subject of his leaving the fort when he walked Priscilla back to her — his — quarters. He had no doubt she would look after the children well in his absence. She was a nurturer at heart. How often had he marveled at her ability to corral and direct the twins, loving them, spoiling them a bit, but disciplining them when they needed it? She was so good with them, not like him, swimming in murky water, overwhelmed at times, swamped by guilt at others.

He'd been lucky — make that *blessed* — to have Priscilla all but dropped into his lap. He could leave on patrol with no worries about the twins. Things couldn't have worked out better.

Priscilla breathlessly thanked her partner, grateful that the post band had stopped for refreshments. She couldn't remember this soldier's name. There had been so many partners tonight. To her disappointment, after the first dance, Elliot had stayed away. Once, she'd spied him dancing with Fern, and once with Mrs. Bracken, but most of the time he stood in the corner with a group of men in blue, talking and watching. She searched the room now but couldn't locate him.

"Enjoying yourself?"

Priscilla jumped, and Elliot laughed.

"Yes, very much. And you?"

He smiled, tilting his head. "Things started out very well, faded a bit, but they're looking up now. I wanted to ask you to reserve the last waltz for me. It will be an early night, so they'll call out the last dance before midnight."

She accepted the cup he offered her. The punch was tart, and she winced. Someone had purchased some lemons and limes from one of the local farmers, and the result, while refreshing, could use a bit more sweetness. Still, the ladies of the fort never ceased to amaze her with their ingenuity. Priscilla never would have dreamed they could come up with even this much way out here in the very center of nowhere.

"I hope I can last until midnight. These boys are certainly . . . enthusiastic . . . about dancing. I was glad Corporal Matthews asked me to sit out a song with him, since he couldn't dance with his broken leg."

"Is that all he asked you?"

Her eyebrows rose. "What are you getting after?"

"He said he was going to ask about courting you. The man's quite besotted, you know. And he's not the only one. How many marriage proposals have you had this evening?"

"Stop teasing. Corporal Matthews did ask, and I turned him down, as you knew I would. He isn't in love with me. He's just lonely, as are most of the men out here. They're starved for a little womanly attention, that's all. I imagine if they knew the real me, beyond the dress and the hair and the perfume, they'd run for the hills rather than offer marriage." She rolled her eyes. "If they were back in civilization with a dozen girls to choose from, I wouldn't even make their top ten."

"Hmm, I shall, of course, have to disagree. I believe if the men here knew the real you, there might be bloodshed, the winner tossing you over his shoulder and making off with you." His gray eyes pierced her, making her breath hitch in her throat.

"Present company excluded of course." She toyed with her fan. If things weren't so at odds between them, if they didn't have the future of the children to sort out, would he want to court her?

"Hmm. I foresee trouble along this path of conversation. I'd best reserve my comments on that subject until a time and place where there aren't so many listening ears."

Silly to be so thrilled that he didn't make an immediate denial. He was only teasing, after all. It was a light and entertaining evening, and in keeping with the holiday mood, he was flirting a bit. She'd best be careful. In the festive atmosphere, she could almost believe their differences could be overcome.

The time flew, and just before midnight, as Elliot had promised, the last dance was called. She went into his arms, and she felt as if she was coming home. Her other dance partners had been just that, dance partners. Elliot was something far different. His hand at the small of her back seemed firmer, warmer, and his arm stronger about her. Their steps melded perfectly, and when he pivoted her, she was safe and secure following his lead. The smell of shaving soap and chemicals and Elliot enveloped her. When the music finally came to an end, she was reluctant to leave his embrace.

He must've been reluctant, too, for he held her, standing still, looking down into her face. His pale eyes mesmerized her. What was he thinking? Could he read her mind? Did he know how perilously close she was to abandoning all her previously held ideas about military life?

As applause for the band erupted around them, his arms dropped away and he stepped back with a bow, breaking the invisible tension holding them captive. She sucked in a deep breath and added her applause.

They took their leave of the Brackens, thanking them for the hospitality. Stepping out into the cool night air, Priscilla took in the stars in the inky sky, and the sound of the wind across the desert plain, sights and sounds she would forever equate with her visit here to Fort Bliss. In the city you could never see so many stars, and the largest open space was the city park.

Mrs. Crane stepped out after them, her voice intruding on the quiet as she commented on the music, the food, and the company. Major Crane followed her along the path toward Officers' Quarters, but her voice carried across the parade ground.

"I'm glad we're leaving this place. And I'm glad you're not going on this latest patrol either. Three weeks or a month away? And liable to get killed for your trouble? I imagine Lieutenant Dunn isn't pleased to have to go so soon after his wedding. And what are we supposed to do here without a doctor for a month with Major Ryder out on patrol? If you think for a minute I'm going to take my ailments to that grizzle-haired old man who helps in the infirmary, you can forget it."

Priscilla halted on the gravel path as she assimilated Mrs. Crane's words. "A patrol?" She sought Elliot's eyes. "You're leaving?"

He nodded. "In the morning. We'll be out for three or four weeks."

Fear rose up Priscilla's windpipe and tightened her throat. "When, exactly, were you going to tell me?" Her voice rose and several heads turned her way. Forcing down the panic, she modulated her voice and spoke through clenched teeth. "When were you going to tell me you planned to be gone for a month?"

"It probably won't be a full month, and I only found out about it tonight. Rather than pull you out of the dance to explain, I thought I'd let you enjoy yourself. I planned to tell you when I said good night." He tugged her elbow. "I'd rather not have this conversation on the parade ground with half the regiment listening on."

She followed him, head down, feet striking the path much too hard for her dancing shoes to protect the soles of her feet. But she couldn't keep silent. "What about your obligations here? What about the hospital and the children?" *And me?*

"Samson will look after the hospital, and I'm hoping you will continue to look after the children."

How could he be so calm? Didn't he know what could happen to him out there? He could be killed, and then where would she and the children be? Her father had gone out on a simple patrol and never come back. All sorts of danger lurked outside the fort's perimeter, from the elements, from wild animals, from hostile Indians.

"Why do *you* have to go? There are plenty of other men here. Men without your obligations." There were plenty of single men with no families dependent upon them. Of course, Elliot was technically single, but he had the twins to consider.

"I go because I'm ordered to go. That's how it works. You know that. This is a frontier fort. Patrols must go out, and I must go when it is my turn. That's the army way."

The army. First, last, and always. They called, men went. And their families just had to deal with it. "And what happens if you don't come back?"

He sighed. "That won't happen."

"You don't know that." *My father didn't come back.*

"If I don't come back, then you will take the children back to Cincinnati to live with you. You'll get just what you wanted."

Tears flooded her eyes, and she jerked her elbow from his grasp. "Elliot Ryder, that's the most barbaric thing you've ever said to me. This is exactly what I would expect of a military man, putting his job ahead of everything else and leaving those who care about him to muddle on alone." She stalked away, eager to get to her room so she could throw herself on the bed and give vent to the tears and terror ripping at her heart.

He grabbed her by the arms just before her hand grasped the doorknob. "Priscilla, wait."

"What for?" Angry tears burned her eyes, and she blinked hard, refusing to cry in front of him. "You've made your choice clear. You'll put yourself in danger regardless of those who are depending on you. The army comes first. And you may wish to live that way, but I don't, and I don't believe the children should have to either."

His eyes hardened. "Typical woman attitude. I should've known better. You and Muriel are cut from the same cloth."

He dropped his hold on her and stepped

back, the coldness in his eyes leaching the warmth from her bones. Without a word he spun on his heel and left her standing on the doorstep, startled out of her need to cry.

Who was Muriel?

CHAPTER ELEVEN

Elliot tightened the cinch on his saddle and tried to put the memory of three pairs of anguished eyes out of his mind. Anyone would think he was leaving them forever instead of three measly weeks.

Tessa's tears and neck-wrenching hug had been bad, but Timothy's stoic stare had been worse. And worst of all had been Priscilla's poor act of pretending nothing was wrong, that she didn't care one way or another, and he could please himself.

Didn't they understand he had no choice but to go? He was a soldier. It was his job. He'd taken an oath. The men on the patrol needed him. Harry was counting on him for guidance. The rest of the troop needed him in case of a medical emergency. And they might even need his ability with a gun should they run into trouble.

He stifled a yawn. Sleep had eluded him for hours last night.

Last night. Hmm.

Things had begun so well, with Priscilla happy and glowing, dancing and laughing, and having a good time. He'd let his guard down. He'd let himself believe that Priscilla was nothing like Muriel, that maybe she *could* be happy with a career soldier. He'd even spent a few satisfying minutes anticipating perhaps kissing her good night.

A rueful chuckle disrupted his yawn. Mad as she was right now, he'd be better off kissing his horse. Taking up the reins he turned Bill's head toward him. "Want a kiss, old boy?"

Bill blew down his nose and tossed his head, making his bit jingle. Stamping restlessly, he shifted his weight, eager to be on his way. All around them in the predawn, soldiers loaded their gear and led their horses in circles waiting for the signal to mount. Leather creaked, boots and hooves stamped, and horses whinnied. Elliot couldn't deny the surge of pleasure that shot through him. The call to adventure.

"Looks like we're all set." Harry led his stocky bay gelding beside Elliot. "The pack horses are loaded, canteens filled, ammunition stowed."

"I'm ready when you are." Elliot checked his cinch once more.

The lieutenant signaled the bugler who blasted out the call to mount. Elliot swung astride Bill, relieved to finally be on the way, and feeling guilty because of it. A little time away from the demands of the kids and the chaotic feelings Priscilla set up in him would be a blessing. He could clear his head, get some perspective, and really analyze things.

They rode two abreast through the early-morning air, holding the horses back to a steady walk that matched the pace of the oxen pulling the loaded wagons of the civilian train. Elliot rode beside a young private named Phelps who was making his first venture beyond the boundaries of the fort since his arrival just a week before. For the first hour, his head was on a swivel, scanning in every direction, even behind him, as if expecting an Apache warrior to rise up from behind every scrubby bush and attack.

"Relax, son. You're so tense, you're going to snap." Elliot removed his canteen from his saddle and took a drink. Not because he was thirsty but to put the green soldier at ease. "There are no hostiles this close to the fort."

"But Major Crane said they could pop up anywhere. He said a couple of men got ambushed right on this very trail." The boy's throat lurched and white ringed his irises.

"Did Major Crane mention that the attack happened more than a hundred miles from here? And did he mention that the teamsters who got ambushed had accosted a young Kickapoo girl at a trading post in El Paso, and that if someone hadn't intervened, they would've hauled her off and violated her?" Elliot's muscles clenched at the memory. Every time something like this happened, it set the peace effort back.

"He didn't mention that, sir."

"Try to get all your facts before making assumptions, Soldier."

Late in the afternoon they met up with another wagon train headed east. Long before they reached it, the plumes of dust kicked up by hundreds of oxen colored the sky a muddy yellow-brown.

"Four abreast?" Phelps stood in his stirrups to get a better look.

"They travel like that for protection, especially if no troops are with them. With four wagons abreast they can form up a circle in a hurry should they come under attack. They corral the spare livestock inside the circle. Often it's the cattle and horses the Indians are after, though the horses more than the cows."

Harry Dunn, at the head of the line of troopers, signaled for the soldiers to pull off to the right to let the wagons pass on the trail. Whips cracked, men shouted, oxen lowed, wagons creaked and rattled. The men from both wagon trains shouted greetings to one another.

"Sure is a dusty, noisy way to travel, isn't it, sir?" Phelps asked.

"That it is. Teamsters are some of the toughest men I've ever encountered. Good to have on your side in a fight, but trouble if you try to oppose them."

The leader of the oncoming train rode over to converse with Harry, and Elliot nudged Bill out of line to join them.

"Any trouble along the way?" Harry asked.

"No, none to speak of. Not Indian trouble, anyway. We heard about the two most recent killings." The trail boss leaned over his horse's mane and spit a long stream of tobacco juice into the grass. "We've kept a close eye out. Indian trouble tends to come in bunches, and them getting started this early in the year has me a little leery. But we've got plenty of guns and the men to use them." He patted his sidearm. In addition to the pistol, a rifle hung in a scabbard under his thigh and a wicked knife jutted from the top of his boot. "I've been over this trail more than a dozen times and managed to keep my hair, and I aim to do it this time, too."

The hair in question hung down his back in a long, dust-covered braid, a fitting match for the chest-length beard in the front. Buckskins, so worn they were shiny in places, clad his muscular frame. He looked as if he'd crossed more than a few hills and won more than a few fights in his time.

For six days, the patrol kept to the slow pace of the westbound wagons, stopping to make camp early enough to pitch their tents while some light remained. The teamsters drank and caroused late each night, and Harry and Elliot, as the officers in the company, kept a sharp lookout to make sure none of the enlisted men joined them.

Finally, after nearly a week, the time came to part company. The train would continue west alone, and the patrol would make a wide north and east arc before returning to Fort Bliss.

When the last wagon had rolled past, Harry bid the trail boss farewell, and the troop changed course for the north. That evening, Harry wisely made camp earlier than usual in a small glade with a clear stream running through it. The men set about pitching tents.

Elliot, as a ranking officer, had a tent to himself, packed by one of the supply mules.

The enlisted men slept two to a tent, each man packing half the tent on his saddle.

Legs protesting after the long day in the saddle, Elliot dismounted and waited for circulation to return to his limbs. When a soldier came to take his horse, Elliot waved him away. "I'll see to him, Private."

Unbuckling the girth, Elliot lifted the saddle and blanket from Bill's sweaty back. "You're in better shape than I am, old son. And you'll eat better tonight than I will. Oats for you. Nothing but salt pork and beans for me."

By the time he'd cared for his horse, partaken of the less than glamorous fare, and found his tent, Elliot was more than ready to sleep. Clouds had rolled in, and to the west, low thunder rumbled. Ah, trail life. Not that rain wasn't welcome anytime in the desert, but why did it have to fall when he was sleeping out?

Before entering his tent, he swept the perimeter of the camp. Pickets had been placed about fifty yards out, standing guard. Harry had tethered the horses in the center of the encampment, safeguarding them against being stolen in the night.

A fat raindrop hit Elliot on the cheek. It was going to be a rather miserable night. Hopefully a rainy night or two would be all the excitement they encountered while away from the fort.

Priscilla held her shawl over her head and splashed through the puddles, hopping up the steps to the commanding officer's house. The rain had come down for a week, and the drizzle had invaded every corner of her existence. Her clothes, the bed sheets, her papers . . . and her attitude were all damp.

"Oh, goodness me, you're bound to be soaked." Mrs. Bracken met her at the front door. "It's just so odd, all this rain. The desert will be beautiful next week, but until then, it's a nuisance. Hang your shawl up and come in. All the ladies are here."

"I'm sorry to be late. I was helping Samson at the hospital. Several of the men have come down with a digestive upset." Not to mention that the twins had been especially difficult. Out of character for the normally placid Timothy, the boy had pitched a fit at breakfast.

"But you like oatmeal." Priscilla had brushed the hair off her face with her forearm.

"No, I don't. I want pancakes."

"I don't have any pancakes, and I don't have time to make them. If you don't want

281

oatmeal, you'll just have to wait until lunch."

Timothy crossed his arms and stuck his lower lip out.

"If Timothy doesn't have to eat his, I'm not eating mine either." Tessa pushed her bowl away from her, hard enough to send the crockery off the edge of the table and onto the floor with a cracking splat.

Her blue eyes widened for an instant before narrowing. Though scared for a moment, she'd obviously decided to bluff by being angry instead.

Priscilla wanted to sit down at the table, put her head down, and indulge in a good cry. Nothing had been right since Elliot had gone away. The children had picked up on the fact that something was wrong, growing more difficult and emotional each day, especially Tessa, who was so sensitive to the moods around her. To have Timothy go off the rails this way was just too much. And yet she couldn't break down in front of the kids.

In the end, Tessa had cleaned up her mess, Timothy had eaten a few bites of his oatmeal, and Priscilla had held onto her temper and her patience. Though each of those outcomes had been a close-run thing.

She shook water droplets off her hair and followed Mrs. Bracken into the front parlor.

Nothing had changed in the austere room since the first day Priscilla had arrived at the fort except a bucket in the corner catching a steady drip from the roof. *Ping! Ping! Ping!*

Half a dozen women sat on the horsehair furniture with teacups in their hands.

Fern moved over and patted the place beside her. Unfortunately, this put Priscilla between Fern and Mrs. Crane. Priscilla set her bag down at her feet.

"I'm so glad you came." Fern squeezed her hand.

"Now that everyone's here, I'd like to unveil a project I've been thinking about." Mrs. Bracken stood beside the empty fireplace. "I asked you all to bring your knitting needles and scissors along because I'd like to start a weekly afternoon knitting bee. As most of you know, our soldiers are not the best equipped when it comes to clothing." She smiled at Mrs. Dillon, the quartermaster's wife. "Not that this is in any way the fault of our supply officer. No, the blame lies in Washington where they don't give a decent clothing allowance per man. It is my hope that this month we, the ladies of Fort Bliss, can knit enough socks to see the men through this next year."

She put them to work with yarn from the

sutler's store. Priscilla settled in, her needles clicking, letting some of the stress of the day bleed away as conversation flowed around her.

"You must be counting the days until you head back home." Mrs. Crane dug into her sewing bag for her needles. "I know I am. We've received word that our transfer will come through at the end of August. I understand that's when you'll be leaving, too. Perhaps we'll be able to travel together, at least as far as Fort Worth or even Kansas City."

The end of August. When she'd first arrived, she'd thought the end of summer far off, but now, with only a few weeks until she had to be back at work at the catalog company, Priscilla couldn't believe how quickly the time had flown. She smiled and nodded to Mrs. Crane, which was apparently all the encouragement the woman needed.

"You must miss your life in the city. I know I do. What was it you did there again?"

"I am a fashion illustrator for a mail-order catalog company. The Carterson Ladies' Emporium Catalog. I draw most of the illustrations and have charge of the overall look of the publication. It keeps me quite busy. When I return, I am hoping to put a deposit down on a house. I've rented until now, but I want a house, a place to put down roots." *And raise the children.* Though for some odd reason, she found it difficult to recall the appeal of her life in Cincinnati where she lived alone. The tumult of having children around her, even on tough mornings like today, seemed preferable.

"Imagine that. I suppose, if you *have* to work for a living, being an artist is better than factory work or being domestic help. I've never had to keep myself, having married Major Crane when I was seventeen. Still, some girls aren't cut out for marriage. It's good you have a way to take care of yourself when you leave since you're a spinster."

Priscilla kept her attention on her work, casting on stitches for a sock. Fern muttered and shifted, and her heart warmed that her friend would take umbrage on her behalf.

"And here you are taking care of the children while Major Ryder is gone. Have you two come to an agreement about them? Will you be taking them with you when you go?"

Every eye in the room focused on her, and she lowered her knitting needles. "We're working on it." *And by working on it, I mean he's still refusing to budge.*

"You know," Mrs. Crane went on, "you could always call upon the wisdom of Solomon. You could split them up. You take Tessa with you and leave Timothy with Major Ryder. This life is much better suited for a boy than a girl. Imagine the advantages you could give Tessa if you took her in hand and brought her to live with you in Ohio. She's on the very edge of running completely wild out here, but there you could train her properly to be a young lady."

Priscilla set her jaw. Hot anger coursed through her, and her knitting fell to her lap unheeded. With all the protectiveness of a mother bear for her cubs, she lit into Mrs. Crane. "The matter is entirely between Major Ryder and myself, but I can tell you right now we wouldn't dream of separating the twins. Whether they stay or whether they go is no concern of yours, but whatever our decision, the children will remain together. As to Tessa, she's a delightful child, imaginative and sensitive. She's generous with her affection, and she'll defend anyone she thinks is being ill-treated. She's even tried to be nice to you, though she'll be the first to admit it's not easy."

No one moved, and Priscilla swallowed. Shocked that she'd let fly all her thoughts and feelings, she was now at a loss. Should she apologize? She wasn't sorry. The very idea of separating the twins was barbaric. And Mrs. Crane's attack on Tessa's behavior was beyond the bounds of propriety. Still, Priscilla should've held her tongue.

All pretense of working was given up as the women in the room looked at one another.

Mrs. Bracken cleared her throat, breaking the strained silence. "Fern, how are you doing with Harry gone this first time?"

Everyone seemed to relax a fraction and handwork was taken up again. Priscilla bent over her work, her face hot and her vision blurred.

"I know it's only been a little while, but it seems forever since Harry left. He was so torn, excited to go but not wanting to leave me. I felt so bad for him. He was trying so hard not to let on how enthusiastic he was about leading his first patrol." Fern pulled some slack up from her yarn ball. "I'm glad you invited us all here today. I've been going crazy with boredom. I can only clean our hallway room so many times. I've read and written letters and played solitaire until I'm ready to scream. The rain makes it worse, having to stay inside."

"I remember those days when Mr.

Bracken was a young lieutenant, before the War. We were stationed in California." The commander's wife chuckled. "Have I ever told you about my first foray into frontier cooking? One of the hunting parties had brought back a deer, and we received a nice piece. I thought I would roast it with some vegetables." She knitted while she talked, her needles a clacking blur. "We had no fresh vegetables, but I had several dehydrated vegetable cakes among our rations. When I asked one of the cooks how to use them, he said you just dropped some in boiling water. It seemed simple enough, so I filled my biggest kettle and plopped a cake in the water."

Mrs. Dillon snickered. "You didn't."

"Too right I did. The whole cake. Then I left it to simmer while I ran to the sutler's store for some canned peaches to make a cobbler."

Several of the ladies had stopped knitting once more, shaking their heads and smiling. Priscilla raised her eyebrows at Fern, who was giggling as much as anyone and then turned back to Mrs. Bracken, puzzled and feeling left out of the joke.

"Imagine my surprise when I returned to find that vegetable cake had swollen to ten times its previous size and was threatening to take over our cabin. I dipped out pot after pot of the horrible vegetables, filled every bowl and basin I had, and still couldn't get to the end of them. We ate vegetables for days, and in the end I had to throw most of them out. Poor Samuel. To this day he still teases me about that."

Fern leaned over to Priscilla. "A quarter cup of the dried vegetables, reconstituted, would be enough to feed a family of five. An entire cake must be enough for thirty helpings or more?"

Grateful that Mrs. Bracken's diversion had worked and the tense moment with Mrs. Crane had passed, Priscilla joined in the laughter. And yet, she felt on the outside of this group. Part of them but not part. The way she'd felt all summer. These women were bound together by their common experience, by their love of their husbands and their love of the regiment. With the exception of Mrs. Crane, every one of them embraced the life out here, proud of their men and proud to serve with them.

They took a break for more tea. Mrs. Crane, recovered from Priscilla's rebuke, launched into speech about what she would do when she and her husband arrived at his new posting at an ammunition depot in

Virginia. "I won't miss the privations, the quarters, the food, the danger. We're finally going to live a civilized life away from all of this."

Unhappiness rolled from her in waves. Most of the other ladies moved away from her, leaving Mrs. Bracken to entertain her outspoken guest. Something Elliot had said to Priscilla came back to her, about how Mrs. Bracken had learned to be content and Mrs. Crane hadn't. Just like her mother hadn't learned to be content.

Had Priscilla? Was contentment finding a suitable situation, or was suiting yourself to whatever situation in which you found yourself?

Priscilla returned to her seat beside Fern. "Do you want to go with me to the sutler's store tomorrow? I want to pick out some material to make new trousers for Timothy. He's outgrowing the ones he's got. I've let them out as much as I can."

"I'd love to. I need some more quilting thread."

"How's the quilt coming?"

"I'm hoping to have it done by the time Harry returns. I miss him so much, especially in the evenings. At least there's plenty of time to quilt." She sighed then blushed.

"I know how you feel. I've spent so many

evenings working on the herbal journal with Elliot, that after dinner, I don't know what to do with myself." She kept her voice low so as not to be overheard.

Fern gave her a searching look. "I've been hoping you and Elliot might make a match of it. It's the perfect solution, you know. The children would have a proper family again, and you seemed so . . . compatible . . . at the dance."

Priscilla clenched her hands in her lap. "I can't marry Elliot. He's made it clear he intends to stay in the army, and I can't live my life by the bugle and drum, knowing that no matter the danger, when the army calls, he'll go. Even now, having him out on patrol is eating me alive. I'm filled with dread at the thought that he might not come back."

"My dear." Mrs. Bracken's worn hand came to rest on her shoulder, and Priscilla realized she'd been overheard. "I'll agree with you, the danger to our men isn't easy to bear. Many's the time I've lain awake at night wondering where my husband was, if he was safe, if he would come back to me. But I've learned through the years that my faith grows the most when it is tested. I have to trust that God loves my husband even more than I do and that He has everything under control. It isn't until I'm willing to let God be God that I can get any peace. My job isn't to keep my husband safe. My job is to support him in his calling, to create as peaceful and pleasant a home as I can for him wherever we happen to be living, and to trust God to take care of him and me."

She settled into her seat and took up her knitting. "When the colonel is fulfilling his duties and keeping his oath of service, I know he's right where God wants him to be. And there is no safer place, be it in the city or the out on the prairie or in the high desert."

Several of the ladies nodded. Priscilla mulled her words. The only woman not in agreement seemed to be Mrs. Crane, whose pinched-lipped expression showed plainly what she thought. Of the two camps in the room, it galled Priscilla that she'd been acting more like Mrs. Crane than Mrs. Bracken.

Fern spoke without looking up, and though she didn't address Priscilla particularly, Priscilla had the feeling she was speaking for her benefit.

"I wouldn't want Harry to be anything else. He loves being an officer, and he feels he's following God's call on his life. When he obeys an order, no matter how difficult, he's keeping his oath, his word. I wouldn't want to be married to a man who didn't keep his promises, or who ran at the first sign of trouble. If a man feels he's following God's call, and he's given his pledge, then nobody should ask him to be or do differently."

The words dropped into Priscilla's mind and settled there for her to ponder.

Lord, help me to trust You. Please give me peace about Elliot's safety. Help me to know that if he's in the center of Your will, there is no safer place for him to be.

Chapter Twelve

The bullets started flying on the third Monday of the patrol, when they were a day's ride north of the fort. Up to that point the patrol had been an exercise in boredom. After swinging north almost to Las Cruces and encountering no Indians, the troop had finally turned south, crossing the open plains between the Organ and Franklin Mountains and striking into the heart of the Kickapoo summer territory. Though they found several abandoned camping grounds, they saw very few Indians, and those only from a distance.

Phelps was disgusted. "I came to fight Indians, and we've seen hardly any. And those we saw were so far away you can't even hardly tell they are Indians."

"Be glad, son. If you see an Indian up close out here, things are liable to get lively." Elliot scanned the miles of yucca and creosote and cactus around them. With all the rain, the desert had bloomed, and riots of color blared from every plant.

By tomorrow night, the patrol might be back at the fort. His eagerness to return surprised him, but then again, this was the first time he'd had something, or rather someone to return to.

They topped a chalky, sandy rise, one of hundreds they'd encountered in the past three weeks, when Harry threw up his arm to halt the column. The smell of smoke drifted toward them, and Elliot tensed. At Harry's motion, he rode forward and surveyed the valley below.

A wagon smoldered beside a humpy little adobe house, and a brown and white cow lay on its side, riddled with arrows. Elliot raised his field glasses, as did the sergeant on Harry's other side, sweeping the area. The cornfield had been set ablaze, and half a dozen Indians rode in circles whooping and shaking their lances. In the midst of their circle, a man sprawled on the ground and a woman, her hair streaming over her shoulders, huddled over him. The attackers poked at her with the tips of their lances, jeering and yelling, but she wouldn't let go of the man.

"Charge!" Harry gave the command, drawing his saber and pointing down the hill. The bugler blew the command and the column fanned out and raced toward the little hut.

At the sound of the bugle, the Indians below broke off, racing toward the south-west. Harry in the lead, the troopers followed. Elliot put Bill into a gallop, and Harry pointed to the homesteaders with his sword, motioning for Elliot to stop and help them while the rest of the patrol gave chase to the fleeing Indians.

Elliot pulled his horse to a stop as soldiers streamed by on his left. When they'd passed, he swung from the saddle, unbuckling his medical bag and racing to the fallen man. The woman clung to the man, and Elliot had to pry her fingers away so he could assess the man's condition. Blood covered the ground around them, and dirt caked his wound.

He pushed the woman aside, and she jerked away from his touch and ran into the house, slamming the door. If she could run, she couldn't be too injured, and the man needed his attention first.

"Sir, can you hear me?" Elliot peeled back the man's shirt to reveal a nasty puncture wound just above his right hip bone. A war lance. He needed to stop the bleeding if it wasn't already too late.

The man groaned, his hands trying to clutch his hip. Elliot grabbed a gauze pad from his bag and pressed it hard on the wound, eliciting another groan from the man who scrunched his eyelids closed, pale and sweating. "My wife."

"She's in the house. I'll check on her soon." Elliot dug in his bag for his bottle of alcohol.

At the sound of approaching hoofbeats, Elliot whirled, reaching for his sidearm, but relaxing when he saw a soldier approaching.

"The lieutenant sent me back to help you and keep a lookout." Private Phelps slid from the saddle.

"Good, hold this bandage hard on this wound. I have to check the woman." Elliot stood and gave a quick look at the horizon. The only thing moving was the wind in the yucca and the quickly dissipating dust clouds churned up by the passage of so many horses.

The house was dark and smelled of damp earth. He ducked under the lintel and squinted to make out shapes in the gloom. Sobs came from a huddle in the corner.

"Ma'am, I'm Major Ryder. I'm the post surgeon from over at Fort Bliss. Are you hurt, ma'am?" He approached slowly, squatting beside the crudely-constructed bed-stead.

She didn't give him an answer but continued to sob, and when he touched her shoulder, she shot away from him, cringing and putting her hands over her head as if to protect herself from a blow.

"Easy, ma'am. It's all right. They've gone. I'm not going to hurt you." He kept his tone low and soothing, as if speaking to Tessa after she'd had a bad dream. "I'm a doctor. Your man's outside hurt, and I need to tend to him, but first, I have to know if you're injured." He couldn't see anywhere that she might be bleeding, but it was so dark in the corner of this earthen hut, he couldn't be sure.

More sobs, and mumbling he couldn't understand. White skin on her shoulder stood out in the gloom where her dress had been torn, and her dark hair had come out of its pins and covered her face, though he caught the glitter of her eyes through the strands.

"I'll be back then, after I see to your husband." He eased toward the door and went outside. The woman didn't appear to be in physical pain, and he hadn't been able to spot any blood anywhere, so he'd have to tend to the more urgent wound before seeing what he could do for her.

He knelt beside his patient. "Soldier, keep the pressure on that wound, then I'm going to need you to find me some water and start a fire. I think there's a cookstove in the house, but the woman in there is pretty hysterical, so it might be better to start a fire out here." He sorted through his instruments and medicaments.

Dosing the wounded man with some laudanum for the pain, he then peeked under the edge of the blood-soaked bandage. "Get your bedroll and mine off our saddles." Gray, sweating, and cold, the injured man was going into shock.

Elliot worked as quickly as he could, cleaning and packing the wound. The puncture was so deep, he couldn't just sew it up. It would have to fill in from the bottom of the wound, and the packing would need to be changed twice a day. He couldn't see the woman being able to deal with that any time soon. He'd have to take him back to the fort.

Private Phelps proved himself efficient, following Elliot's orders quickly. When the patient murmured something, the private leaned over him and whispered back. Elliot dug in his bag for a packet of dried comfrey. He soaked the leaves in a pan of water and then pressed them into the wound, covering it with cotton bandages.

"Thank you for your help, Private Phelps. Cover him with those blankets. When you're done, stoke up that fire. I need to brew some medicine and see if we can spoon it into him. Meanwhile, I'll go check on the woman again." Cramped from kneeling for so long, Elliot pressed his hands to his back and stretched. "And keep an eye out. With soldiers on their tail, I doubt any of the Indians will double back, but we'd look awfully foolish if we didn't at least consider the possibility."

Entering the adobe house once more, he took the time to light the lantern sitting on the rough-sawn table. The sobbing had subsided, but the woman hadn't moved from the bed.

He knelt once more on the hard-packed dirt. "Ma'am?"

She didn't stir. Gently, he eased the hair off her face and found her sound asleep. Her mind had suffered too many shocks and had closed down. A bruise had developed high on her left cheekbone, and another on her upper arm. Distinct finger marks stood out on her pale skin. Someone had grabbed her hard. Elliot pulled the quilt up from the end of the bed and drew it over her. She and her man would both need to come to the fort. Her husband would need care for the next couple of weeks, and she couldn't stay here alone.

Throughout the afternoon, Elliot and Private Phelps watched over their patients. Elliot dug in his pack and produced some herbs which he sprinkled into a cup of hot water.

"What is that stuff?" Phelps wrinkled his nose.

"Garden nightshade." Elliot let the leaves steep, covering the cup with a cloth to hold in some of the steam.

"Nightshade? Ain't that a poison?"

"You're thinking of belladonna, known as deadly nightshade. That *is* a poison. This is garden nightshade, which is in the same family. It's a sedative and a narcotic. It will reduce his pain and keep him asleep when we transfer him onto a travois and haul him back to the fort."

"How far away do you reckon the lieutenant will go chasing those Kickapoo?" Shielding his eyes, Phelps checked the location of the late-afternoon sun.

"Those weren't Kickapoo. They were Kiowa. Either way, I'm hoping he'll be back by nightfall." Elliot didn't voice his concerns, but he had plenty. Harry had been on the frontier for less than a year, and he hadn't seen any skirmishes with hostile Indians. Though Elliot knew he was needed here, he couldn't help but pray that his fellow soldiers wouldn't be in need of his services should they actually catch up to the band they were chasing. How he wished he had Samson along with him. He'd have left him here and gone with Harry just in case.

"She's growing like a weed in the spring rain, Maybelle." Priscilla cuddled Brigit against her shoulder.

"That she is. Sleeps good, too. Which is a blessing, considering as how I've got more laundry customers than ever." Maybelle Dugan bent over her washboard. "It's a blessing and a curse. Where are your young'uns?"

Priscilla smiled, though a streak of pain ran through her chest. Her young'uns. "They're helping out at the bakery. They love punching down the dough, and the baker seems to enjoy their company."

A shout went up from the guardhouse at the end of Suds Row. Maybelle straightened, pressing her wet hands to the small of her back. "Looks like someone's coming." She shaded her eyes.

"That's not teamsters." Not enough dust

kicked up behind the riders to be one of the wagon trains heading up or down the Camino Real. The black dots on the horizon grew and separated, becoming distinct. Riders on horseback.

"Is it the patrol returning?" Priscilla's heart leapt.

"From the way men are scrambling, I'd say that's unlikely." Maybelle dried her hands on her apron.

Soldiers ran, rifles in hand to the north side of the fort. As the riders grew closer, she could see they were Indians.

Priscilla handed Brigit over to her mother. "I'd best go find the twins." She held up her hem and hurried along the front of the quartermaster's warehouse and around the parade ground toward the shops building. The smells of leather, hot metal, and baking bread greeted her as she drew closer. The saddler, the blacksmith, and the baker all leaned out of their doorways.

"It appears we're having a visit from some Indians." Priscilla waved toward the north. "Are the twins still here?"

Two yellow heads popped out of the doorway under the elbows of the baker who was wiping his hands on his apron. "Aunt Priscilla, we can't leave now. It's time to put all the dough in the pans."

"I'm sorry, kiddos," Priscilla said, "but we've got visitors coming, and we need to get back to our quarters."

Tessa's eyes widened. "Visitors?"

"Come on, I'll explain on the way." She held out her hands for them, grateful when they obeyed. "Thank you, Mr. Preston. I appreciate you letting them help."

The baker nodded. "Anytime. They're great kids." He stepped back inside and closed his door.

"Who's coming? Is it Fern coming for dinner again like last night?" Tessa swung on Priscilla's hand, skipping along, her bonnet dangling by its strings down her back. Her curls tossed as she hopped.

"No, there's a band of Indians coming. I don't know who they are, but you know what Colonel Bracken has said. When we see Indians coming, all civilians are to get inside and wait until the all clear is given."

Timothy glanced up. "Then we're going to be inside for the rest of the summer."

"What do you mean?"

"Dusty says there will be a lot of Indians coming into the fort over the next few weeks because of the annuity payments that are due."

"What annuity payments?"

The boy gave her a pitying look and spoke

as if he were a schoolmaster instructing a child. "Last fall, a whole bunch of tribes signed the Medicine Lodge Treaty. Kiowa, Comanche, Plains Apache, Kickapoo, Arapaho. Medicine Lodge is up in Kansas. All the chiefs were there, even Quanah Parker and Pekhotah and Little Raven and Satanta. The treaty says the government will pay the Indians in money and trade goods, and the Indians agree to move out of some of their land and stop fighting the white men and live on reservations."

"Why are they here then?"

He shrugged. "Not all the Indians stay on the reservations all the time. Anyway, some of the tribes come here to get their annuity payments. Dusty says it's going to get a little tricky, since the money and supplies to pay them haven't shown up yet. We could be completely surrounded by Indians waiting to get paid if it doesn't arrive soon."

The idea of the fort surrounded by potentially hostile Indians and Elliot being away sent a chill through her. They needed him here.

Samson emerged from the hospital and walked toward them, his lined face grave. "You children go into the house. I need to have me a word with Miss Priscilla."

They went up the steps to their quarters

but hesitated at the top. He shooed them inside. "Git, now. This talkin's for grown-ups, not for little ears."

When they were safely inside, Samson shook his white head. "Miss Priscilla, it's bad. We's got three cases of the cholera in the infirmary and shore to be more to come."

"Cholera?" She swallowed, trembling at the word.

"Yes, ma'am. I'm going to need some help, what with Mistah Elliot bein' gone. I got an orderly, but he isn't hardly worth the powder it would take to blow him up when it comes to nursin' sick men."

"What about the children?"

"I believe now might be a good time for them to maybe stay over in the officers' quarters with one of the ladies. We want to keep them away from the cholera, that's for sure." He rubbed his hands down his face. "I believe it's going to be a long few days."

Priscilla went into the house to find the children, trying to formulate a plan and wishing even more that Elliot would return. "I need you each to pack a bag to tide you over a few days. There's some sickness at the infirmary, and Samson needs my help to take care of the men. You're going to be staying over at the officers' quarters."

"But where?" Timothy asked. "The officers' quarters are all full up. Miss Fern's in
the hallway, and Mrs. Bracken doesn't have
a spare room to be had. You remember what
Uncle Elliot said when you first got here?
You'd be staying with Mrs. Bracken if she
had room instead of turning him out of his
bed and making him sleep with that old
buffalo Sergeant Plover."

"We'll figure out something when we get
over to Officers' Quarters." Was Elliot still
chagrinned at being forced out of his home?
Poor man. He hadn't asked for any of this.
Not to parent these children, not to have
her dumped in his lap, none of it. And if
she stopped to think about it, he had han-
dled it all rather well. He certainly cared for
the children, and though he wouldn't give
them up to her, he had been kind to her in
every other way.

Mrs. Bracken agreed that the children
should stay away from the hospital for the
next little while and agreed to find lodging
for them. "Don't you worry. Just go help
Samson. I'll find a place for the little ones
to sleep, and we'll take care of them until
this is over. I do wish Major Ryder and the
rest of the patrol would return." She leaned
over to whisper to Priscilla. "The colonel is
just the teensiest bit worried. He's anticipat-

ing the arrival of many more Indians over the next week or so and the additional thirty troopers would be a help."

Priscilla nodded, her chest tightening. "They should be back any day now, shouldn't they? It's been more than three weeks already."

Mrs. Bracken patted her arm. "That it has. I'm sure you'd like Major Ryder to return as much as any of us." Her smile was encouraging and the tilt of her head invited a confidence.

But Priscilla wasn't ready to give any confidences regarding Elliot Ryder. The truth was, she wasn't sure what to think in that regard. It was as if through proximity and kindness and his sometimes exasperating reasonableness — not to mention his charm and exceedingly handsome looks — he had slowly torn down her resistance to all things military.

And his absence had magnified his presence in her thoughts. Each day without him at the fort had stretched out like the Texas desert, empty and dry. His space at the dinner table, his desk in the surgery, his spot on the edge of Timothy's bed for evening prayers, every place empty of his presence but so full of memories and his essence.

She filled some of her loneliness for his

company by working on the herbal journal. Every night after the children were asleep, she'd spread his notes and her art case on the kitchen table. She sketched and added color and dimension to the drawings he'd approved as accurate. When those ran out, she organized his notes and began the task of rewriting them in a better, more legible hand. Sitting at his table at night, transcribing his notes, she could almost hear his voice, enthusiastic about his subject matter. She could almost see his face, eyes shining in the glow of the lamps, bending to sniff the aroma of one of his herbs or scratching out a definition in his rapid scrawl. As each day passed, she realized more and more how she'd come to rely on and care for him.

And what was she going to do about that? She was slated to leave for Cincinnati soon. He was adamant the children would be staying with him, and though the thought of leaving them here was unbearably painful, she knew without a doubt that leaving Elliot would be just as hard.

Heaven help her, she'd fallen in love with a military man.

"Yes, Mrs. Bracken, I'll be glad to have him back."

CHAPTER THIRTEEN

The patrol returned to the adobe house where Elliot and Private Phelps waited, but not unscathed. One trooper had taken an arrow to the thigh; another's horse had stumbled, throwing him and fracturing his collarbone; but worst of all, Harry Dunn had been shot.

They rode in, supporting the wounded, just after dark.

"What happened?" Elliot caught Harry as he fell from the saddle.

"Ambushed. Followed them into a canyon." Harry mumbled and his head lolled.

Sergeant Plover helped him carry the lieutenant to a pallet by the fire. "I tried to head him off, but he charged right into that blind break. They were waiting for us." Blood had dried on the side of his face from a cut high on his cheekbone. "When the shooting stopped, we retreated and they climbed out the narrow end of the canyon

310

and rode off to the west."

Guilt pricked Elliot. Harry was green when it came to Indian fighting, and he'd fallen for a fairly elementary tactic. If Elliot had been there, might he have been able to keep Harry from racing into that ambush? He thrust aside those thoughts as counterproductive and set to work.

As the only other officer in the group, Elliot was in charge. "Set up pickets, fifty yards out. I want a water detail sent to the creek. Every canteen and every bucket you can find around here gets filled. Corporal Rhodes, see that every man takes care of his horse and his equipment, then assign the watches. And find someone to take care of the lieutenant's mount as well. We'll need more fuel for the fire, and everybody get some food in their bellies." He grabbed his medical bag.

"You, Phelps, you're with me. Stir up that fire and start heating water. I'm going to have to go after this bullet." Unbuttoning Harry's tunic, Elliot assessed the damage in the light of a lantern. Harry's white undershirt was soaked with blood along the left side. When Elliot looked up, Private Phelps had unsheathed a wicked-looking knife.

"You want me to cut that shirt off?"

"Yes. And when you're done, wash your

hands. I'm going to need you to hand me instruments." Elliot poured a bottle of whiskey into a basin and dunked his hands in the liquid. "Where's Sergeant Plover?"

"Here, sir." The stocky, red-faced man lumbered over. His legs were so bowed, he could never have stopped a pig in a lane, and his barrel chest strained the buttons on his shirt.

"There are two civilians in the house. Assign one soldier to watch over them and report to me if there is any change in their conditions. And get me more light. I can't work in the dark."

"Yes, sir." Plover snapped out a salute.

Elliot knelt to examine Harry's wound more closely. The bullet had gone into his side just below the left ribcage. Using the torn shirt, he wiped the seeping blood away.

"Private Phelps, hold that lantern higher. Harry, can you hear me?"

Harry grunted, his jaw locked against the pain.

"I'm going to have to get that bullet out. I'm going to give you something to knock you out for a while." He reached for his laudanum bottle and shook it trying to assess how much he had left. He needed to save some for the trooper with the nasty leg wound.

"You have any more of that nightshade stuff you gave the other fellow?" Phelps asked.

"No, just what we brewed up. We'll give whatever's left of that to the soldier with the broken collarbone."

The bullet had gone deep, and Elliot had to cut it out. His probes located it, but he couldn't grasp it with his forceps. The whole procedure took longer than he'd hoped, but he was thankful he'd opened Harry up, for the bullet had nicked his spleen and he'd been bleeding rather badly. Examining the bullet in the firelight, he shook his head. A heavy musket ball from some antique muzzle-loading firearm.

Inserting sutures while kneeling on the ground in the dark wasn't his idea of the best way to practice medicine, but field conditions were rarely good. His training during the War stood him in good stead. When Elliot finished and had Harry bandaged up, he turned his attention to the trooper with the arrow in his leg. The shaft had gone deep through the fleshy part of the back of his leg. Elliot could feel the arrowhead not far beneath the skin of the inside of the man's thigh.

"Am I going to lose the leg, Major?" he asked through gritted teeth, his hands clutching his leg just above the still-protruding arrow.

"Not if I have anything to say about it." Elliot filled a spoon with the last of his laudanum and held it to the trooper's lips.

He gulped the medicine and made a nasty face. "You trying to poison me?"

"It's a good thing it tastes bad, or you'd grow too fond of it." Elliot turned to Phelps. "Where's that knife of yours?"

"Here, sir." He produced the bowie knife.

"Cut this pant leg so I can see what I'm doing."

When the man's leg lay bare, Elliot surveyed the situation. He didn't touch the arrow, but every time he probed the skin near it, the trooper stiffened and groaned.

Elliot turned to Phelps. "Gentle as you can, cut the shaft of that arrow about an inch away from his leg. I'll hold it as still as possible."

The injured man shrunk back, his eyes wide. "You going to yank it out?"

"No, Soldier. It's too deep for that, and I'd do a lot of damage trying to pull it back through the arrow track. It's so far in, I'm going to push it through the other side."

The young man squeezed his eyes shut and began to pray. Phelps had the shaft sawn through in a matter of seconds.

"Always good to keep your knife sharp, sir," he said by way of an answer.

"Here, bite down on this." Elliot took the sawn-off arrow shaft and put it between his patient's teeth. Using his scalpel, he made a shallow cut on the inside of the thigh over the arrowhead and quickly, because it was best done quickly, he pushed the arrow through.

The man cried out, but the sound was muffled by the wood he bit down on.

"There, Soldier. It's done. We'll wrap it up tight, and barring infection, you should heal just fine."

Though the trooper's eyes watered, he nodded and relaxed a fraction. The laudanum really wasn't enough to push the pain very far away, but it would help some. And by tomorrow night, they would be back at the fort where Elliot would have his fully-stocked surgery at his disposal. He poured the rest of the whiskey onto the wounds and wrapped the leg in strips of cotton bandage.

"Sergeant Plover, see what you can do about fashioning some travois to carry our wounded. Don't forget the civilians in the house. They're coming with us, too. The woman should be able to ride." Fatigue pulled at Elliot, but he ignored it and went on to clean the abrasions on the man whose horse had fallen. Using strips of canvas cut from one of the tents, Elliot fashioned a sort of brace that pulled the man's shoulders back and allowed the ends of the broken bone to come into alignment.

"It will be sore, but you should be fine. Try to get some rest." He dosed the man with the last of his garden nightshade tea.

He checked on all his patients one more time. The settler felt a bit warm, which was better than his gray, cold sweat of before, but might be a harbinger of infection setting in. Elliot bathed the man's face and hands with cool water and let him rest. The woman hadn't stirred, but when he checked on her, he noticed a slight swelling to her abdomen. She was with child. They'd have to be careful with her. Shocks such as she'd suffered could cause her to lose the baby.

By midnight, he was ready to drop. He hadn't been this tired since the War when he'd stood at a table for hours as wounded men were brought in one after the other. At least that horrific experience had prepared him somewhat for this.

"You should try to rest, sir." Phelps pushed a cup of hot coffee into his hands. "I can watch out for the wounded and wake you if there's any change."

Elliot rubbed at his scratchy eyes. The coffee smelled good, though he winced at the strong, bitter taste. "Wake me in two hours and I'll take a turn. Watch their breathing, particularly the lieutenant's. If it gets shallow or he starts laboring, let me know."

With his bedroll in use to cover one of his patients, Elliot lay down on the bare ground and put his head on his saddle. He'd slept rougher and in more hostile territory than this.

He hardly knew when he fell asleep, but it seemed he'd only been out for a few moments when someone shook his shoulder.

"Sir, it's been two hours." Phelps bent over him.

The edges of the very vivid dream he'd been having began to blur and dissipate until the images vanished and he blinked, his jaw nearly cracking with an enormous yawn.

"Any change?"

"No, sir. Everything's quiet. The picket guard just swapped, so it's sometime around two, I guess." Phelps yawned, which made Elliot yawn again.

"Get some sleep then. We'll have a big day tomorrow."

Sitting by Harry's side, Elliot poked at the bed of coals and ashes. A heavy weight sat in his chest, a remnant from the dream he'd had. No doubt his thoughts of the War had stirred up old memories. He'd been returning home from battle, eager to see his love and hold her in his arms again. Confident of his reception, he'd swept into her house, ready at that moment to rush her to the altar and begin their married life together.

Only when he opened the door, it wasn't Muriel standing there.

It was Priscilla.

Priscilla stepped outside into the cool, fresh predawn air and stuffed the dirty linens into one of the washtubs that had been hauled over to the infirmary and filled with water. A fire blazed under a kettle, and Gilda poked at the boiling sheets with a wooden paddle. Of all the laundresses, only Gilda had come over to help with the sickness. Maybelle would've come, but when she offered, Priscilla had refused outright. She couldn't expose her infant to something as deadly and decimating as cholera.

"Two more cases have come in. That makes six." Priscilla grabbed the lye soap and scrubbed her hands. "It's all I can do to keep up."

"We'll be seeing more of them. The cholera hops from one to the next." Gilda added another stick to the fire and dusted her hands. "A messy disease."

"It is that. Between the flux and the vomiting, I'm changing sheets and rinsing bowls constantly."

"Sure wish the doc would get back."

"As do I." Pale pink streaked the eastern sky. Soon Reveille would blow and another day would start. Would this be the day when the patrol returned?

"You should get some sleep. You've been up all night." Gilda lifted a dripping sheet from a tub of soapy water and tossed it into the boiling kettle.

"Samson made me lie down on one of the cots for a couple of hours around midnight. I got a little sleep."

The laundress snorted. "Not enough."

"No, but neither did Samson, and we're needed. Speaking of which, I'd best get back inside."

"I'll bring you clean sheets as soon as they're dry." Gilda waved to the rows of damp linens drying on the makeshift lines that had been strung for her use. At least the hot, desert air would have the sheets dry as dust in less than an hour.

Priscilla entered the infirmary and walked over to one of the windows to open it. As hard as she tried to keep up, the smells of the sickness were taking over the room.

"Miss Priscilla, if you look in the cabinet marked *S* in the surgery, you'll find a bundle of dried sweetgrass." Samson lifted a bucket of water and refilled a pitcher. "We could burn some in here to help with the odors."

She went into the surgery, feeling again Elliot's absence in the place where he should be. She went to the medicine cabinets. Beneath the shelves of glass jars, he'd stored larger quantities of some herbs as well as surgical equipment and supplies. She found the right cabinet and withdrew the burlap-wrapped packet of aromatic grass.

"Just put it in that metal bucket and light it. That's what Major Ryder did the last time we had the cholera in here." Samson barely looked up from bathing a patient's face and chest. They'd given up on nightshirts for the sick men. It was all they could do to keep up with clean bedding. Each of the stricken soldiers wore only cotton drawers and lay under a sheet and light blanket.

Priscilla stuffed the dry stalks into the pail, breathing in the sweet fragrance that bloomed each time she touched the grasses. She set the bucket in the middle of the room and lit it. Within a minute, most of the grass had been consumed and the room smelled much better.

"Too bad that's the last of it. I have a feeling we're going to need it again."

"The major taught me a few more tricks, and there's some I taught him. We can try them later. For now, we have to get some fluids into these boys. With all they're bringing up and putting out, they's getting dehydrated."

Six of the nine beds in the ward were occupied. "Last summer, when the cholera got bad, we had twelve beds in here, and two men to a bed. Major Ryder had tents set up outside for the rest of them. I don't think he slept for a week." Samson rubbed his hands on a towel. "We'll probably have a new patient or two coming in soon. Sick call is in about half an hour. I'm gonna go brew some more barley water and see if we can't get some of it to stay inside these po' boys."

Samson's prediction proved correct. They did get another patient in the beginning throes of cholera. They settled him in a bed, and Priscilla laid a cool cloth on his forehead.

"I feel terrible, ma'am." He cradled his stomach. "I don't remember ever feeling this awful."

"Shh. Just sip this. It will help to settle your stomach." She held a cup of birch bark tea to his lips. From her hours working through Elliot's herbal journal, she'd absorbed so much information, and while it helped her now, she missed Elliot's calm certainty, his steadiness. The weak tea, smelling faintly of wintergreen, had been steeped from the bark of a birch tree, and according to his notes would soothe the lining of the stomach.

Another soldier moaned and grabbed the basin beside the bed, retching and gagging. He'd thrown up so much already, there was nothing left to bring up. His skin had taken on a sunken, dry pallor. But each time she gave him something to drink, it showed up in the basin only moments later.

Still, she had to try something, so she headed outside.

"Gilda, go find one of the men and send them to the sutler's for every bit of peppermint candy he has. When you get back, boil me a sheet. One of the ones you've got drying on the line. Boil it in clean wash water and bring it to me. It's fine to bring it to me wet." She didn't know if she was doing the right thing, but anything had to be better than watching these boys dry up and waste away. How she wished Elliot would return. Not only would she know he was safe, but he could take over here. It was one thing to be helping him, another altogether to be in charge. Though Samson had far more experience, because she was white, the soldiers, both ill and well, looked to her for guidance.

When a soldier returned with the candy, she met him at the door and took them. "Thank you, Private. Is there any word about the patrol?"

"No ma'am."

She quelled her disappointment. "Go find your sergeant and tell him I need you seconded to the infirmary to help out. Tell him I need you and two more men."

"Yes, ma'am." He snapped to attention and caught himself half-way to saluting. With a sheepish grin, he lowered his hand and hurried away.

"Samson, take that candy and smash it to powder, then mix it in some water until it dissolves." Priscilla sorted out some clean bowls and lined them up on the work table in the center of the room.

Gilda came in with a basket. "Here's your wet sheet. I let it boil for a good long while."

"Thank you. Grab the shears off the table across the hall and cut the sheet into squares about the size of a man's handkerchief.

"Samson, pour a little of the peppermint water into each of these bowls."

Gilda returned with the damp squares. "It ain't too tidy a job, but I figured fast was better than neat."

"Thank you." Priscilla took the squares. Folding one into quarters, she dunked a corner of cloth into the water. "Let the men suck on the cloth. Those that are too weak, squeeze just a few drops at a time into their mouths. Hopefully it will absorb slowly enough that they won't retch it right up again. Peppermint is supposed to be good for a bilious stomach. I guess we'll find out."

The three soldiers she'd asked for arrived, and she set them to dosing the sick men with the flavored water. Gilda came and went with clean sheets, carrying away the soiled ones, doing the work of at least two women without complaint. Samson and Priscilla worked on, bathing hot skin, turning pillows, holding basins, scrubbing, dosing, worrying, praying.

By late afternoon, Priscilla's arms, head, and back ached, and she felt as if someone had thrown a handful of sand into her eyes. But the sick men had responded better than she'd hoped to the peppermint water, and they'd received no new patients throughout the day.

When she finally managed a few minutes to herself, she stepped outside and around the building to sink into the shade on the east side. The adobe wall had soaked up the sunshine and was warm against her shoulders as she leaned back and closed her eyes. Her dress was a mess. Sometime during the day she'd caught her heel in the ruffle and ripped it. Rather than waste time changing, she'd taken a pair of Elliot's bandage scissors and cut it off all the way around to keep it from dragging the floor and tripping her up. She'd rolled up the sleeves, creating creases and wrinkles, and though she'd worn a big apron all day and changed it several times, the purple poplin bore stains and smudges that might never come out.

Gilda rounded the corner holding two cups of tea. "Here, love. If anyone ever deserved this, you do."

"I think you do as well. We wouldn't have made it through the day without you." Priscilla took the mug and breathed in the steam. "I was just sitting here looking at my sorry dress. You know, if this had happened when I first arrived, I'd have been horrified and devastated that my dress was ruined." She took a sip. "Now I don't care. There are other things more important than clothes."

"Life out here has a way of sorting out our needs from our wants, that's for sure."

Gilda tucked a wayward, wiry curl back into her haphazard bun. "Look at that bunch there." She gestured to yet another group of Indians riding toward the fort. "They've been coming like ants to spilled honey all day. There must be three hundred of them camped along the river. The quartermaster started handing out some of the annuity goods today, but from what I hear, he's uneasy about it."

"Why's that? Because he's afraid he'll run out before the rest of the supplies get here?"

"Well, there is that, but some of the annuity goods are guns and ammunition. The Indians are supposed to use them for hunting game to feed themselves. The quartermaster is afraid they'll start using them for hunting bluecoats for sport."

The group of Indians grew closer. Though they were still a good distance away, Priscilla could see they were dragging travois behind some of the horses, and at least two of them rode double. She stood and shaded her eyes against the lowering sun. The strains of a bugle reached her at the same time as the realization that those riders coming in weren't Indians.

"It's the patrol!" Her heart leapt to her throat. The travois could only mean one thing. They had wounded.

Gilda saved Priscilla's teacup as it fell from nerveless hands. "You go. I'll tell Samson to prepare the surgery."

Priscilla gathered her skirts and ran toward the incoming troops. If he had been hurt, if he was dead, she didn't know how she would stand it.

CHAPTER FOURTEEN

Elliot adjusted his hold on the woman from the homestead. He carried her in front of him in the saddle at the head of the procession. She hadn't said a word all day. Each time he offered her his canteen, she drank, but he couldn't persuade her to eat anything. Her eyes stared blankly out of her pale face, and Elliot worried over her state of mind. When he asked if the attackers had hurt her, she shook her head and wouldn't meet his eyes. She didn't act as if she was in pain physically, and he was loathe to subject her to a thorough examination at this point. Best to get her back to the fort and in the company of some of the women who might be able to reach beyond the walls her mind had thrown up to keep out the frightening memories.

Her husband rode on one of the travois, as did Harry Dunn. The homesteader had awakened in pain at dawn. His wound had stiffened up, and when Elliot had removed the packing from the puncture, the agony to his patient had been so severe, Elliot had broken out his medicinal whiskey and dosed the man to deaden the pain. The man spoke with a clipped British accent, said his name was Oliver Essex, his wife was Matilda, but beyond that, he was in too much pain to chatter.

Harry had been more stoic and refused whiskey. He'd lost a lot of blood, and the jouncing, bouncing drag of the travois wasn't doing him any favors, but he bore it in silence. Elliot turned his horse back from the front time and again to check on them.

The trooper with the arrow wound had declared himself fit to ride, though from his ashen expression and the way his hands were fisted in his mount's mane, he might be rethinking his choice. He would be stiff and sore for a while, but barring complications from an infection, he'd be fighting fit again before the fall rains.

Elliot's other patient, the private with the broken collarbone, was gutting out the ride with gritted teeth and his arm strapped to his chest.

The sun beat down on them, and a baking, summer wind gusted like heat from an open oven door. The air around them wavered in the blistering temperatures, and the horses raised dust with every step. Each man wore a layer of reddish-gray dirt that obscured their blue uniforms. Elliot insisted they stop frequently to offer water to the wounded men.

"Major," a corporal drew his horse alongside Elliot's. "I scouted ahead like you ordered. We're about three miles from the fort, and there are Indians camping along the Rio Grande. Lots of Indians. Mostly west of the fort, from what I could see."

Elliot removed his hat and swiped at his forehead with his arm. "They're here to get their annuity money and supplies. I doubt they'd stir up trouble this close to the fort, but just to be on the safe side, let's swing a little wide and come in from the east."

"Yes, sir."

When Fort Bliss finally emerged from the shimmering heat waves, the men grinned and straightened in the saddle, and the horses picked up the pace. Elliot knew he couldn't let up on his vigilance just yet. He ran the medical procedures he would need to accomplish through his mind, listed the equipment and medicines, prioritizing his patients.

As soon as the wounded were squared away, he would be free to see the twins. And

Priscilla. How had she fared in his absence? A tiny niggle of doubt had been pestering him the whole trip, and it rose up again. Would she be there when he got back? She wouldn't have packed up the kids and left the minute his back was turned.

Smoke from dozens of Indian campfires smeared the blue sky, and wickiups had sprung up in bunches, crowded around the adobe dwellings of the town of El Paso. The patrol would have to ride through at least one Indian camp in order to reach the outskirts of the fort.

"They're cozied right up to the picket lines." Private Phelps, whose horse dragged Harry's travois, motioned toward the perimeter of the fort.

Sergeant Plover, riding just ahead of them, turned in the saddle. "What are the odds that the very scoundrels we chased up that wash yesterday are now camping along the river waiting for a government handout?" He hacked and spit into the sand.

At his words the woman in Elliot's arms reared up, pushing at his wrists, twisting in his grasp until she was clutching the front of his shirt. White ringed her eyes, and the cords on her neck stood out. She didn't make a sound, but her desperation was clear.

"Shh, you'll be okay. Nobody's going to hurt you." Elliot scowled at Plover over her head, and the big sergeant ducked and faced the front. The woman didn't relax entirely at his soothing words, but she did turn around again in the saddle, her back stiff and her hands clutching his forearms.

They rode through the Indian camp, and as Elliot recognized faces, he realized it was Chief Pekhotah's band of Kickapoo. As the patrol passed, the Indians stared. Kennekuk emerged from one of the wickiups, and Elliot nodded. Niganithat, the man who had won the horse race and tried to buy Priscilla, sat cross-legged before a fire, sharpening a long knife on a whetstone. His black eyes bored into Elliot's, and a superior smirk tugged at his thin lips. He was bare to the waist, and sweat glistened on his skin.

Chief Pekhotah sat beside him, smoking a pipe, his wrinkled face sober as always. He held up his hand, palm outward in a silent greeting. Elliot returned the gesture but didn't stop. He had to get his wounded to the hospital.

Fort Bliss had never looked so good to Elliot. He gave the signal to the bugler to announce their arrival, grateful to have the trip coming to an end. In spite of all he had been through and what he still needed to do, he had come to a decision on this patrol.

He was ready to face his feelings about Priscilla and get his questions answered. The dream he'd had as an idealistic young army doctor still lingered in his mind, that of coming home from battle to the woman he loved. He had the oddest sense of déjà vu, and he couldn't help but wonder if he was brave enough to risk his heart again. What if Priscilla stuck to her guns about having nothing to do with the military ever again? What if she left him like Muriel had?

At the sound of the bugle, soldiers and civilians emerged from the fort buildings. The beleaguered patrol splashed across the irrigation ditch and up the south bank, coming to a stop between the shops building and the quartermaster's warehouse.

Colonel Bracken strode toward them, flanked by Captain Dillon and Major Crane. Elliot dismounted, motioning for the woman to stay in the saddle, and led his horse to the front of the group.

"Colonel." He saluted.

"Major." Colonel Bracken returned the salute, his eyes grave. "We're glad you're back. How did it go?"

"We ran into a bit of trouble. I've some wounded here, Colonel, that I'd like to get over to the hospital. When they're squared away, I can give you a report."

Bracken nodded, tugging the end of his goatee. "We've had a bit of trouble here ourselves. As you can see, we're up to our epaulettes in Indians, and there's been a bit of a crisis —" He broke off.

Feet pounded the dirt, and Elliot looked away from the colonel. He blinked. Racing toward him from the direction of the hospital came Priscilla. Her hair had come loose and waved behind her like a brown flag, and bless him if she didn't have quite a bit of petticoat showing at her hem.

His first thought was joy at her eagerness. His second was fear that her racing toward him had nothing to do with him and everything to do with the twins. Were they hurt? Were they sick? His third thought was what a blatant breach of protocol would unfold if she didn't stop and wait until he'd been dismissed by his superior officer before approaching

Priscilla must've had the same thought, because she stopped cold about ten feet away, her chest heaving and her cheeks bright. She looked him over from hat to boots, her gaze lingering over his beard and travel-stained clothing. As if satisfying herself that he was all in one piece, she stepped back and folded her hands waiting her turn. He blew out a breath and returned his attention to the colonel.

The older man's lips twitched. "Major, tend your wounded. There's been quite a lot going on here in your absence. I'm sure Miss Hutchens can fill you in on her part of it. I'll be awaiting your report, but don't come before your patients are seen to."

"Yes, sir."

Duty first. He understood that. He only hoped Priscilla would as well. He saluted his commanding officer and turned to issue orders to his men.

"Sergeant Plover, get these patients over to the infirmary. The rest of you men see to your horses and equipment and get some chow." He turned to Priscilla. "Miss Hutchens, would you find Fern and bring her to the infirmary? Then I could use your help with Mrs. Essex here."

"What's happened? Are you all right?" Priscilla's hand went to her throat, and her face lost all color. Private Phelps walked his horse slowly by with Harry lying on the travois.

"I'm fine. We ran into a little trouble, and I have some patients to tend. I'll tell you about it all later. Now, go get Fern. She'll want to be at the hospital. Harry's been wounded, but I think he'll be fine." He smiled and reached out to touch her cheek with the back of his hand, wishing he wasn't wearing gloves so he could feel her soft skin. What on earth had happened to her dress? She looked as if she'd spent the day hanging over a washtub. Yet she smelled like peppermint? Perhaps she'd been baking. "We'll catch up on everything later. Are the twins all right?"

"They're fine. Elliot, there's something I need to tell you."

"Not now, Priscilla. Duty first. I'm sorry, but that's the way it is."

She set her lips in a thin line that scored his heart, nodded and turned away to go get Fern, and he led his tired horse toward the hospital. If they were to have any hope of a future together, she was going to have to come to terms with his place in the army. What he wanted to do and what he had to do were often two separate things, and his oath to the army came first. He shook his head, too tired himself to worry. They'd sort it out later.

Samson greeted him at the hospital door. Wrinkles seemed to have multiplied in his dark face, and his eyes were bloodshot. He held a wet cloth that dripped gently onto the steps.

"Are you sick? What's wrong?" Elliot

reached up to help Mrs. Essex from his saddle. "What's going on around here? First Priscilla looks done in, and now you. We ran into some trouble along the way. I've got wounded to treat, and I need your help."

"We've had our share of trouble here, too. They's seven cases of cholera in the ward."

Elliot's shoulders sagged. Cholera. "How bad?"

"The cholera's never good. But Miz Priscilla's been helping me tend 'em, and we haven't lost any yet, though a couple are lookin' mighty wobbly. I'm glad you're back."

Priscilla, tending a cholera ward? There weren't too many illnesses as unpleasant to treat as cholera, and yet she'd stepped in to aid the sick? He shook his head. When Elliot had first seen her, all lace and silk and city notions, he had assumed she would never last out here, and yet, not only had she lasted and adapted, she'd actually flourished. Samson cleared his throat, breaking Elliot out of his reverie.

He turned to Private Phelps. "We're going to need some beds brought over. We'll turn my surgery into a separate ward and keep the cholera patients away from the wounded. Help get everyone inside, and then go fetch some cots and blankets." He

337

scrubbed his hand down his scruffy face. He hadn't shaved since leaving the fort over three weeks ago, and the beard irritated him. A bath, a shave, some decent food, and a clean bed all beckoned him, but the patients came first.

He helped Mrs. Essex up the steps and handed her over to the care of Samson before returning outside. "She'll want to be with her husband for now. Give her some tea with a bit of chamomile and lavender in it to calm her."

Elliot returned outside to supervise the transporting of the wounded into his dispensary. For now they could lie on the floor. Anything to get them out of the sun. Beds would arrive soon, and Elliot could make the men more comfortable. He ducked under the arm of his arrow-wounded patient to help him up the steps. Fern arrived at a run, tears streaming down her cheeks. She flew to Harry's side on the travois, heedless of the dirt she knelt in, with eyes only for her husband.

"Oh, Harry, is it bad? What happened?" She stroked his sweat-drenched face.

Harry reached up and caught her hand. "It's not bad. Elliot fixed me up." His voice sounded thin and strained. "You sure are a sight for these old eyes, Fern." He raised her hand to his cracked, dry lips.

Her eyes sought out Elliot's for confirmation, biting her bottom lip, her brow furrowed.

"He's bled a lot, but with rest he should get better. He'll need a lot of care, but I expect you can help out with that. Private Phelps, help him inside."

Phelps helped Harry sit up, stand, and put Harry's arm across his shoulder. Fern eased up under his other arm, careful of his bandaged side.

"Bring him into the surgery. Put him on the table, and I'll redress that wound. Bunks will arrive soon."

Elliot brought his man into the surgery and settled him into his desk chair, breathing deeply of the herbal medicinal smell. Another smell, unfamiliar in this setting brought him up short. "Is someone baking a cake? It smells like Christmas candy in here."

Samson chuckled as he draped a clean sheet over the surgical table and eased Harry's tunic off before gently laying him back. He folded the dusty blue garment and placed it under Harry's head. "No, sir, that's Miz Priscilla's doing. You know how rank things can smell when the cholera's about. She soaked some pumice stones in vanilla then put them in tin cups on top of the lamp chimneys. It works a treat at fighting off the bad smells. We burned up all your sweetgrass the first day. That Miz Priscilla's a wonder. Been here the whole time looking after the sick. I had to force her to rest for a while last night."

Elliot removed his hat and hung it on a peg by the door. "What about the twins?" He'd expected them to come pelting out of the house or come tumbling out of the stables at the first sound of the bugle.

"They's staying over in the officers' quarters. Miz Priscilla took 'em over there first thing yesterday when we realized we had the cholera here. She wanted them seen to and away from the sickness."

Fern, who held Harry's hand and brushed her fingers down his cheek and over his hair repeatedly, spoke without looking up. "I watched them during the day. They slept on pallets in the Cranes' quarters last night. It was the only place that had room."

Samson, efficient as always, brought a tray of supplies for Elliot and then left to brew up the tea Elliot wanted for Mrs. Essex.

Elliot set about cleaning and re-bandaging Harry's wound, and when Samson returned with the chamomile and lavender tea, Elliot took a cup and handed it to Fern. "Make sure he drinks all of this. It will help him sleep."

Mrs. Essex sat beside her husband, still dazed, but she took a cup of the tea from Samson and sipped at it. Her husband was in a bad way, feverish and flushed. Elliot went to the dispensary shelves for some feverfew and ginger, but as he reached up for a glass jar, his hand stopped in midair. Someone had soaked off all his old labels and put on new, tidy, legible ones.

Priscilla. It had to be. Elliot shook his head, smiling, as he prepared medicine to help reduce a fever.

When everyone had been treated, Elliot quickly refilled his medical bag with fresh supplies. One never knew when someone might be in need, and an empty bag would be useless to him.

"Where do you want these beds, Major?" A soldier stood in the doorway holding a folded cot under his arm.

"Samson, you're in charge here. Get everyone settled. Fern will help you." Elliot washed at the corner basin and dried his hands on the roller towel. "I'm going to check the patients across the hall." He didn't say the word *cholera* because he didn't want to alarm the wounded.

Priscilla bent over one of the beds, sponging the face and neck of a sick soldier. She straightened and brushed the hair off her forehead with the back of her wrist. With a sigh, she dropped the cloth into a basin on the table and pressed her hands to her lower back. She picked up a cup with a cloth hanging from it and squeezed a few drops of liquid into the patient's mouth. "Sleep now, Private. I'll be here to watch over you."

Elliot paused in the doorway, taking in the sight. Priscilla wore a smudged apron and wrinkled dress that appeared several inches too short, her hair was twisted into a hasty knot at her nape and several pins had loosened, and tiredness ringed her eyes.

She'd never looked more beautiful to him.

When she left, she would be taking his heart with her.

Even unwashed, unshaven, and exhausted, the sight of Elliot safe and unharmed sent warm sparks shooting through Priscilla's chest. The tension of the last three weeks drained away as he walked into the ward.

"What is that you're giving them?" He took the cup from her hand and looked into it, raising it to his nose and inhaling. "Peppermint?"

She shrugged and nodded. "Crushed peppermint candy dissolved in water. We're just dropping into their mouths or letting them suck it off cloths. Every time they drank even a few swallows of water, they'd bring it right back up again. This method seems to be slow enough to be absorbed better. And the mint is to help settle their stomachs. We've been using barley and rice water and birch tea as well."

"That's brilliant. You're a natural nurse. I don't know that I would've thought of that."

She swayed as a wave of fatigue swept over her.

He took the cup from her hand, set it on the side table, and grabbed her arms. "You're ready to drop."

"No," she shook her head. "I had a rest. It's just . . ."

"Just?" His gray eyes searched hers.

"Relief, I guess." His hands were warm on her arms, steady and firm and so comforting. "I'm glad you're back safe."

"So you were worried about me?"

"Of course."

A satisfied smile touched his lips. "That's good to know. Let's take these patients one by one. You can apprise me of their conditions, and then you're going straight to bed."

Bunk by bunk, she walked him through each patient's current condition, the treatment he'd had, and the results of the treatment. Two cases had her very worried.

"They've had such bad cramping. It started as stomach cramps, but then it turned to muscle cramps as well. Samson has been giving them laudanum and that seems to help but not for long. They've continued to decline, and I'm having a hard time getting more than a few drops of water into them at a time. Private Watson here is barely conscious most of the time."

Elliot took her hand, and she drew strength from his light clasp. "Priscilla, you've done all you can do and more. The fact that only two are critical is amazing. The things you've tried, the way you've coped. How did you know to use these remedies?"

"The herbal journal. And Samson. And common sense." She laughed a little. "And sheer desperation. Gilda has been a rock. She's washed sheets and carried water and scrubbed basins. It's been a team effort. Not to mention Fern taking the twins." Taking the cloth off the edge of the basin once more, she dipped it and bathed Private Watson's pinched face. "The kids are going to be so glad to see you. They've missed you so much."

"I can't wait to see them, too."

"You'll have to go over to officer country.

They're under strict orders to stay away. The colonel himself laid down the law. With the cholera, they're forbidden to come anywhere near the hospital. And with the increase in Indians camping around the fort, he's decided it would be best if the women and children limited their time out of doors." She pinched the bridge of her nose.

"Now that you've given me a status update for these men, you're going to go to bed. You're ready to drop."

"I can stay. Everyone's tired. What about Gilda and Samson?"

"I'm sending them to bed, too. I've got a young trooper with me, Private Phelps, who has shown some ability in tending patients, and I'll have Fern to watch over Harry."

"How is Harry?" She'd been so focused on her cholera patients, she had almost forgotten about Harry.

"He's going to be fine, I think. He lost a lot of blood, and he's going to hurt for a while, but he'll pull through. He's got a lot to live for. That sure helps."

"Fern's second-worst nightmare, him coming home wounded."

"Second worst?"

"The worst would be if he never came home at all. All the women who had men on this patrol watched and waited and worried the entire time." She wrung out the cloth and laid it on the edge of the washbasin. Her hands were red and raw from spending so much time in the water.

Elliot scrubbed the back of his neck with his palm. "We're both too tired to go into all that. For now, I need you to take Mrs. Essex, the homesteader's wife we brought back with us, over to the house. She's in the family way, and she's had quite an upset. We came up on their place as they were being attacked by a band of Kiowa. Her husband has a lance wound, and she's in shock, hasn't said a word to anyone in more than a day. I don't think she's been badly hurt, but I didn't want to traumatize her by subjecting her to a thorough examination. She's not bleeding anywhere, so I think she's more frightened than anything. You can put her to sleep in Tessa's bed. Then I want you to sleep."

Just having him there, taking charge, caring for her, cracked some of the tight control she'd kept on her emotions the last three weeks. Hot tears pricked her eyes. Before she disgraced herself entirely and threw herself into his arms for a good sob, she nodded, gave his hand a squeeze, and went to find Mrs. Essex.

The woman sat on a canvas stool, staring at the floor. Her bedraggled calico dress hung on her, and her hands lay limp in her lap. Priscilla squatted so their eyes were on the same level.

"Mrs. Essex, I'm Priscilla Hutchens. If you'll come with me, I have a place for you to wash and rest."

The woman's dark brown eyes focused and her chin came up. She darted a look at the cot where a large man lay, bandaged and slack. A pinkish-red stained the white wrappings, and a flush rode his cheeks above his beard.

"Is this your husband?"

She nodded.

"He's under the best of care, and I'm sure he'd want you to take care of yourself and your little one." Priscilla grasped the woman's elbow and helped her stand. "The house isn't far, and Major Ryder will send someone if anything here changes."

Priscilla carried a bucket of clean water from the hospital to the doctor's quarters. When Samson had first diagnosed cholera, Colonel Bracken had detailed two men to keep the hospital supplied with water hauled from the river. Priscilla had never really appreciated a supply of fresh water at hand, but as she staggered up the house steps with the heavy bucket, she sent up a prayer of thankfulness.

Once inside, Priscilla helped the woman wash and change into a clean nightgown. With giving her best two gowns to Maybelle and now loaning one to Mrs. Essex, she would be down to her last bit of nightwear. Priscilla shrugged. She was thankful to have enough to share.

Tucking the weary, compliant woman into bed was much like putting Tessa to sleep at night. Except for the silence part. Tessa talked from sunup to sundown and even in her sleep sometimes. Priscilla shook her head, a smile tugging at her lips. She missed that little sprite. And Timothy, too. How often as she tended patients and waited for Elliot to return had she missed them at her elbows, missed their chatter, turned to ask them a question or to tell them something, only to remember at the last minute that they were across the compound and mustn't come home until the all clear had been given?

Priscilla stroked Mrs. Essex's hair, much as if she were Tessa. "It's going to be all right. You sleep now, and you'll feel a lot better when you wake up. Before I go, though, can you tell me your name?" Elliot had mentioned that she hadn't said a word since they'd found her, but perhaps in the calm of this adobe house with only another woman present she might feel safe enough.

As if the kind words had cut the drawstring on a bag stuffed with emotions, tears filled the woman's eyes, and a sob clawed its way up her throat. Her shoulders shook. Priscilla sat on the side of the bed and hugged her close. The gut-wrenching sobs continued, and the woman clutched at Priscilla, gasping and jerking.

"Shhhhh, you're safe now. It's all right." Priscilla repeated those words over and over.

The poor woman's tears soaked Priscilla's apron, but after a time, her grip began to ease and the sobs to subside. Priscilla laid her back on the pillow, ducked into the kitchen for a clean towel and a pitcher of water, and returned to bathe her face.

"Matilda." The whisper leaked out of the woman's lips.

"Your name is Matilda?"

She nodded, biting her lip.

"That's a beautiful name. You go to sleep, Matilda. You're safe here."

Before Priscilla made it to the doorway, the woman was asleep.

Unbuttoning her own battered dress, she let it fall to the floor of her room. Ton weights pulled at her eyelids, and she performed only a sketchy wash before slipping into her nightgown and falling into bed.

She had just enough strength left to whisper a prayer before sleep claimed her.

"Thank You, Jesus, for bringing him home."

CHAPTER FIFTEEN

Priscilla awoke at dawn refreshed and ready to take over nursing duties once more. Knowing Elliot was safe within the protection of the fort had given her the best night's sleep she'd gotten in almost a month.

She picked up her dress from the day before, holding it up ruefully and examining the chopped hem, the stains, and the bedraggled collar and sleeves. Fit only for the ragbag. Donning her dark blue skirt and pin-tucked white blouse, she made sure she had a clean apron to protect both.

Matilda Essex slept on, and Priscilla left her that way to return to the hospital.

And Elliot.

The strains of the bugle blowing Reveille drifted through the morning air as the post began to stir to life. Soon she'd hear Stable Call, and the soldiers would head out to feed and curry their horses. Mess Call and

Sick Call would follow, and they'd see if there were any new patients. Hopefully, the cholera had reached as far as it was going to this time, and the rest of the fort would be spared.

Fatigue Call, Water Call, Adjutant Call, Drill Call. Strange how her days had fallen into the pattern of the bugle calls. At first the rigidness of the schedule had irked her, but now she found a certain security in the rhythm of her days.

Halfway to the hospital, she changed her mind about her destination and headed toward the parade ground. She couldn't wait any longer to check on the twins. The hole their absence left in her days was too great. As soon as the cholera scare was over, she would have them back in their own home quicker than she could say Carterson Ladies' Emporium Catalog.

Entering the south officers' quarters, she could smell bacon frying. The curtain sectioning off Fern and Harry's hallway quarters was open and empty of people. Fern had no doubt spent the night at the hospital with Harry. Anxiety pressed on Priscilla's heart. Fern must be tired and hungry. Priscilla would relieve her as soon as she'd had a talk with the twins. Then Fern could at least get some fresh air and food and a change of clothes.

Priscilla tapped on Major and Mrs. Crane's door. Mrs. Crane yanked it open wearing her wrapper and her hair tied up in a kerchief. "I told you two to stay put —" She broke off when she saw Priscilla.

"Good morning, Mrs. Crane. I'm sorry to disturb you so early, but I was hoping to see the twins."

"So was I." Her lips puckered and pinched. "The minute they heard this morning that the major and the patrol had returned, they up and offed like the devil himself was chasing them. You just missed them. I imagine they've gone to the hospital, though they've got strict orders to stay away. Those two are the most ill-behaved, precocious, outspoken pair —"

The thought of the twins near the hospital had Priscilla turning away from Mrs. Crane's sputtering. "Thank you for taking care of them. Hopefully we'll get the all clear soon, and you won't have the burden any longer." She spoke over her shoulder as she headed outside.

Mrs. Crane was definitely not a morning person, and not the one Priscilla would've chosen to take in the twins. The sooner she had them out of there the better. And the sooner she headed them off so they didn't go inside the infirmary the better, too.

Skirting the parade ground, she hurried toward the hospital. Several times she was greeted by familiar faces. Matthews came out of the barracks, his crutches replaced with a cane.

"Morning, ma'am. If you're looking for the twins, I just saw them race past along the back of the barracks. Heading to the hospital, they were."

"Good morning, and yes, I'm looking for them. Thank you." She smiled and waved. Rounding the end of the building, she stopped.

Elliot knelt in the dirt ten yards away, his arms around the twins. They hugged his neck, and even from this distance she could tell Tessa was talking.

Tears pricked Priscilla's eyes at their warm reunion. Everything had been wrong in the twins' lives when he went away, and with all the chaos and her needing to be at the hospital, the poor little mites hadn't had anyone to temper the wind for them. She drew close, and Elliot looked up.

He'd shaved his beard and put on clean clothes. His face was thinner, and he looked tired but happy, too. "Good morning, Priscilla."

She couldn't speak for the happiness in

her heart, so she nodded. Tessa broke away from Elliot and launched herself at Priscilla. "He came back."

"He did."

"Does this mean we can come home? I don't like staying with Mrs. Crane."

"Soon, cherub." She bent and cupped Tessa's cheek. "There's still sickness in the hospital, and it would be safer for you to be away from it. Probably for only a few more days."

Tessa huffed but didn't argue. When she found out she couldn't spend the day with Fern, she'd be even more miffed, but there was no help for it.

Elliot lifted her up on his arm and pressed his forehead to hers. "It's so good to see you all. I missed you something fierce."

"Did you really?" She fingered the epaulette on his shoulder.

"Just as soon as Lieutenant Dunn gets better, you ask him. He'll tell you I talked about you the whole time." He bounced her a couple of times. "Every man out there talked about how he couldn't wait to get back to his family." Though he was talking to Tessa, his eyes were on Priscilla. She grew warm and tingly. There was so much she needed to say to him, so much she'd come to realize, but now, with the hospital full of sick and wounded, with the fort surrounded by Indians waiting for their trade goods and growing restless, it didn't seem the right time.

"I know you want to move back to our quarters, kids, but for your own good, you need to stay where you are a little while longer. I think I've discovered the source of the cholera, and it didn't come from inside the fort, but just to be sure, you need to steer clear of the hospital for the next day or so. But, to make it up to you, Corporal Rhodes is going to take you for a ride this afternoon."

The twins beamed, and Tessa hugged his neck.

"You have to obey him. No fooling around. There are several Kickapoo and Kiowa tribes camped along the Rio Grande. They shouldn't cause you any trouble, because they know if they kicked up any dust right now, they can whistle for their money and supplies. Still, you listen to what the corporal says, got it?" Elliot's voice had taken on the military-orders tone that had so irritated Priscilla when she'd first arrived. Now it sounded like perfect common sense.

"Go get your breakfast, and report to the stables at Fatigue Call." Putting Tessa on the ground, he gave her a friendly swat on the backside. "Timothy, you watch out for your sister on your ride, and when you get back, come to the hospital yard and I'll come outside to get your report."

Timothy snapped off a salute. "Yes, sir." Mouth split in a wide grin, he and Tessa scampered off.

Which left Priscilla and Elliot standing in the morning sunshine. He regarded her with his light, gray eyes.

"You've done well. They look like they've weathered the last few weeks fine."

"They're wonderful kids. They missed you terribly, but they're so . . . I don't know . . . stalwart? They were proud that you were out on patrol, even when they were complaining about your absence. They were restless and content all at the same time." An attitude that Priscilla found fascinating, and also found herself adopting, especially after the knitting party at Mrs. Bracken's house.

"They're children of the regiment." Pride tinged his voice.

She couldn't hold his gaze. All the feelings she had for him, all the things that had changed inside her, were too new, too sudden. She swallowed and studied the columns of smoke rising from the wickiups on the other side of the creek.

"How is Mrs. Essex?"

Grateful for a new topic, she smiled. "Sleeping."

He nodded. "Did she say anything to you?"

"She told me her name and cried until my heart broke. Whatever happened before you rode onto the scene must've scared her terribly."

Elliot stroked his mustache. "She must've been sure she'd be killed or kidnapped. And she would've been if we hadn't come along."

"Then it's good you did. How are the rest of the patients?"

Sadness invaded his expression. "We lost Private Watson last night."

She closed her eyes against the pain. So young. And he'd tried to be so brave in spite of the agony he'd been suffering. *Why, Lord? Why would You take someone with so much promise, and in such a terrible way?*

This loss hit her harder than the loss of the young man who had been kicked by the horse. She hadn't known that young man, though is passing left her saddened. But she had known Private Watson for days, had worried over him, tended him, prayed for him, and soothed him to the best of her abilities. A hard lump formed in her throat.

"It's hard, isn't it?" Elliot asked. "When

you invest so much of yourself into their welfare only to have them slip away? You did the best you could. Nobody could've done more." He reached for her hand. As his fingers touched hers she began to understand a little of how difficult his job was and how good he was at it. "Priscilla, there's so much we need to say to each other, so many things to get straightened out, but right now we're both needed. When things settle down, we're going to have a long talk." He squeezed her hand. "We'll sort everything out. I promise."

Hope burst in her chest at the warmth in his voice. She nodded and followed him into the hospital.

Priscilla emptied another basin out the back door. All day she'd tended sick men. Midmorning she'd gone to check on Matilda Essex, and finding her awake, had brought her over to the hospital to sit with her husband. He lay on a cot in the surgery, flushed with fever.

"Bathe his face with cool cloths to help bring down his temperature. Talk to him and let him know you're here." Priscilla set a pan of cool water on the floor beside his bed.

Fern was rolling new bandages she'd cut

from a sheet, keeping busy. Harry lay quietly on his bed.

"How is he?"

"He's doing well." She snipped off some stray threads. "Whatever herbs Elliot is giving him for the pain are working. His sleep is much more peaceful. And it's quieter in here now that the other two wounded are well enough to return to the barracks. The one with the broken collarbone is a talker. My head was ringing. But I think he was talking to take his mind off the pain in his shoulder, poor man. How is it going across the hall?"

"No new cases, thank the Lord. Only one death so far, and Elliot thinks the rest will recover, though it will be a long convalescence. They're all down to skin and bones, and so quickly, too." She propped the empty basin on her hip. "But they're on the mend. The cramping has lessened. Elliot's mixed up a tonic to replace the salts and things that they lost."

"You and Elliot are working well together. Have you sorted out what you're going to do about the children's future?"

Priscilla tugged on her lower lip. "Not yet. Things have been at sixes and sevens since he got back. He says we'll have a talk when things calm down."

"You don't have long before you're supposed to return home. Only a couple of weeks?"

"I know." The time factor weighed heavily on her shoulders. She was in love with Elliot, but what if he couldn't or wouldn't return her love? He'd told Priscilla in no uncertain terms that he had no intention of marrying. Did he still stand by that?

Of course, she'd told him in no uncertain terms that she would never marry a military man.

And then there was the woman he'd mentioned only once. Muriel. Who was she and what did she mean to Elliot?

If only they could get all these patients well and have that talk, she would know where she stood.

Walking into the hallway, she was so preoccupied with her thoughts, she didn't realize anyone was standing in the doorway until she collided with him. Giving a yelp, she sprang back, the metal basin clanking to the floor.

Niganithat reached out for her, grasping her arms to steady her. Behind him, Kennekuk entered the hospital.

Priscilla jerked away from the man who had offered to buy her for a horse and five dogs, hitting the wall and putting her hand to her throat.

"What's going on out there?" Elliot called from the cholera ward. "Did you drop something?"

"Um, Elliot, we have visitors." She strove to keep her composure, but Niganithat's piercing eyes pinned her in place and chased chills up her arms.

"Kennekuk, Niganithat, welcome." Elliot held out his hand.

"We have brought you gifts." The medicine man held a buckskin packet in one arm and pointed to the large bundle on the floor beside the other Kickapoo man. "We have been told sickness has come and your men are not good. I have brought you things to help."

"You are a good friend." Elliot accepted the gift, peeling back the hide covering to reveal bundles of dried herbs. "I have used many of my supplies treating the sick, and I was in need of more."

Priscilla reached down for the pan she'd dropped, not taking her eyes from Niganithat, who continued to stare at her.

He said something in Kickapoo that made Elliot look up from his plants. His eyebrows rose, and he shook his head.

"No, Niganithat, she is still not for sale."

He scowled and spoke again. At his words,

Elliot's mouth fell open. Kennekuk shook his head and spoke harshly, his finger jabbing the air. Niganithat clenched his fists, his words flying.

Priscilla held the metal basin before her like a shield. All three men engaged in heated words, and she wished she could understand them. Niganithat towered over Elliot and Kennekuk, his open shirt showing a well-muscled chest. He stood, rigid, his body quivering, but finally, he threw up his hands, glared toward Priscilla, and stomped out.

Kennekuk, shook Elliot's hand once more, and followed.

She sagged against the adobe wall, staring out the open doorway. "What just happened?"

Elliot drew a deep breath. "He offered for you again."

"That part I gathered. What made Kennekuk so angry?"

"When I turned Niganithat down again, he changed his offer. He asked for Tessa instead."

"Tessa?" Her voice squeaked.

"He likes her yellow hair. His first wife is childless and wants him to bring her a child. That's why he's eager to take another wife, and why he'd like to have Tessa. Kennekuk took exception to this idea, as did I." He frowned. "I told him no, he couldn't have you or her, not at any price. Kennekuk told him he had offended by asking."

Unease swirled in her middle. "He wouldn't do anything . . . rash, would he?"

"Kennekuk will settle him down. I don't know why he's being so unreasonable about this. He really must've taken a shine to you two." Elliot bent and picked up the bundles of herbs.

Priscilla set her metal pan on the table in the hallway. "I'll feel better when these annuity goods are delivered. The Indians will leave then, won't they?"

He nodded. "At the officers' meeting this morning, Colonel Bracken said he'd received word that the goods were on their way and would be here in a day or two. Things will calm down, and you and I can have that talk we've been putting off."

Impatience jabbed at her. "Let's have it now, Elliot. There's so much I need to tell you. So much has changed for me."

"Priscilla, not just now. I've thought all of this out, and I want to talk without distractions. I've got a ward full of recovering cholera patients, several wounded men, and here we are in a hallway up to our eyeballs in duties." He gestured with Kennekuk's gifts. "Tonight, when everything's quieted down. Right now, I have to fill out some reports, sort these herbs and get them put away, and I want you to give each of the men another dose of rice water. I sent Samson to his quarters to rest, and I don't want to leave the sick men unattended."

"Tonight then."

He paused and brushed the backs of his fingers down her cheek. "Thank you for understanding. I don't know how I would get through this without you."

Warmed and encouraged by his words, she returned to the ward. Stoking the fire in the little stove, she set the pot of rice on top and covered it with water. While that cooked, she could remake the beds with the clean sheets Gilda had brought in earlier.

Tonight. Things would be settled tonight. One way or another. The idea scared and thrilled her. She busied herself with her patients to keep her mind off what was coming.

She'd just dished up a portion of the rice water when little feet pounded up the steps and into the hall. Dropping the ladle into the pot, she headed out to shoo the children away. What were they doing here anyway? They were supposed to be in the care of Corporal Rhodes. She started scolding even before she got out of the ward.

"Tessa and Timothy, I know you're excited to see your Uncle Elliot, but what did we tell you about coming to the hospital?" She stepped into the hallway expecting to see their happy faces and hear Tessa's chatter.

But only Timothy raced to her, wrapping his arms around her waist, panting, eyes enormous.

"She's gone. Tessa's gone."

CHAPTER SIXTEEN

"Gone?" Priscilla knelt and grabbed Timothy by the upper arms. "What do you mean gone? Where?"

He shook his head. "I don't know. I can't find her."

"Didn't you go riding with Corporal Rhodes?"

"He couldn't take us after all. Major Crane ordered him to have the entire stable cleaned out and the hay in the stack yard restacked by afternoon Stable Call."

Which probably made Tessa mad, not being able to go on her ride. She was probably getting her revenge by hiding somewhere in the fort.

Elliot emerged from the infirmary. "What's going on? Timothy?" His eyebrows arrowed together. "What are you doing in here?" He checked his watch. "You're back from your ride sooner than I anticipated, but I told you to wait for me in the yard, not to come into the hospital."

"I know, sir, but it's Tessa. She's gone. I can't find her anywhere."

The desperate edge to his voice sent unease scampering through Priscilla again, but she forced it down. She got to her feet, wiping her hands on her apron. "I imagine she's hiding from you. You know how she likes to play hide and seek."

"No." He shook his head. "It's been too long. When we couldn't go on the ride, we decided to play behind Colonel Bracken's house, seeing who could walk the farthest on the fence rail. Tessa wanted to get her kepi. Mrs. Crane wouldn't let her wear it this morning. She said it was a boy's hat, and she took it away from Tess. I waited a long time for Tessa to come back from Mrs. Crane's, but she never did." He drew a deep breath, his chest expanding and his shoulders rising. "When I went to find her, Mrs. Crane said she'd come in, but she'd left a long time ago."

Elliot rolled his eyes. "She's probably at the stables or the bakery. Or one of the laundress's kids talked her into coming over to play."

Samson ambled up the steps and through the open doorway. "Hello, Mr. Timothy." His smile brightened his face. He looked more rested than he'd looked in days.

"Samson," Elliot reached for his hat on the peg just inside the surgery. "Take over the sick ward. Tessa's wandered off somewhere, and Priscilla and I are going to go find her. Fern is in the surgery with Harry and Mr. and Mrs. Essex if you need any help."

Priscilla pulled her apron strings and dragged the covering off, tossing it on a hook by the door. "I'll check with the laundresses. You'd best check the shops. She's probably there. Timothy, you come with me." Irritation warred with agitation. She didn't have time to be traipsing off after Tessa. A smidgen of guilt poked her. She'd spent so much time at the hospital, turning over the care of the kids to others. If she'd been watching Tess, this wouldn't have happened.

Neither Maybelle nor Gilda had seen Tessa. Gilda put her hands on her ample hips. "Not like her to disappear, is it?"

"No, it isn't." Priscilla shaded her eyes, surveying the landscape behind Suds Row. Clusters of adobe dwellings, temporary Indian camps, orchards, all the way to the river. "She's never done it before."

"I'll help you look for her. Maybelle!" Gilda shouted through Maybelle's open door. "Watch my fire. I'm helping Miz Priscilla look for Tess."

By the time she and Timothy had made it all the way around the fort to the stables, Priscilla's uneasiness had grown to alarm. Corporal Rhodes had nothing to allay her fears.

"Wingfoot is gone." He kicked the stall divider. "I never saw her take him. I was busy in the stack yard."

Timothy went into Sooty's stall and backed him out.

"Where are you going, young man?" Priscilla took hold of the halter.

"I'm going to find her." His jaw was set, his legs sturdy, his hands fisted.

"Not on your tintype, buddy. Put that horse away. I'm not having you traipsing across the countryside and getting lost."

"She's my sister. I have to find her. I know the places she'd go." He stood his ground.

Elliot stomped toward them, exasperation in every stride. "She's not in the shops or the commissary. Nobody I talked to remembered seeing her. She must be hiding somewhere here in the stables."

Corporal Rhodes stepped up. "I'm afraid not, sir. Her pony's missing."

Elliot smacked his folded gloves into his palm. "How long ago?"

"I don't know, sir. Wingfoot was here at morning Stable Call. Tessa helped me feed and water him. I haven't seen either of them since then." He stood at attention, his eyes miserable.

"Elliot, you don't think . . ." Priscilla stepped forward and put her hand on his arm, loathe to give voice to her fears but compelled by necessity.

"What?" His gray eyes bored into hers, the tension in his face transmitting to her.

"Niganithat was awfully angry when he left. You don't think he would just take her, would he?"

Grimness tightened the skin around his mouth. "Corporal, saddle my horse and one for Miss Hutchens." He knelt before his nephew. "Timothy, find Sergeant Plover and send him here to the stables. Then you get to Mrs. Bracken's house and stay there until I or Aunt Priscilla fetch you. And don't worry. We'll find her." He straightened. "I'll notify Colonel Bracken of the situation. Priscilla, go get my medical bag and some provisions. Samson will know what to pack. Go now. It's already past noon."

Priscilla ran along the back of the barracks buildings to the hospital. She arrived gasping. "Samson, I need Elliot's medical bag and some supplies. Tessa's taken her pony

371

and ridden away from the fort somewhere. We're going to search for her."

His eyes widened, and his mouth went slack. With a trembling hand he rubbed the top of his frizzled hair. "That po' child. What can she be thinkin'? I'll get what you need. You might want to go get a change of clothes for Miss Tessa, and a blanket, in case you need it."

Fern caught her at the door. "Oh, Priscilla, I overheard you. Tessa's lost? I'll be praying. You'll find her."

A bugle call ripped through the air. Company B's Assembly Call. Sergeant Plover's company.

Rushing, Priscilla tried to think of everything she might need to take, but trying not to include so much that it would slow her down. Rolling a clean set of clothes into a blanket, tying up some biscuits and jerky into a cloth bundle, and grabbing an extra canteen from a peg by the door, she kept up a running prayer.

"Lord, please watch over her. I don't know why she'd break the rules like this. She knows better than to run off. If she's been taken, by Niganithat or someone else, please keep her safe. Help her to know we're coming."

The prayer didn't stop while she ran back

to the hospital for Elliot's medical kit and on to the stable with her burdens. Elliot was sliding his rifle into his scabbard. Around him, at least twenty soldiers from Company B saddled their mounts.

She panted to a stop. "Here's what Samson sent."

He took his medical bag and tied it behind his saddle. "Pray to God I don't need it. Did you bring some food?"

"Yes. And some things for Tessa for when we find her." Her hands shook.

"Rhodes saddled Applejack for you." He took her elbow. "It's highly unusual for you to be allowed to ride with us, but the colonel agrees that when we find Tessa, having a woman along will be best. You will stay with me at all times."

She nodded.

He turned to the men. "We've no way of knowing which direction she went. The ground is too churned up around the fort to pick up her trail. Farther out you might find signs of her passing. She's riding a little pinto with a short stride. She's a good rider, and she's fearless. Major Crane, take four men with you and head west along the river. Sergeant Plover, you and your men take the east. Corporal Rhodes, and you four" — he pointed — "you'll ride into the camps. Miss

Hutchens and I will head north with Privates Wagner and Thompkins. We'll go to Chief Pekhotah's camp first, and if we don't find her there, we'll fan out. All of you, search the camps first, but don't stir up trouble. We're not accusing anyone, we're just looking for a lost girl. If you cut her sign or if you find her, send one man back to the fort with the news. They'll recall the other searchers."

Each squad headed out, faces grim, determination in every line. How grateful Priscilla was for them, and for their military discipline. Surely, with so many capable men searching for her, Tess would be found soon.

Elliot checked his saber and his side arm then boosted Priscilla into the saddle. Applejack snorted and sidled, eager to go. Elliot swung himself aboard Bill's back and lifted the reins. "Let's go."

Elliot set a brisk pace. He'd chosen Pekhotah's camp for himself. He wanted to see for himself that Niganithat hadn't taken Tessa, and if not, he wanted to enlist Kennekuk's help in the search.

Pekhotah had moved his band close to the northeast boundary of the fort, near the irrigation ditch soldiers had dug the first year

Fort Bliss had been at this location. The ditch fed water from the Rio Grande to the fort to be used for watering the horses and gardens. Everything but drinking water. For drinking water, men hauled barrels every day from the river and strained the water through cloth to help purify it.

As Elliot and Priscilla and the two troopers approached Pekhotah's camp, Elliot slowed Bill to a walk. Their approach did not go unnoticed, and several warriors rode out to meet them.

"Stay close to me," Elliot ordered, looking at Priscilla.

She drew Applejack alongside Bill, keeping his nose at Bill's flank. The kids had been right about Priscilla. She could certainly ride. Even in that sidesaddle, she had total control of her mount, well-balanced and confident.

He spoke in his limited Kickapoo. "We are missing a little girl." He leaned over his saddle and showed how tall Tessa was. "She's riding a spotted pony. Have you seen her?"

They looked at one another, wary, but shook their heads.

"I must speak to Kennekuk."

"No go into camp." Their leader spoke English.

"I must."

"He come to you. You not go to him."
They shook up their reins and turned back
to the camp.

"Fine." But why didn't they want him in
camp? He'd been welcome there before.
Were they harboring Niganithat and Tess?

Elliot dug out his field glasses to survey
the group of bark and pole wickiups. Studying every corner of the camp he could see,
and spending a long time on the herd of
horses grazing at the far end, he came to
the conclusion that Wingfoot wasn't among
the animals.

"Do you see anything?" Priscilla's voice
was tight.

"No sign of Tessa."

"There's Kennekuk."

The medicine man rode out toward them
on a tall gray horse. He stopped thirty yards
away.

"Wait here," Elliot told Priscilla.

"I'm coming with you. I want to hear what
he has to say." She legged Applejack into a
walk beside Bill.

They approached Kennekuk slowly, leaving the two troopers behind.

"Hello, friend." Elliot held up his hand.

"I did not know you were coming. You are
still angry from this morning?" Kennekuk's

face gave nothing away.

"I am not angry, friend. I came to you because I knew you would want to know and would want to help me. Tessa has gone from the fort. We can't find her."

He nodded. "You are right. I want to know. We have not seen her here. If we had, I would have brought her back to you. She is on a horse?"

"That's right. On her pony. We searched the fort for her, but she's gone. At least two hours now, maybe more."

"I will come with you." He wheeled his horse and then paused. "Niganithat is not in camp. He did not return with me when we left the fort. He rode away alone. He was very angry that you would not give him the woman or the girl."

Elliot fought the fear growing in his mind. Niganithat wasn't in camp.

They rejoined the two soldiers waiting for them and headed out into the desert. A hot, summer wind flowed over the yucca and cactus. Lather frothed from the horses' hides, and the sunshine forced Elliot to squint against the intense glare. His heart alternated with clogging his throat and filling his boots.

Where are you, Tessa? Why'd you leave the safety of the fort? You know better. Do you have any water? It's broiling out here. Lord, please watch over her, keep her safe, help us find her, perhaps one of the other groups has already found her. Please, Lord, let her be safe. What was I thinking trying to raise children here on the frontier? They'd be so much better off back east where it's civilized. Priscilla was right. If I'd listened to her when she first arrived, she would've taken them with her to Cincinnati and Tessa wouldn't be lost in this never-ending cactus patch.

On his right, Priscilla on Applejack, must be thinking the same thing. If he hadn't been so stubborn, so sure that his way was right, Tessa would be safe right now.

A thousand different dangers lurked on the frontier, and any one of them could result in injury or death. It was difficult on grown men trained to deal with the peril. What chance did a precocious seven-year-old child have? His little girl was so small, so defenseless.

His little girl.

Tessa was that. From the moment Rebekah had entrusted him with their care, Tessa and Timothy had become his. They'd crawled right into his heart. And because he loved them, when he found Tessa, he would do what was best for the twins. No matter that it would be the most difficult, painful thing he'd ever done. He would let them go.

Priscilla shaded her eyes. They'd ridden for two hours with no sign of Tessa. Could she have gotten this far? Applejack leaned forward heading up a slight grade. Flecks of lather flew back from his neck where the reins rubbed, landing on her skirt and soaking in. Her throat was parched, but she refused to drink from her canteen until she couldn't stand it anymore. The next water might be miles from here, and she didn't want to run short, especially since Tessa would no doubt be thirsty when they found her.

She glanced ahead to where Elliot rode. The poor man. The anguish in his eyes broke her heart. No matter what else, he loved and cared for the twins as if they were his own children. He would never forgive himself if something happened to Tessa.

What had possessed her to run off?

A whistle pierced the air. Elliot swung his arm, motioning her to come. Had he found something? She booted Applejack in the ribs and galloped closer, her heart in her throat.

"Did you find something?"

He shook his head. "No, but she couldn't have gotten this far, not on Wingfoot. We'll swing a little farther east and head back in the direction of the fort. Wagner, you and Thompkins turn to the west a bit. We'll separate here to cover more ground, but you two stay within sight of each other. And keep a lookout. There's still a renegade band of Kiowa in the area. If you don't find her in the next couple of hours, return to the fort for reinforcements."

"Why didn't the colonel send more men than just part of Company B?" Wagner took a slug from his canteen and wiped his mouth with the back of his hand.

"The trade goods for the annuities were arriving today. Captain Dillon and the rest of the quartermaster's department advised having an armed guard to show a little force when they started handing out the supplies. There are always a few squabbles and skirmishes, and part of the trade goods is bullets and guns. Colonel Bracken didn't want to leave the fort exposed to a superior armed force just to chase down one little girl." Elliot raised his field glasses to his eyes and swept the desert to the north one more time. "I understand his point."

Priscilla understood it, too, but she didn't like it. Her heart cried out for the colonel to empty the fort and the camps and make people search until Tessa was found.

Elliot stowed his field glasses and removed his hat, running his fingers through his sweat-soaked hair. Priscilla wanted to reach out and touch his hand, assure him that they would find Tessa, that she would be all right, but she hesitated. If she gave in to the impulse to comfort him, she might just throw herself in his arms and cry out her fears and frustration.

Kennekuk sat his horse, silent, staring at the northeastern horizon.

"What do you think?" Elliot asked him.

"These Kiowa. You have seen them?"

"They attacked a homestead about thirty miles that way." He waved to the northwest. "Our patrol came on them before they could finish off the homesteaders, but they got away."

Priscilla closed her eyes, swaying in the saddle as dizziness swirled in her head. What if these same renegades had come upon Tessa? Elliot grabbed her shoulder.

"Are you all right?"

She pulled her eyes open, blinking. "I'm fine." Though she wasn't. She wouldn't be fine until she was holding Tessa in her arms.

He squeezed her shoulder, and she drew strength from his grip. "Drink some of your water, then let's ride. We're burning daylight."

Kennekuk saw the horse and rider first. The medicine man pointed, drawing her attention to the dark blot on the horizon. Elliot must've seen it at the same moment, for he put Bill into a run. Priscilla followed on Applejack, leaving Kennekuk behind as her big horse's stride ate up the ground.

Straining her eyes against the wind created by their speed, Priscilla leaned over Applejack's neck. The blot in the distance grew larger, but heat waves rippled and flickered, changing the aspect, so she couldn't tell how far away it was or if it was getting nearer or farther away. Bill, carrying Elliot, galloped ahead, and she followed, praying, praying, praying.

At last, she could tell. It was a single horse and rider, and they were coming this way.

Her heart tripped. That horse. She'd seen it before. A tall, rangy pinto. Not Wingfoot, nor was the rider Tessa. That was the horse that Niganithat had ridden in the horserace the day they'd visited Pekhotah's camp. Niganithat was astride, and he held something ahead of him. Sunshine glinted off something bright gold in his arms

That had to be Tessa.

Niganithat must've spied them, for he wheeled his mount and the horse leapt into a run. Elliot shouted and took off after him.

Determined not to be left behind, Priscilla urged her horse on, the thundering of Applejack's hooves warring with the thundering of her heart in her ears.

Elliot leaned over Bill's neck, and she realized how much he'd been holding his horse back during the first race between Bill and that pinto. The huge chestnut's strides lengthened, and he closed the distance faster than she would've imagined possible.

A pop reached her ears. Elliot had drawn his gun and was firing into the air. Her heart tripped. Surely he wouldn't try to shoot Niganithat. That would endanger Tessa. They thundered down a slope. Niganithat's horse leapt creosote bushes and yucca plants, swerving and agile. Prairie chickens and jackrabbits bounded out of their path as Elliot gave chase.

High on the wind, a little girl's scream floated.

Applejack faltered, nearing exhaustion after being pushed all day. Priscilla hated to urge him on, but she had to get to Tess. Where was Kennekuk?

Elliot was almost on top of them when Niganithat whirled his horse, racing back toward Priscilla. She pulled up, not knowing which way to turn, but wanting to keep him at bay long enough for Elliot to get there. Why hadn't she thought to ask for a firearm? The notion of having to defend herself against an attacker hadn't crossed her mind when she'd set out.

Applejack's sides heaved like bellows in the blacksmith's shop, and he responded sluggishly to her command to angle right. Niganithat jerked his horse to a stop, his eyes wild. Tessa sat before him, tears streaking her face, and a long cut on her cheek coated with dried blood. What had he done to her?

Rage filled Priscilla, and her mothering, protective instincts charged to the front. How dare he harm her child? For Tessa was just that: her child.

Elliot, galloped near, his gun pointed at the Kickapoo warrior's head.

Tessa hiccupped and held out her hands. "Aunt Priscilla!" Niganithat's arm tightened around the little girl.

"Let her go." Sleet had nothing on the coldness in Elliot's voice.

"Do not shoot." White ringed Niganithat's eyes. He held up one hand, keeping the other around Tessa's middle. He spoke again, in rapid Kickapoo to Kennekuk who had ridden up behind Priscilla. She dared a quick look at the medicine man. He held his rifle at the ready, his face a mask of fury.

"Put her down. Priscilla, stay back," Elliot ordered when she started toward them.

Kennekuk barked at Niganithat, who shook his head, firing back a response. They exchanged words a few more times before Kennekuk lowered his rifle.

"My friend." Kennekuk rode between Elliot and his quarry. "Put your gun away."

"No. He stole a child. My child. I want her back, now." Elliot maneuvered Bill so as to get a clean shot at Niganithat if necessary.

"He says he found her and was returning her to the fort. He did not steal her."

"I don't believe him. He wanted her, and he took her." His hands shook.

"Uncle Elliot?" Tessa's voice broke on another hiccup. "He's telling the truth. He was bringing me back."

They stood, frozen, as what Tessa said sank in. Elliot still looked angry enough to shoot Niganithat, and the man seemed to understand his peril. As long as he had Tessa in his arms, Elliot wouldn't risk it, but the minute he gave the little girl up, he'd be shot.

"Did you run away from the fort all by yourself, Tessa?" Priscilla asked.

The little girl hung her head. "Yes." Her shoulders bobbed.

"Then how'd you end up with her, Ni-ganithat?" Elliot's eyes bored holes in the Indian's. "Where's her pony?"

"I found her. I would not harm her. I was bringing her back."

"Then why did you run when we spotted you?" Elliot's aim never wavered.

"I did not know who it was. If it was other soldiers from the fort, they would shoot me before I could tell what happened."

Through it all, Kennekuk interpreted but kept his rifle trained on his tribesman.

Priscilla dropped from the saddle and let her reins trail. "Enough of this. Niganithat, please, let me have her. Elliot, put your gun away." She held up her arms, and Tessa dove into them.

Pressing her cheek to the child's hair, she savored the feel against her skin as relief at finding her alive coursed through her and made her weak. She sagged to the ground with Tessa in her embrace. "Poor, baby. Are you hurt?" She cupped her hands on Tessa's cheeks and examined her. "What happened to your face?"

"Wingfoot stumbled and I went clean over his head. I saw stars, and when I sat up, I couldn't find him." Her words clogged in her throat with her tears, and she flung her skinny arms around Priscilla's neck. Elliot swung from the saddle and squatted beside them, rubbing Tessa's shoulder.

"What were you doing out here in the first place? You know better than to leave the fort." Priscilla couldn't keep the censure out of her voice now that Tessa had been found and was safe.

"I was hiding."

"From whom?" She stared hard at Niganithat over Tessa's head. If he had threatened her in any way, scared her into running, Priscilla would trample him into dust.

"From you. And Uncle Elliot." The little girl's voice was muffled against Priscilla's bodice.

Priscilla and Elliot's gazes collided, and his brows rose.

"From us? Why?"

She leaned back. "Because of what Mrs. Crane said. She said you were leaving soon." Her finger jabbed Priscilla in the shoulder. "She said you and Uncle Elliot had been fighting all summer over what to do with me and Timothy, and if you had any sense at all, you'd do what the Bible said and split us up. She said I should go east with Aunt Priscilla, and Timothy should stay here with Uncle Elliot." A fresh torrent of tears streamed down her face. "And Uncle Elliot says we always have to do what the Bible says. I don't want to leave Timothy. And I don't want you to leave us, Aunt Priscilla." She collapsed against Priscilla once more, sobs shaking her.

Priscilla closed her eyes against the anger at Mrs. Crane for her thoughtless words, and against the pain and fear they had caused Tessa. Rocking the little girl, she whispered soothing words against her sunwarmed hair.

"We need to get back to the fort. It will be dark soon." Elliot lifted Tessa from Priscilla's lap. "Mount up, Priscilla, and I'll hand her up to you." His grim demeanor gave Priscilla no reassurance as to what he was thinking. Surely he wouldn't contemplate Mrs. Crane's notion of splitting up the twins. Was he considering punishing Tessa for running away?

Priscilla took Tessa into her arms. Uncorking her canteen, she let Tessa drink. "Not too much, or you'll be sick. You can have more in a little while."

Tessa lowered the canteen, pressed her cheek into Priscilla's bodice and promptly fell asleep. Priscilla brushed the tousled curls off her temples and dropped a kiss onto her warm little head.

The ride back to the fort was made in silence. A mile or so north of the Pekhotah's camp, Kennekuk and Niganithat pulled their horses up.

"We will stop here, friend." Kennekuk leaned over to clasp forearms with Elliot. "It would not go well for us to ride into the fort with you. Major Crane might not understand that we had not stolen the child."

"Thank you for your help." Elliot turned to Niganithat. "And thank you for finding Tessa."

Niganithat took Elliot's hand. He spoke in Kickapoo, and Kennekuk translated. "I was very angry when you would not give me the woman or the girl, and I was angry with Kennekuk when he would not take my side. But I was wrong. They belong to you. If they were mine, I would not give them up either." He lifted his reins, nudged his big pinto in the ribs, and rode away.

The adobe buildings of Fort Bliss had never looked more beautiful to Priscilla. Weariness had settled into Priscilla's bones like an ache. Elliot hadn't spoken to her, and his expression didn't encourage conversation, even if Priscilla had the strength. Was he blaming her for Tessa getting lost? If she hadn't come to the fort, if she hadn't insisted on taking the children from him, none of this would've happened.

The sun was a pink memory quickly turning to gray on the horizon when they were challenged by the first picket guard. "I'm sure glad you found her, sir. The men were gearing up to search again in the morning."

They rode toward the hospital. Lamplight streamed from the windows. "Take her to my quarters. I'll get the horses seen to, check on my patients in the hospital, and find Timothy. We've got a few things to settle, and I want it done tonight." Elliot was as grim and unbending as the day she arrived at the fort.

Tessa woke up as Elliot carried her into the house. He set her on a chair, did a cursory examination, and stood. "Priscilla, wash that cut well when you bathe her. I'll be back soon."

Priscilla swallowed against the lump in her throat and set to tending Tessa.

An hour later, freshly scrubbed and fed, Tessa sat up in her cot, picking at the sheet. Her hair was drying into a halo of curls, and Priscilla's chest ached with love for the little girl. Tessa eased back against her pillows, listless and quiet.

"You need a good rest. You'll feel better in the morning."

Boots clomped on the steps, and Timothy barreled into the room. His parfleche slapped against his leg, and he skidded to a stop beside Tessa's bed. "That was a dumb thing to do, running off."

Tessa nodded. She glanced up at Elliot who stood in the bedroom doorway, and lowered her eyes.

"It *was* a dumb thing to do, and Tessa knows it, Tim." Elliot unbuttoned his navy tunic and shrugged out of it, revealing a wrinkled, sweat-stained shirt pinned to his shoulders by his suspenders. "I don't think she'll make the same mistake again." He leaned against the door frame.

Timothy sidled over to Priscilla where she sat on the edge of Tessa's bed, and she put her arm around his waist.

"Corporal Rhodes sent word that Wingfoot showed up about a half hour ago. He's one tired pony, but he doesn't seem to be hurt. And the other search parties have returned as well." He rubbed his hands down his face. "You caused a lot of trouble, Miss Tessa. And put not just yourself, but other people in danger. Men had to leave their duties, leave the fort less protected than it should've been, and you caused your aunt and me considerable worry."

Tessa nodded, two new tear tracks appearing on her cheeks. Priscilla handed her a clean handkerchief, biting back what she wanted to say. Couldn't he see she was sorry? Did he have to lay the responsibility for the safety of the fort on the shoulders of a repentant little girl? She sent him a pleading look, but he wasn't watching her.

"Tessa, I owe you and Timothy an apology." He gripped his hands together, his shoulders bowed. "I haven't done right by you. You've been troopers, and I've treated you badly. If I hadn't been so selfish, none of this would've happened."

Priscilla's arm fell away from Timothy as the little boy went to his uncle.

"You haven't treated us bad." He put his hand on Elliot's laced fingers and looked up into his uncle's face. "You're the best uncle we could ever have."

Tessa smeared the tears with the handkerchief, nodding. "The best."

"Thanks, kids. I didn't realize until today how on edge you two must've been, not knowing what would happen when Priscilla's visit here came to an end. I didn't realize you two knew that there was even a question as to whether you'd be moving east or not." He ruffled Timothy's hair and walked over to tweak one of Tessa's curls. "You two are sharper than a new scalpel." He took a seat on Timothy's bed, his elbows on his knees.

"Tessa, I'm sorry that Mrs. Crane scared you with the idea that we might separate you two. I can tell you that will never happen as long as I can prevent it. You two belong together." He took a deep breath. "That's why I've come to the decision to let you both go with your aunt Priscilla."

Priscilla's head snapped up. "You've what?"

"I realized when we were chasing all over the countryside, hoping to get to Tessa before renegade Indians found her, that she would never be in that kind of danger if I hadn't been so stubborn. If I had let you take the twins east when you first arrived here, they wouldn't be exposed to cholera, they wouldn't be surrounded by Indian camps that might get out of control, and Tessa wouldn't have felt the need to run away, straight out onto an unforgiving desert." Anguish bracketed his gray eyes. He sucked in another deep breath. "I love you kids, and it will about kill me to let you go, but I have to do what is best for you." He stood and walked out, leaving Priscilla and the twins staring toward the open door.

She slipped off the bed to her knees, gathering the twins close, bringing their heads to hers. "Listen to me. I don't want you to worry. Your uncle is upset right now.

He was very worried about Tessa, and he doesn't know what he's saying. You two wait here, and promise me that you won't worry. I'm going to go talk to him. You won't be leaving here." She hugged them tight, planted a kiss on each golden head, and stood.

Her heart stampeded in her chest, and her mind scrambled for what to think, what to say when she found Elliot.

He wasn't in the kitchen. He wasn't in the yard. She checked the hospital, where Samson and Fern had everything under control. Neither had seen Elliot.

She finally spotted him behind the hospital. He'd hooked his thumbs into his waistband at the base of his spine, and his head was tipped back to study the multitude of stars scattered like seed pearls across the indigo sky.

"Elliot." She put her hand on his shoulder, warm and firm under her palm.

"You win, Priscilla. You were right. This is no place to raise children."

The dejection in his voice irked her. "I think this is the perfect place to raise children."

Starlight bathed his features, and he turned to her, his brows down, his eyes wary.

"I'm serious. How could you think I would be so heartless as to take those children away from you? You're their uncle and their guardian. It was their parents' wish that you raise them, and you're going to live up to that responsibility."

He took hold of her arms. "But what about the dangers? I can't watch over them like I should, not when I have to go out on patrol, not when there are wounded or sick men who need my attention. I can't make a home for them like they deserve."

She decided to lay it on the line. Either he would accept what she had to offer, or he would turn her down, but either way, the twins would stay with him because it was the right thing to do.

"I had a lot of time to think while you were out on patrol. Every night when I worked on the herbal journal, I thought about you and the children and your life out here. I would open my art case, and there was that picture I'd drawn of the house of my dreams with the ivy growing up the side and the wide windows, and that inviting porch. For such a long time that was my vision of home, that I was blinded to reality." She stepped closer and took hold of the front of his shirt. "Elliot, I realized, as I was worrying over you and praying you came home safely, that home isn't a building. Home is family and the ties of love that bind them together. Home is made in people's hearts. I watched Fern make a home of a corner of a hallway, and Mrs. Bracken create a home from dirt floors and adobe walls. Even the Kickapoo women make homes out of poles and bark. And why? Because that is where the people they love are." Her fingertips brushed his temple, down his cheek, and along his neck to lie against his chest. She gathered every shred of her courage.

"Elliot, the truth is, you and the twins have made a home in my heart. I never thought I would say this to a military man, but I love you. I'm proud of you for being a major in the cavalry, and if you'll let me, I'll do my best to make a home for you and the children, no matter where the army might send us."

He went perfectly still. His heart throbbed under her palm, and she searched his eyes for a response to her pledge. He brought his hands up to cover hers, squeezing them, pressing them hard against the wall of his chest.

"Are you sure? You're not overwrought because of what happened today?" His voice was raspy, his stare demanding.

She shook her head, her lips parting. "No. I've wanted to tell you for a while, but there was so much to do, so many sick people to tend. You were so busy, and then Tessa was lost . . ."

He took her face between his palms. "You love me?" His face was only inches from hers. He seemed to be trying to look into her very heart. "You love *me*?"

"With all my heart." Her skin tingled at his touch, and her breath caught in her throat as he moved even closer.

"Priscilla, Priscilla," he whispered against her lips, his fingers diving into her hair and loosening her hairpins, letting his mouth trail over her jawline and down the column of her neck, sending heat spiraling up her middle. The brush of his mustache against her skin chased tingles through her blood and made her heart soar. "Say it again."

"I love you, Major Ryder."

His arms shot around her, gathering her to him until she could barely breathe. Her arms went around his neck and her hands cupped the back of his head. He slanted his mouth over hers in a fierce kiss, as if he'd opened the gate on feelings too long penned up. Priscilla kissed him back with all the love in her heart, waves of happiness crashing over her. Her knees turned to water, and her toes curled inside her shoes.

He didn't break the kiss off abruptly, rather withdrawing slowly with murmurs and nuzzles of his nose against hers. He finally let her go, only to cup her face between his palms again.

"Can this be true? Am I dreaming?" he asked.

"If you are, then I am, too, and I don't want to wake up." His face, so close, so dear, swam in her vision as tears of joy sprang to her eyes. She stroked his neck, his shoulders, his arms, unable to get enough of him, thrilling in the freedom to express her love for him this way.

He kissed her again. "When?"

"When?" She shook her head, puzzled.

"When will you marry me? Is tomorrow too soon?"

"Tomorrow?"

"I don't see any point in waiting. Do you?"

"I . . . I don't know." Things had changed so fast, she was still trying to catch up.

"We'll turn the proceedings over to Mrs. Bracken, and she'll have everything whipped into shape before first Fatigue Call, if I know her. And the twins —" His grip tightened. "Oh, the twins. They think they're leaving with you."

She put her fingers over his lips, thrilling

at the softness and the brush of his mustache. "Shhh. They're fine. I told them they wouldn't be leaving. I just didn't tell them I'd be staying."

"They're going to be beside themselves. Tessa told me the day you arrived that I should marry you. She's going to be quite cock-a-hoop when she hears that I'm following her orders."

Priscilla gave him a rueful smile. "I was so angry with you that day. I didn't know how to get you to see reason. And I was the one that was all wrong. I hated the very thought of the children belonging to you and the regiment."

"We both have some things to regret, but that's all in the past. I love you, Priscilla. I've loved you for weeks and weeks. I just didn't want to admit it to myself." He brushed a kiss across her brow. "You haven't answered my question. Will you marry me tomorrow?"

She hugged him close, breathing in the smells of medicine, herbs, sunshine and that indefinable something that was just Elliot. "Yes. Oh, yes, Elliot."

The strains of a bugle came to them on the night air. Taps. Time for lights out.

"The kids will be anxious. We'd best go tell them the good news." He laced his fingers with hers, raising her hand to his lips.

"They won't sleep, they'll be so excited."

He chuckled. "I won't blame them. I might be too excited myself."

Her heart soared. "I doubt I'll need Reveille to wake me up tomorrow either."

As the moon rose high over the desert, he walked her to his — soon to be their — quarters. Stopping on the steps, he smoothed the hair back from her temples. "Thank you, Priscilla. Thank you for taking me and the twins on. I'll do my best to be a good husband to you and a good father to them."

"Thank you for loving me. Thank you for giving me a home in your heart." She raised her lips to his.

A giggle broke their kiss, and they turned to see two little towheads peeking around the door.

"I told you so." Tessa elbowed Timothy. "You owe me a quarter."

ABOUT THE AUTHOR

Erica Vetsch is a transplanted Kansan now residing in Minnesota. She loves books and history, and is blessed to be able to combine the two by writing historical romances. Whenever she's not following flights of fancy in her fictional world, she's the company bookkeeper for the family lumber business, mother of two, an avid museum patron, and wife to a man who is her total opposite and soul mate. Erica loves to hear from readers. You can sign up for her quarterly newsletter at www.ericavetsch.com.

And you can email her at ericavetsch@gmail.com or contact her on her author Facebook page.